JULIA JARRETT

Westmount Island: The Complete Trilogy

Copyright © 2021 by Julia Jarrett

All rights reserved. No part of this publication may be reproduced, stored or transmitted in any form or by any means, electronic, mechanical, photocopying, recording, scanning, or otherwise without written permission from the publisher. It is illegal to copy this book, post it to a website, or distribute it by any other means without permission.

This novel is entirely a work of fiction. The names, characters and incidents portrayed in it are the work of the author's imagination. Any resemblance to actual persons, living or dead, events or localities is entirely coincidental.

Julia Jarrett asserts the moral right to be identified as the author of this work.

First edition

Editing by CM Wheary

This book was professionally typeset on Reedsy.
Find out more at reedsy.com

Contents

Acknowledgement   vi

I   Falling Fast

1	Ella	3
2	Marcus	7
3	Ella	12
4	Marcus	20
5	Ella	28
6	Marcus	34
7	Ella	46
8	Ella	53
9	Marcus	61
10	Ella	67
11	Marcus	73

II Falling Again

12	Kayla	83
13	Sam	88
14	Kayla	95
15	Kayla	102
16	Sam	106
17	Kayla	109
18	Sam	115
19	Kayla	122
20	Sam	130
21	Kayla	136
22	Sam	141
23	Kayla	149
24	Sam	155

III Falling Forever

25	Mac	163
26	Tawny	167
27	Mac	172
28	Tawny	177
29	Mac	183
30	Tawny	188
31	Mac	197
32	Tawny	202
33	Mac	209
34	Tawny	216
35	Mac	222
36	Tawny	226
37	Mac	233
38	Tawny	240

About the Author	245
Also by Julia Jarrett	246

Acknowledgement

As with all of my books, this one would not have been possible without the unwavering support of my husband. He is my real-life book boyfriend, and the best man I know.

And, my KKSB sisters. Your love, support, encouragement and inspiration makes this writing journey so much better.

I

Falling Fast

1

Ella

The spray from the ferry boat wake is a fine mist, cool on my skin, as I watch the peaks of Westmount Island draw closer. It could have been a poignant moment, if not for the wind whipping my long hair into such a frenzy it starts to slap me on the cheek.

"Oh, for fudge's sake," I mutter to myself as I try in vain to twist it back from my face. What I wouldn't give for a hair tie. But they're in my car, on the vehicle deck, and even after just two days away I am so homesick for my island, there's no way I want to go down there and miss this view.

A chuckle from behind makes me turn, ready to glare at whoever is mocking me. But when my eyes land on him, a glare is the last thing on my mind.

"Holy shiitake," I breathe, most likely cementing my place in his mind as the weird girl who uses food words instead of curse words. What can I say? You can take the kindergarten teacher out of the classroom, but you can't take the goody-goody bone out of the kindergarten teacher. Wait. That doesn't even make sense.

Clearly, the guy in front of me is scrambling my brain.

He's tall, like towering over me tall, which is hard to do when you consider I'm above average height for a woman at five-eight. His eyes match the stormy grey of the water churning below us and his chiseled jaw is quirked into a grin. And yes, that's the first time I have ever said *chiseled jaw.* His body seems to be made of solid muscle, which I can see rippling beneath his shirt, currently plastered to his chest from the wind. Never have I been more grateful for wind.

When he opens his mouth and his voice pours over me, warm like melted chocolate, I'm not sure if I'm drooling, or if it's just more spray from the boat. I try to casually wipe at my face, just in case.

"I'm not sure fudge could hold back your hair, but I've got this if it'll help." He holds out his hand, which has, of all things, a rubber band in it. In his other hand he holds a rolled up piece of paper, I'm guessing that's the source of the rubber band. Part of me winces at the damage it'll do to my hair, the other part is just grateful not to have the strands smacking me anymore.

"Thanks," I say, still unable to meet his penetrating gaze.

"Anytime."

That one word comes out as a rumble, the sound sending a shiver down my spine. Good grief, I can't remember the last time a man affected me like this. I take that back; I can't remember the *first* time a man affected my body with just his voice. Westmount Island has a depressing shortage of hot men my age.

Maybe I can blame my visceral response to him on my mood. After all, I'm not exactly in my normal, more logical, frame of mind right now. I never am when I leave the island, but my sister Tawny insisted I take a weekend and visit some friends.

I've spent the summer helping Tawny run the inn our family has had for generations. It's fun, but exhausting dealing with so many different people, with so many different demands. And with the school year rapidly approaching, it's almost time for me to go back to my regular job teaching the littles of the island. I love my work, there's nothing more rewarding than watching a child play and create and develop into an awesome tiny human. But it is also exhausting. So every year, I take the last three weeks of summer off for myself and do whatever I want. Which normally means hiking around the island and lots of reading. But when Tawny suggested I go visit some old friends from school, I listened. A weekend on the mainland was meant to be a fun break, a chance to connect with friends and live the life of a typical twenty-seven-year-old. Instead, I'm tired and drained from the hustle and bustle of the city. Yes, after just forty-eight hours away, I'm happy to be home. Call me a small-town girl; I don't care. I'm ready for my cozy cottage and maybe even a hot bath. What I'm not ready for is this gorgeous hunk of a man standing in front of me, eyeing me like I'm some tasty treat he wants to lick all over.

Where did that come from? I'm no prude, but my love life has always been more vanilla than any other flavor. Even if I wanted to change it, as I mentioned, the options are limited on the island.

I blink back to the present moment, aware that he's been talking while I've been lost in my dirty little fantasies about ice cream and licking.

"...at this old inn, so if you have suggestions on where to eat, that would be great." He looks at me expectantly and I hurry to fill in the blanks, hoping I'm making the right assumption about what he was asking.

"Oh! My older sister owns an inn. The inn, I mean. The inn you're staying at. There's only one. Well, I guess my sisters and I all technically own it, but Tawny's the only one who works there. Anyway, it's really cute and I'm sure you'll like it. The restaurant there is great. Good food, really good." I let my voice trail off, feeling the heat on my cheeks as I cast my gaze downward in embarrassment. I hate it when I ramble, but it's inevitable. When I get nervous, my mouth takes over and I babble like it's my last chance to say anything, ever.

When I finally look up, he's grinning at me appreciatively. I don't miss the way his gaze travels up and down my body. How could I, when my body is suddenly hot, as if he's shooting laser beams from his eyes.

His seductive voice rolls over me yet again, and I shiver involuntarily. "Would you care to join me for dinner at the really good restaurant?"

I know he's teasing me for my rambling, but my jaw drops, and I hurry to close it before he thinks I'm a total country bumpkin. What the hell is going on here? Is this Adonis of a man asking me out? I'm nothing special, just Ella Michaels, kindergarten teacher from Westmount Island. My family has been on the island for generations, so I guess you could say we're well known there, but the three of us – my two sisters and I, we're just regular people. This guy – he is anything but regular. He's got this air of importance surrounding him. He's not cocky, he's confident. Like he knows his purpose and nothing will stand in his way.

Is that purpose now dinner with me? The thought makes me shiver.

Once again, I realize he's waiting for my reply. I groan inwardly; I am so easily distracted by him I must come across as a total idiot. Regardless, I fumble out a response that sounds somewhat normal.

"Dinner. Yes, that would be good, I eat."

Did I mention that normal for me is social awkwardness for anyone else? Yet for some strange reason, he seems to like it, judging by the way his eyes crinkle at the corners as his smile widens.

"Perfect. I also eat." He winks at me. *Winks* at me.

"I'm Marcus. It's nice to meet you…" Now his voice trails off, but this time I know what to say.

"Ella. My name is Ella."

2

Marcus

Ella.

Well, fuck me if she doesn't look like she should have woodland animals singing songs around her and braiding her hair. Thanks to my college friend Brooks, and his seven-year-old daughter, I am a lot more familiar with Disney princesses than any single guy wants to be.

I flash her another smile, loving the way she twists her hands nervously. She's stunning, adorable, sexy, and a whole host of other adjectives my brain is too fuzzy to think of right now. I felt a pull to her the instant she walked out onto the deck, and any hint of frustration and impatience I felt over having to come to this damn island was gone. Her long brown hair shone in the sun, strands of chocolate and mahogany and gold all weaving together. When she spoke, with her ridiculous food substitutions for swear words, I couldn't have held back my chuckle if you'd threatened to cut off my dick.

Suddenly this trip doesn't seem like such a fucking hassle. Honestly, if Robert, the property developer I sometimes partner with, hadn't convinced me this island was the perfect place for a new resort community that could lead to a massive payday, there was no goddamn way I would be here. It's not like I need the money, but I do need a new challenge.

Anyway, spending a day on a tiny island is not my first choice of how to spend a workday. Give me the chaos of the city any day over a sleepy little island town. Peace and solitude? My idea of hell. I wasn't meant to be the one making the trip, but Robert's current girlfriend is a major bitch and is demanding his presence at some gala tonight.

This was meant to only be a one-day trip, and if I had kept to my schedule and made it on the first ferry this morning, I probably would have scouted the proposed site and been home in time to put another couple of hours in at the office. Instead, I missed the first boat, thanks to a last-minute conference call with Shanghai, and ended up with an arrival time that leaves no time to tour the site today, and no place to stay tonight. I had planned on my assistant figuring it out, but she called in sick. A quick google search told me there was only one hotel on the whole island, thankfully with a room available.

If I believed in fate, I'd say it was conspiring to get me here, now, with Ella.

"So, dinner at the inn tonight, say around seven?"

I don't miss the panic that flashes across her face, and briefly I wonder if she's rethinking her decision to let me take her out. I'm determined to convince her to join me, no matter what. A fling with a beautiful girl is just what I need to make this trip bearable, and I'll be damned if she hasn't found a way under my skin. It's as if something in me craves something in her, but what? I haven't even touched her, so why am I so desperate to keep her with me?

"Well," she begins hesitantly, and my lips quirk up again at her nerves. God, she's adorable, and all I want to do is kiss away her worry. And if a kiss lands us in bed together, all the better.

"The thing is, if my sister sees us together, she'll be watching us like a hawk all evening. She's nosy," she blurts out. Another sinful blush covers her cheeks as I feel the grin stretching across my face. Damn, it feels good to smile this freely. "Not that there'll be anything for her to watch. I mean, I don't think you're going to do anything...oh cheese-us, I should just stop talking."

"No, please continue," I laugh, oddly turned on by her awkward, fumbling way. "A big sister watching me eat isn't high on my list of things to experience tonight." I turn my gaze to her, letting my eyes roam her curvy body, trapped in a light blue sundress that whips in the wind. She's innocence and sin all mixed together, and I want more. And I always get what I want.

"If we aren't going to eat at the inn, where do you recommend two people enjoy a quiet meal together when just getting to know each other?"

I can tell that my forthright nature intrigues her from the way her sea glass green eyes darken.

"Getting to know each other? Is that what we're doing?"

"I hope so, Ella." This time even I can hear the sincerity in my voice. It's such a change from the cold, calculating persona I have to play every single day at work. I feel that version of me falling away, much like a snake sheds its skin. Ella, with her sweetness and light, is bringing out a side of me I thought was gone – the man my mom raised me to be, who doesn't let arrogance stand in the way of respect and kindness. It takes a toll, playing the cocky asshole who gets shit done, but my business needs me to be that way.

As I watch, she takes a deep breath in, and squares her shoulders. I wonder what inner monologue is going through her mind, but whatever she says to herself, it works.

"I'd like that. Do you eat seafood?"

I nod.

"Okay, we'll go down to the wharf and get salmon burgers from the diner, then I'll show you a spot on the beach that not many people go to."

A burger on the beach. I almost laugh out loud at how insane that sounds to me, Marcus Ryder, successful business owner, multi-millionaire, with a condo in the city, a chalet up in the mountains, three cars – all luxury models, of course – and I'm going on a date with a woman I can't seem to pull myself away from, to have burgers on the beach. Despite the complete deviation from my normal life, it feels right.

"Sounds great," I reply with a smile. And it does.

I think for a moment. I need to explore the island and get a feel for it. What better way than with a local? And if it gives me more time with this intriguing woman, that's even better.

"What are the chances you'd also be willing to give me a bit of a tour of the downtown area? I've never been here before, but I'm interested to see what Westmount Island has to offer. Aside from beautiful women, that is." I'm piling on the charm and hoping it doesn't scare her away. She's timid, but I can sense a fire inside of her that seems to be growing. "And you seem like you would be pretty familiar with what there is to see around here."

She laughs lightly, and flushes again. God, I want to see what that looks like on her when she's spread out on my bed, naked.

"You could say that. My family has lived here for generations."

"Wow. Your family must be a big deal around here. What do your parents do?"

A shadow falls over her face and instantly I know I've said something I shouldn't have.

"My parents died ten years ago. It's just my sisters and I here now."

She's quiet and subdued, as if the light that was beaming from her has been turned off, and I am desperate to turn it back on. Without a second thought, I take the two steps I need to be right in front of her and pull her into my chest. She's rigid for only a second before she melts into my arms with a soft sigh. At first, I'm taken aback by how fucking amazing she feels against my body. Then I register her smell, sweet like vanilla and honeysuckle. Her hair tickles my nose and my lips drift down to press a kiss to her head. This is madness, I just met this woman, she shouldn't feel so perfect in my arms. She isn't pulling away, and neither am I. Something is drawing us together with a force stronger than anything we could hope to control. Unfortunately, I eventually feel her draw back slightly and I let her go. But the second she is out of my arms I feel an ache in my chest that is unfamiliar and unpleasant. As if my body knows I need her.

"I'm sorry, that was, well, I've never, you're a stranger, so..." She is back to her delightfully awkward self, stumbling over her words and I reach out a hand to grasp hers.

"Don't apologize, Ella, I wanted to comfort you." It's the honest truth, even if it, too, sounds awkward and strange.

"Thank you." Her free hand fidgets with her dress, and her eyes won't meet mine. I'm wracking my brain on how to help her relax, when we're both startled by the foghorn on the ferry, notifying us we're nearing the dock on the island. She drops my hand as we walk down the stairs to the vehicle deck.

"Where should I pick you up for dinner?" I ask, desperate to cling to some confirmation that I'm not about to lose her. These moments together have felt so fleeting and yet so monumentally important, I can't let her go.

"Oh, I'll meet you at the inn," she replies, but the fact that she won't meet my eye tells me there's something she isn't telling me.

Before I can get her number, or any way to find her again, she's gone, hurrying down the narrow aisle between cars. It's a small ferry, so I keep sight of her until she stops at what must be her car. She turns back and waves, and her smile tells me everything I need to know.

She's mine.

3

Ella

What. Am. I. Doing.

This is not like me. Not at all. I'm quiet, have a few friends and my sisters, but don't really enjoy chatting up strangers. It's part of why working at the inn is so draining for me. I'm much more of an introvert.

But I just spent the better part of an hour flirting – yes, *flirting*, with the sexiest man I have ever seen. What's more, he flirted back. And asked me to dinner. And I said yes. And...cue freak out.

I calm my breathing and try to pull the rubber band from my hair without it tangling too badly, and I think about how to approach the rest of the day.

He said he wants a tour of the island, and I wonder why. He doesn't strike me as someone who would move here; truthfully, we get very few new residents each year. Ever since the ferry company decreased service to our island, more and more people have had to move away to the mainland for work. It's why our community is slowly fading and it's the root of my deepest fear – that the beautiful island I call home will wither away if we don't get an influx of money and people to revitalize us. We also need an alternative to the ferry service that's run by some bigwigs who don't give a hoot about us. There were rumors that some big property developer wanted to build some luxury cottages somewhere, which was met with mixed reviews. Some people thought it was a great idea, a way to bring some life back to the island, but others were understandably concerned that it might make our island lose its quaint, small town feel. I'm undecided. We need to stimulate the economy, but I don't want to lose our community to some big developer who won't appreciate our relaxed and friendly way of life.

But that's not the crisis I should be focusing on right now. Nope, the current problem is a big, tall drink of water as my grandmother would call him, waiting for me to show him around my island. Why is he here? I suppose that should have been my first question, but I hadn't wanted to burst our little bubble on the ferry. Still, guys like him don't show up on Westmount Island for no reason. We've got a vibrant tourist season all summer, but it's more for young families and retirees, or as my twin sister Kayla calls them, "newlyweds and nearly deads". Of the two of us, she's more sarcastic and outgoing, in case it wasn't obvious. I miss her so much. But she's off living her dream as a travel photographer. I think she's somewhere in Alaska right now, hopefully not being eaten by bears.

Anyway. What to do about Marcus. Maybe I should have told him that my cottage is right next to the inn he'll be staying at, but I didn't for some reason. There'll be no hiding it when we both pull into the same driveway, however, and maybe that's a good thing. It'll be easy to meet up later. But what if he changes his mind about me between now and when we get to the inn? How embarrassing would that be if I'm all eager to show him around and he's all *yeah, no thanks, I'm good, you weirdo.*

Deep breaths, Ella. Deep breaths. Remember the hug. There was definitely...something in that hug. Something that felt unbelievably right, like my soul was breathing a sigh of relief. I've read about soul mates in the romance novels I'm addicted to, but never once did I think they existed in real life, or that I would ever find one. But that's what it felt like when I was in Marcus's arms. As if a part of me had been missing and was now found. I snort at myself and how ridiculous I sound. I'm infatuated with a man I just met.

But what if it's not ridiculous...what if he is someone worth getting close to? I felt a part of myself stir awake when I was talking to him. A sensual side, a part of me that longs to be seen as more than just goofy Ella Michaels who's always got finger paints in her hair from the kids she teaches. It felt like Marcus saw that in me.

The cars start moving off the ferry, and as I drive off, a glance in my rearview mirror shows a sleek black sports car has managed to pull up behind me. Marcus. His hair flops over his forehead in a way that's both youthful and sexy as anything. I want to run my fingers through it, push it back from his face, and feel the strands between my fingers.

I shake myself out of yet another fantasy involving this mystery man and give him a small wave. We drive off the ferry and Harold, who is manning the deck today, gives me a cheerful salute and I don't miss his curious stare at the man behind me. I hope Marcus is prepared for a lot of curious stares while he's here. A single guy in a car like that is going to stand out on the island.

The drive to the inn is short, only about ten minutes. I drive past the main parking lot and pull to a stop in front of my cottage. I climb out of my car just as he does the same. I'm not sure what to do now, but Marcus solves that by strolling over, with a smile on his face.

"Why Ella, are you following me?" His eyes are dancing, so I know he's teasing me again. I can't hide my blush, however.

"No! Technically I was in front so you were following me. But I, well, I live here." I gesture to my home as my words spill out.

If anything, his grin goes wider as he follows my finger, which is pointing to my cottage. It's insane, but he seems charmed by my inability to be anything but awkward.

"So close. Isn't that...perfect. I hope you'll show me your cottage sometime."

His voice is barely more than a murmur, but the heat behind the words is intense.

"I, well, sure. If you really want to see it." I stammer out. His eyes haven't left mine; his gaze is soft, but warm and inviting. I'm starting to believe he's just as drawn to me as I am to him.

"When shall we meet up for my tour?" he asks, casually placing his hands in his pockets. This somehow tightens his pants around his... considerable bulge, and I hear myself gasp under my breath. When I look up, there's a twinkle in his eye as if he caught me looking. I feel the heat rush over my face, but somehow keep a straight face when I reply.

"Give me an hour, and I'll meet you back here." I'm impressed by how normal that sounded. Maybe I'm finally getting some control.

"Perfect. I'll see you soon, Ella."

Gah, there's that sexy voice again, oozing over me. The way he says my name...if swooning were a real thing, I would be doing it.

I watch him turn and walk back to the front door of the inn, appreciating the view.

I love my cottage. It used to be my parents' until they had us three girls and they had to move to a bigger house in town. When they died, we stayed in that house for a while, but the memories were too hard for me to handle. So I asked my grandmother, who was still running the inn at the time, if I could have the old cottage. She agreed and I've been here ever since. Tawny still lives in the house; she says she likes being there. Kayla stays with one of us when she's in town, which isn't often these days.

I unlock my front door and step inside, taking a deep breath filled with the comfort and relief of being home. This is my sanctuary.

I make my way through my tiny living room, leaving my suitcase at the end of the hall that leads to my bedroom and bathroom. In the kitchen, I fill the kettle to make some herbal tea, and fill a pitcher of water for my plants. Kayla calls my cottage a greenhouse library and she's not wrong. Plants cover almost every available surface, and where there aren't plants, there's a pile of books. I've loved to read since I was a young child. I never bothered with getting a TV; I'd much rather escape into an imaginary world between the pages of a book than on a screen. My shelves are full and for Christmas two years ago, my sisters bought me an e-reader that is packed with books waiting for me to read. My dream is to someday open a library on the island. Right now, there's nothing, unless you go to the mainland. For that reason, I have collected a huge stock of children's books, and I run my own sort of library from the school. But it's not the same. It's one of those things that I hope will happen in time if the island can return to being the fantastic place to live that it used to be.

The kettle whistles and I pour hot water over some peppermint tea leaves. As it steeps, I water the jungle and grab a proper hair tie from my bedside table to twist my hair into a messy bun. I'll return Marcus's rubber band this afternoon. *Right, because the sexy guy with the expensive car is definitely going to miss a rubber band.*

Tea in hand, I head out to my favorite spot on the entire property. My back porch is my private oasis. I've got a private view of the pond from here and right now all the wildflowers are in full bloom. My dad built the porch swing and I absolutely love sitting in it. I feel like they're with me, but not in the sad way I feel when I'm at the house we grew up in. No, this place is full of love and joy, not grief.

I've barely had time to take a drink before my phone vibrates with a text message from my sister.

TAWNY: So, care to tell me why our hunky new guest says you're taking him on a tour of the island?

So much for hoping Marcus wouldn't say anything to my sister...

ELLA: It's no big deal. We met on the ferry, he wants a tour guide, I agreed to help. Stop overreacting.

TAWNY: I'm not overreacting, I'm just reacting. Who is he? Do you even know his last name? Because I do, and I'm about to google the heck out of him

ELLA: DON'T YOU DARE. Stop, Tawny, just stop. I like this guy, and I don't need you digging up his life story just because you think some stranger is going to come in here and...

ELLA: You know what? I don't even know WHAT you could be worried about.

ELLA: He's a hot guy. Who happens to be attracted to me. Let me have this, Tawny. Please.

TAWNY: Fine. But I still want to google him.

ELLA: Walk away from the Google.

TAWNY: Ugh. I just want you to be safe, Ella.

ELLA: I'm twenty-seven, pretty sure I'm capable of going out on a date.

TAWNY: A DATE? I thought it was a TOUR

ELLA: OMG calm down. It is a tour. And dinner...*covers ears*

TAWNY: DINNER?!?!?!?! ELLA JEAN MICHAELS! WHAT ARE YOU DOING?

ELLA: Wow, you middle named me. Geez Tawny.

ELLA: I'm taking Marcus on a tour of the island and then he's taking me for dinner. That's it, that's all. So just relax, big sis.

TAWNY: Don't do anything I wouldn't do.

ELLA: *Snort* right. Okay. So, I can do basically anything.

TAWNY: You know what I mean. Just be careful. And text me when you get home.

ELLA: Love you, sis.

TAWNY: Love you too.

And that, ladies and gentlemen, is my sister in her prime. Overprotective and apparently incapable of remembering all the trouble she got into when she was younger. The stories of the chaos Tawny and her best friend Mac got into are legendary on the island. Mac, or Shawn Macdonald, moved away after he graduated from college. Everyone figured Tawny and Mac would end up realizing they were destined to be together, but Tawny always swore they were just friends. When Mac left, she hid her devastation pretty well, but I knew the truth. Her heart was broken the day he left and it's never fully healed.

But Tawny seems to have forgotten her wild days. She took over at the inn when Grandma was ready to retire and she works seven days a week keeping things going. She's a total control freak, so it works, but man, does she need to lighten up. Especially when it comes to my social life.

With a sigh, I pick up one of the books I'm reading, a regency romance novel, and lose myself in the pages for a short while.

But when my tea is all gone, I glance at my phone to check the time. Oh fudge! I've only got about ten more minutes until I'm supposed to meet Marcus. My heartbeat quickens at the thought of seeing him and I can't help but hope I might have a reason to hug him again. He smelled so good, like the ocean, but in a sexy man way. Hopefully I can manage to get through the afternoon without being even more of a bumbling idiot, but let's face it, awkward should have been my middle name, not Jean. *Sorry Grandma.*

I go inside, put some cash and a lip gloss in my pocket, and grab my sunglasses. With a quick check in the mirror to make sure my hair isn't looking too insane, I head out the door to find Marcus.

When my eyes land on him in the parking lot, I realize that after only an hour, my memory of just how handsome he is had faded. This man is sex on a stick, and I'm filled with a desperate wanting to explore every inch of his gorgeous body.

It's still a mystery as to why he's here, but I think I'm going to enjoy solving it. With a man who looks like he does, who looks *at me* like he does, there's no doubt in my mind.

This is going to be an interesting afternoon.

4

Marcus

Ella walks up to me and I shift my stance in an effort to hide my growing arousal. Fuck, I'm a grown-ass man, I should have more control than this, but something about her gets to me, deeply. And it's not just physically, my soul is calling to me to claim her as my own. Which is fucking insane, after only spending an hour with her. But I've learned in business to always trust my gut, so I guess I should trust it here as well.

I hold myself back from reaching out and pulling her into my arms, aware that she might not be feeling as intensely attracted to me as I am to her, but I can't stop my hand from reaching out to grasp hers. The smile she beams at me is a relief. Maybe she is, in fact, on the same page.

"So, Ella Enchanted, where to first?" I say, and immediately cringe at the ridiculous nickname.

She stops walking, and because we're holding hands, I jerk to a stop as well.

"Oh no, no you don't. Don't you dare compare me to some silly princess. I've heard all the nicknames, and I'll tell you right now, don't use them. Besides, you can't honestly tell me *you* know who

Ella Enchanted is."

She's got some sass in her now, and I like it. But weirdly enough, I also liked nervous Ella.

"Okay, okay, sorry, I blame my buddy's daughter. She's made me watch more kid movies than I can count." I apologize, squeezing her hand and tugging her closer. My other hand reaches up to softly cup her chin. I lift her sunglasses up onto her head so I can see her mesmerizing eyes. "How about I just call you beautiful?"

Her eyes soften, and she smiles. I get the feeling she hasn't been called beautiful before, and I want to pound on my chest like some ridiculous caveman and claim her as mine.

"Come on, let's go."

She sets off down the tree-lined sidewalk of the inn's driveway and I can't hide my surprise.

"I thought we were driving."

Ella just laughs.

"Why? Everything you'll want to see in town is within walking distance. Outside of town is just homes, the nature reserve, a small winery, and some hiking trails." She looks at me shyly and pauses before continuing. But what she says next makes me want to pump my fist and cheer. "I could show you that tomorrow if you're interested."

"There's nothing I want more than to spend another day with you."

Every word is the God's honest truth, and the way she smiles at me says she's pleased to hear my response. But deep inside, I'm aware I have a job to do here as well. At some point I need to scope out the land that Robert wants to develop. His vision is a gated community full of luxury vacation homes, and before arriving here, I would have said it's a great investment. Now I'm not so sure his original plan is going to work. He wants high end with the amenities to service it. The little bit I saw on the way from the ferry to the inn showed a small town, with an old-fashioned main drag lined with small shops.

Not exactly what the rich buyers Robert hopes to attract will want. Still, maybe there's a way to make it work. I consider telling Ella why I'm here. After all, maybe she can help. But I don't want her to look at me differently once she knows I'm here to change her island. For now, I like the fact that we don't have anything between us except attraction.

We walk in silence for a moment, and I find myself enjoying the simplicity of the moment. That realization is jarring, because the Marcus of yesterday would have been itching to move on to the next big thing. Instead, I'm relishing the feel of her hand in mine, the late summer sun on my face, and the surprisingly pleasant quiet. Instead of the cacophony of the city, I hear nature. Birds chirping, trees rustling, and somewhere in the distance is a lawnmower running. Maybe this isn't hell after all.

Ella's melodic voice interrupts my musing.

"So, tell me about yourself. We don't get a lot of young single guys on the island. At least I'm assuming you're single. Oh fudge, I hope you're single because you hugged me and asked me to dinner, and now you're holding my hand and..."

It would seem nervous Ella is back, so I stop her anxious rambling the only way I can think of.

I kiss her.

But this kiss, well, just like everything else with this woman, it's different. What started out as an impulsive means to distract her has now become my new addiction. She melts into me instantly, her arms winding around my neck, and her fingers dragging through my hair as if she's been waiting to do that all afternoon. Her lips are as soft as silk and when she opens for me, my tongue sneaks in to tangle with hers. There's a faint hint of peppermint on her breath as it blends with mine, our mouths fused together perfectly. I want to take it deeper, to devour her, but it's too soon.

Reluctantly, I pull away slightly, and press a chaste kiss to her nose, something I've never done before, but feels right for her.

"I hope that answers the question of whether or not I'm single."

She nods, her eyes still closed, and I lean in, unable to resist kissing her one more time. This time I keep it short and sweet; I just need another taste.

Ella slowly blinks her eyes open, and the smile she gives me makes me feel like the Grinch on Christmas day. I swear my heart grows two sizes, until it feels like it might burst from my chest.

I'm falling for her, after only one hug and one kiss.

"That was..." she trails off, and I'm amused by the fact that my rambling girl is, for once, at a loss for words. Wait. When did I start thinking of her as *my girl*?

But she is. She has to be. Somehow, this captivating woman in front of me has awakened a part of me I didn't know existed. The part that longs for a wife and family, for a home filled with love and laughter, for a life that is dictated by more than just business and work.

"That was the first kiss of many," I answer confidently as I lower my hands from her waist.

"The first of many."

She repeats my words as she looks up at me, and I can see something in her eyes that I suspect is mirrored in my own. A deep sense of completeness, of pure satisfaction and happiness.

I wrap my arm around her shoulders and tug her close into my side. I need to feel more of her against my body, in whatever way I can right now. Granted, what I really want is to turn around and march us back to the inn, find the nearest flat surface, and peel away these clothes so I can truly feel her body against mine. Fuck, that thought awakens my cock, and my pants are starting to feel tight. I try to think of business stats to make it go away, which only helps somewhat.

Soon we've reached the main part of town. Ella explains that the main drag is called Wharf Street, because it leads straight down to the old fishing pier. She takes me straight down there, bypassing all of the storefronts, claiming the only place to start is on the pier.

"So, do you want the history of the island, or just a tour of the town, or both, or something totally different?" Ella somehow manages to blurt that all out without taking a breath.

"Do you talk so quickly all the time?" I ask, pressing a kiss to her head so she knows I mean it nicely.

She gets a faint blush that starts at her chest and I allow myself a moment to enjoy the view.

"Only when I'm nervous." Her voice is so quiet, I almost miss the words. I stop and turn her to face me, moving my hands back to her waist.

"Why do I make you nervous, beautiful Ella?"

She's silent for a moment and won't meet my eyes. She tugs her bottom lip between her teeth, and I want desperately to bend my head down and cover her lips with my own, but I don't. I hold back, sensing that this might be a pivotal moment for us.

Eventually she looks up, and her eyes are shining with something I can't quite identify, but it fills me with an unfamiliar sensation of warmth and happiness.

"You don't make me nervous, Marcus. But the way I feel around you does. This, whatever's between us, it isn't normal. At least, I've never heard of it, except in romance novels. I feel like I'm falling for you, so quickly and so completely, and I can't decide if I should be terrified or ecstatic. So I'm a weird combination of both."

When she lowers her gaze, I can sense the nerves running through her. I admire the bravery it must have taken her to put her feelings out there like that. She's such a contradiction of courageous and shy, and it's a huge turn on. I gently run my hand down her cheek, loving the feel of her pressing into my palm. When I cup her chin, and gently tip her face up to mine, the first thing I do is lean down and kiss her. Once, twice;

soft swipes of my lips against hers. Designed to relax and reassure, not arouse. I know I'm successful when I feel a soft sigh escape from her. I tuck her into my chest, one hand resting on her lower back, the other coming up to cup her head.

"You're right. This is anything but normal for me as well. Fuck, Ella, I haven't been on a date in years," I say honestly. "But despite the crazy fast speed at which I'm also falling for you, I don't want to stop. Do you?" I find myself holding my breath while waiting for her reply. God, what the hell will I do if she feels it is too fast? I want more and more with this woman, hell, I want everything. What if she's not ready for that? I'm a lot, I know. I come with baggage in the form of my business and my work responsibilities. For a small-town girl like Ella, that might not be very appealing, and she doesn't even know about all that yet.

"No, I don't want to stop. I don't think I could, even if I wanted to," she says, and the words are a soothing balm to my worries.

"Good. Then let's just give in to this wild ride, and enjoy our time together," comes my swift reply. She nods at me slowly, and a soft smile stretches across her face. Together we start to walk slowly back toward the town, my arm still holding her close to my side.

When we get to the buildings, Ella perks up. "First on the tour is Seas The Day, our local diner. They've got the best salmon burgers in town; this is where we'll grab dinner later." She gestures to the first storefront, which boasts a bright awning with blue and white stripes. There's tables and chairs set up on the patio out front, and what looks to be a bustle of customers inside.

"Next is Pete's Hardware and Tackle shop."

Again, I'm impressed by how clean and tidy the exterior of the store is. Clearly the residents of Westmount Island pride themselves on their local businesses. This bodes well for any future developments, but I'm still worried that the vibe might be too quaint for what Robert wants to build. My mind starts churning with ways to adapt his idea, and more importantly, convince him to accept the changes.

I hear someone call out Ella's name, and turn to see an older man walking toward us with a big smile. He's wearing a faded ballcap, jeans, and a plaid shirt with – honest to God – suspenders.

"Ella, my dear, I'm so glad I caught you," he calls out cheerfully, before turning and giving me a curious look. "Who's your friend?"

I'm relieved that Ella doesn't pull away from me. Instead I feel her spine stiffen, but her voice is warm and happy when she replies.

"Hi, Mr. Thompson, this is Marcus. He's just visiting the island, so I'm showing him around."

"Humph. Looking mighty cozy for a visitor," comes his suspicious reply. I know I need to win over the locals, so I stick out my hand.

"Marcus Ryder, sir. It's a pleasure to meet you. I must say, I'm charmed by the island and it's inhabitants." I glance down at Ella with a smile, as the older man slowly accepts my handshake.

"George Thompson. Pleasure to meet you as well, Marcus Ryder. What brings you to Westmount?"

Looks like the old guy is still suspicious. Or maybe just protective of Ella. Either way, I understand. But when I tell Ella my real reason for being here, I want to do so when it's just the two of us. So, thinking quickly, I come up with a response that isn't quite a lie, but definitely isn't the whole truth.

"A friend of mine told me it was a beautiful place to visit and suggested I come to check it out, so here I am."

"I see. And just how do you know our Ella?"

"Well, Mr. Thompson, it was lovely to run into you, but I think we need to be going. Bye!" Ella interrupts, tugging me along the sidewalk. I give Mr. Thompson a quick wave goodbye and let her pull me along.

"Well, that was interesting. Is everyone going to be so concerned about my intentions with you?" I tease.

She flashes me a smile that's half grimace.

"Yeah, probably."

I smile back, trying to appear as if that isn't a problem. And really, it isn't. I have no intention of doing anything to hurt Ella, so no matter what it takes, I'll win over her friends and family.

I do love a challenge.

5

Ella

Dang it, I'm so embarrassed. I cannot BELIEVE old Mr. Thompson started grilling Marcus like that. He seemed to take it in stride, but I'm flustered by the interaction. It dawns on me that we'll have a lot of people asking the same question if they see Marcus with his arm around me. After all, my neighbors are used to 'single' Ella, not...'it's complicated' Ella.

Thankfully the rest of our walk down Wharf Street is uninterrupted, but I certainly don't miss the curious stares that are thrown our way like confetti. I'm sure I'll have plenty of questions to answer the next time I'm out alone.

As we meander through the side streets, I fill the silence with some more random facts about Westmount Island. Marcus seems oddly interested in the vacant plot of land on the northern tip, and I agree to go with him tomorrow to take a look at it.

"Tell me something you would change about the island if you could."

I'm slightly taken aback by his question; it's not something I've ever been asked before. But my answer is an easy one.

"A library. I would build a library."

Marcus chuckles at my response, but his next question has me even more curious about his reasons for coming to Westmount Island.

"What about stores, a movie theater, cafés. Don't you wish there were more of those?"

I consider that for a moment, before answering carefully.

"Sure, I mean, a little bit. We're a small town with everything we need. But do I wish there were more choices, of course. But the mainland isn't that far away, and whatever we can't get here, we get there." I shrug. "If anything, better ferry service would be nice."

Marcus nods slowly.

"Why are you asking me this?" I say quietly. He doesn't answer right away, and my suspicion that he's part of the potential development team grows. But I'm not brave enough to ask him that outright, so when he avoids the question, I let it go. For now.

"Just curious, that's all."

Eventually we find ourselves on the road heading back to the inn. The sun is slowly beginning its descent, but with it being the end of summer there's still plenty of light. The glow on Marcus's face is incredible; he looks as if he's lit up from within and it takes my breath away. There's still a part of me that feels this entire day has been a dream, and I'll wake up soon. Oh, how I hope that isn't true. I don't ever want to wake up from this, it's more than a dream. A handsome man, captivating and confident, and completely focused on me. It's a fantasy I never let myself indulge in. I'm filled with a deep longing to see that focus redirected to the bedroom, but don't want to appear too forward. Not that I can't tell he wants the same thing, but it feels fast. Oh, who am I kidding? This whole dang day has felt fast! It's crazy to think it was a mere few hours ago that Marcus offered me the rubber band for my wild hair on the ferry. Now here we are, unable to stop touching and holding onto each other. And here I am, already envisioning him naked and in my bed. *Am I a hussy? Is this what being a hussy feels like? Overheated, aroused, and desperate? Because I think I like it...*

When we reach the front steps of the inn, I look around furtively to make sure my sister isn't spying somewhere. Marcus must realize what I'm doing, because he just chuckles.

"Is the coast clear for me to kiss you, or will your sister have a shotgun pointed my way?"

My shoulders droop as I laugh ruefully. "I'm sorry, I should have warned you about her earlier. I hope she didn't give you too hard of a time."

"Not at all. She was the perfect innkeeper, respectful and polite. But I could tell she might have some big sister claws hidden behind the calm demeanor."

I roll my eyes in response. "Yup, sounds about right. Tawny has a hard time accepting that I'm old enough to make my own decisions in life."

He puts his hands in his pockets, and I instantly miss the connection of his arm around me. "So, what's your decision about kissing me?" he asks casually, but with enough heat behind it to make me shiver.

"Oh, I'm definitely on board with that," I say breathlessly.

Marcus grins, and his hands come up to hold my face as his lips swoop down to mine. Just like the first time, this kiss makes my head swim, my heart speed up, and my legs feel weak. He moves his hands down to hold my hips, and I smile against his lips because it feels like he knew I needed him to hold onto me. Our tongues tangle together, and I'm lost to the sensation of his full lips plundering my mouth. I wonder if he can feel my heart race the way I can feel his.

The sound of the inn door opening breaks us apart, and I look up to see Tawny standing there, her arms crossed as she stares at us.

"Hello Ella, Mr. Ryder, I hope you've had a nice afternoon." Her voice is stern, and I roll my eyes at her attempt to intimidate.

"Relax, Tawny. Everything's fine."

Marcus chuckles and pulls me in front of him, my back against his front where I feel the reason for this position. His rock-hard erection is pressing into my lower back, and I stifle a giggle, knowing he's using me to hide it from my sister.

"Hi Tawny, your sister was a wonderful tour guide. I can see why you love the island so much." His answer is perfectly respectable, and I see Tawny's posture relax. Hopefully she can see the happiness I'm sure is written across my face. She nods, and turns to go back inside, with one final parting shot.

"Yes, the island has a lot of appeal...for the right people."

When the door closes behind her, Marcus lets out a long, slow breath.

"Phew, that was intense. Think I passed the sister inspection?"

I turn in his arms and sneak mine around his waist. "I think so."

He looks down at me with a wry grin. "Good. I want her to like me, but not as much as I want you to like me."

"I think...I think I more than like you."

The joy that emanates from him at this is blinding, and I can feel the answering smile stretch across my face as well.

"That's good. Because I more than like you, Ella," he says softly, then leans down and kisses me again. This kiss feels different, like it's been laced with something special, something that feels suspiciously like a different *L* word. Which should feel insane, but doesn't.

When we break apart, I'm relieved to see his chest heaving just as much as mine is. It's a heady feeling to know I affect him as much as he affects me. I feel powerful, seductive, and wanted.

He breathes in and out slowly. "I'm going to walk inside, hopefully avoid your sister, so she doesn't see the raging hard-on you've given me, and go upstairs to take a cold shower before dinner," Marcus says, his forehead resting on mine.

"Enjoy. I'm going to take a hot shower. A really hot one."

Oh, good gravy, he sounded sexy talking about water temperature, and I sound like a total dweeb. But Marcus just chuckles as if he somehow finds my bizarre response amusing. Then he presses a kiss to my forehead and pulls away. I instantly miss the connection of his body against mine.

"I'll be at your door in an hour, beautiful."

I nod and watch him as he gives me one last devastatingly sexy smile, then turns and walks into the inn. I can only hope Tawny isn't lying in wait, ready to pounce on him and give him the third degree. Thinking quickly, I pull out my phone.

ELLA: LEAVE HIM ALONE

TAWNY: For your information, I'm in my office catching up on invoices.

ELLA: Good. I like him Tawny, like, really like.

TAWNY: I can tell. He really likes you too. Just be careful, I don't want my little sister getting hurt, that's all.

I pocket my phone with a smile and turn to walk toward my cottage. I wish Kayla was home, she would be able to help me make sense of these insane feelings. Sometimes I swear she knows me better than I know myself.

Inside, I turn the heat of the shower up high, until steam billows out the top and fills the small bathroom. As I step under the spray, I think of Marcus and his cold shower, which of course leads to thoughts of Marcus naked. Oh great, now I'm squeezing my legs together to try and ease the ache that comes with that mental image.

"Oh, fudge it," I say aloud to my empty bathroom. Then I close my eyes and let my hand travel down my body until it reaches the spot between my legs that is throbbing. I picture Marcus's hand taking over for mine as I play with my clit, rubbing it the way I know will get me off the fastest. I'm not prepared for how quickly my arousal builds as I let myself imagine Marcus in here with me; that it's his hands teasing me. I can almost hear his voice whispering dirty words in my ear and feel the seductive heat of his body against mine. It's not long before my gasps and moans are bouncing off the walls of the shower and my legs are shaking from the intensity of my release.

Once I regain control of my body, although my heart continues to pound for a few more moments, I quickly finish my shower, dry off, massage some honeysuckle scented lotion into my skin and then spend far too long trying to decide what to wear. Part of me wants to dress up, the other part remembers that the plan is burgers on the beach. Eventually I settle on a pair of jean shorts and a light sweater. But I do take the time to blow dry and straighten my hair, hoping that Marcus will be running his hands over the smooth strands later tonight. By the time I'm done, I look at the clock and realize I only have a few minutes before he'll arrive. I race around my bedroom, putting away my wet towels and straightening the pillows on the bed. Just as I finish, there's a knock on my door.

He's here. And something tells me there will be more than just a kiss between us tonight.

6

Marcus

I'm nervous. Why the fuck am I nervous? I just saw Ella an hour ago, yet even after jacking off to thoughts of her in the shower, I'm still fighting a semi in my pants and I'm desperate to see her again.

She is a part of me now, a part I never knew was missing. I probably shouldn't have asked Ella the questions I did; I'm almost positive she's realized why I'm here. Why I don't just come out and admit it, I don't know. Maybe she could help me figure out a plan for the project without destroying the small-town community vibe that already exists here. But I'm too chickenshit to tell her and risk ruining things between us before they actually happen. My time on the island is short; I have a meeting set with Robert next week to discuss my thoughts on moving ahead with the development here.

I guess it's no surprise I'm nervous.

I'm running out of time with Ella. Time I desperately need to try and figure out if these intense feelings are real, or just a momentary flight of insanity. Who the hell am I kidding, this is more real than anything I've ever experienced.

When Ella opens the door to her cottage, she takes my breath away. She's wearing a simple sweater that hangs off one shoulder and jean shorts that show off her long, tanned legs.

"Damn, you look beautiful," I say hoarsely as I reach out and pull her in close so I can kiss her. She giggles, and it's adorable and sexy at the same time.

"Thanks, you look pretty good yourself."

I smile, happy I had the forethought to pack some casual clothes for the weekend. Burgers on the beach wouldn't work in dress pants, so I changed into some shorts and a lightweight Henley.

"Are we driving or walking?" I ask as Ella lays her head down on my shoulder for the short walk over to where my car happens to be parked.

"Driving, but only because I want to sit in that fancy car of yours," she says, her eyes alight with mischief. She giggles again, and the sound is my undoing. Any chance of self control disappears in an instant.

"I want to do more than drive with you in my car," I growl, and spin her around so I can cage her in between the passenger door and my body. Vaguely I realize that a parking lot in front of the inn isn't the most private of locations, but I can't bring myself to care. The heat radiating between us is unmistakable, and her scent, that fucking sweet smell that is my Ella, is tantalizing. "I want to taste you, Ella. Can I do that?" I say in a low rumble. I've clearly rendered her unable to speak, because all she does is nod and I bend my head to lick a swath along her bare shoulder with a groan.

"Fuck, you taste as good as you smell."

Her answering moan is all the permission I need to keep going, so I keep one hand in place on the car beside her head, but let my other hand trail down her side until I reach the hem of her sweater. Slowly I creep my fingers under the fabric to brush against her satin smooth skin. Her arms come around my shoulders to clutch my head, holding it in place as I nuzzle her neck.

"Marcus..." She whispers, then gasps when my hand reaches the lace of her bra. I lightly run my fingertips over her breast, feeling the perfect weight of it, and I smile when I realize her nipples are standing at attention with arousal.

"You like this, don't you, beautiful? You like me touching you and kissing you," I murmur against her skin.

"Oh yes..." she sighs.

In this intimate moment, Ella is the center of my entire world. Everything around us fades away and all I can see, smell, hear, and feel is her. Unfortunately, such a perfect moment can never last, and we're interrupted by the sound of tires on the gravel driveway. I pull back with a groan, feeling the distance between our bodies like a physical ache.

"I suppose we had better go and get those burgers, or this date isn't going to happen." I say reluctantly.

Ella surprises me with her saucy smirk. "Oh, the date would still happen, we would just skip past dinner and go straight to dessert."

And just like that, my cock is seconds away from exploding out of my pants. Her confidence seems to be growing with every minute we're together, and this sexy seductress is just as hot as the shy and nervous woman from before.

"Don't tempt me, woman," I mock growl.

"Sorry, I want a burger first." Ella winks, then she turns and slides into my car, leaving me breathing heavily in the space where she was seconds before.

"Fuck," I sigh as I walk around and climb into my car. I turn it on, enjoying the purr of the engine. This is my favorite sports car to drive, and from the way Ella is looking at it appreciatively, she's enjoying it, too.

"What kind of car is this anyway?"

"Audi R8 Spyder," I answer, then glance over to see her reaction. It's a relatively well-known sportscar and the price tag isn't a secret, either. She's looking at me quizzically.

"You're a mystery, Marcus. With a car like this, I assume you're well-off, and probably live a very different life from me. I just don't understand what it is you see in me."

My heart cracks listening to Ella compare the two of us, as if my bank account affects who I am as a person. My parents raised me better than that and it's time I remember that fact. I pull the car over to the side of the road and turn to face her.

"You're right, beautiful girl, and also oh, so wrong. Yeah, I've got money. But that's a story for another time. But how can you not see that the car I drive or my dollars in the bank mean nothing when it comes to how I feel about you? You should be a stranger, Ella, we just met earlier today. Instead, you feel like someone I've been waiting for my whole life."

I sit, patiently waiting for her response to my heartfelt words. The play of emotion across her face is mesmerizing. She reaches out one hand and her fingers stroke down my cheek, and I can't help but lean into her touch.

"Marcus..." The way she says my name, full of longing, brings peace to my heart. What she says next is whispered so softly I almost miss it.

"I think I've been waiting my whole life for you, too."

We stay like that for a while, gazing at each other, her hand on my cheek and mine on her thigh, gently stroking her warm skin. But then my stomach lets out a loud rumble, reminding me it's been a long time since I wolfed down a sandwich on the ferry, just moments before I met Ella.

"Good gravy, was that a monster or your stomach?" she laughs, and I chuckle right along with her. My hand drifts back to her thigh, and this feels so comfortable, so easy, as if we've been together for years, not mere hours.

The drive to the diner is short and I'm able to get parking right out front. Ella takes my hand as we walk inside, and it feels good that she's not shy about showing me affection. I don't miss the curious glances that come our way and more than one person asks Ella who I am when they come up to chat with her. She evades the question, saying I'm a friend visiting the island, and that does NOT feel so good. I'm much more than just a friend. I want to be everything to her, a partner, a lover, a friend, and eventually a husband. That thought startles me. *Marriage? Where the fuck did that come from…*but now that the idea is in my head, I can't shake it. I can see Ella walking toward me, outside the inn, a flowing white dress, and flowers in her hair. Our guests will chuckle at the story of how we met and even if it might seem fast, they won't be able to deny how perfect we are together. Fast forward and I can see her belly, swollen with our child, glowing with the love that comes from finding your soul mate. Because that's what she is to me. Ella is my soul mate; I know that by the way my body craves her touch and with the way my heart feels as if it belongs to her.

Suddenly her voice trickles into my consciousness. While I've been fantasizing about our future, Ella has been saying something about pickles.

"No, no pickles. Not for me," I say, still somewhat distracted by the vision of her pregnant.

She grins up at me. "Excellent. I hate pickles. So, do you trust me to order the best salmon burger you've ever had?"

I look down at her, and with one hundred percent sincerity, I reply, "I would trust you with anything."

Her smile softens and she goes up on her toes to press a chaste kiss to my lips. "Does that mean I can drive your car?" she murmurs against my lips.

My head falls back with laughter. This woman, she is something else.

When we reach the front of the line, she steps up to place our order. I whip out my black Amex card and quickly hand it over to pay for dinner. The guy running the till raises his eyebrows and looks me up and down, and I realize they probably don't see a lot of those cards here. I give him a nod and turn with Ella to leave.

We take our food outside and I look at the captivating woman beside me.

"Where to, beautiful?"

She gestures dramatically toward the water. "To the beach!" she announces.

We walk down the street, but instead of going to the public beach, Ella leads me down the road a little bit further before taking a small side path with a sign that reads *private property*.

"Umm, Ella, babe, are we allowed here?" I ask.

She giggles at me and shakes her head. Apparently, that was a silly question to ask. "Of course, we are. The locals put that sign up so that tourists wouldn't come here. We don't bother with the public beach during tourist season; this is the secret beach." She wiggles her eyebrows at me, and I don't know if she's trying to be seductive, but it just looks amusing to me, so I chuckle.

"Alright, lead on."

A moment later, the path opens up onto a stretch of beach with soft, pale sand and large logs providing perfect spots to relax.

"Damn, I forgot a blanket," Ella pouts. "We'll just have to sit on a log to eat. It won't be as comfy as the sand, but oh well."

"I don't plan on being here long enough to worry about a comfortable seat because someone said something about dessert," I reply. Her intake of breath is full of anticipation and arousal, and if I wasn't salivating from the aroma of those burgers, I'd turn her around and march her back to my car, speed the entire way back to the inn, and have my way with her. *Do I really need to eat?* I answer my own question with another loud rumble from my stomach.

We both chuckle at that and find a log to sit on. The view is spectacular from this beach. The blue water of the ocean stretches on for miles. I can hear seagulls in the distance and the gentle sound of waves lapping the shore. It's probably the most tranquil setting I've been to in years, and the press of Ella's leg against mine only adds to the perfection of the moment.

For a while, the silence is broken only by the sounds of us eating our burgers. Ella's little moans and sounds of enjoyment are doing things to me that should be illegal, and she doesn't even realize it. *She's mine...* the thought crosses my mind and feels familiar. We just met, but she's as necessary to my survival as the air I breathe.

I take the last bite of the best salmon burger I've ever had, crumple the wrapper, and toss it into the paper bag they came in. I brush my hands off on my legs and turn to Ella, only to let out a groan at the sight of her licking her fingers one by one.

"Fuck, woman. That's...fuck," I say hoarsely.

She winks at me impishly as she sucks one more finger, letting it go with a pop.

"That's it, dinner's over."

I stand up, grab her hand, and pull her to stand against my body. I press my erection into her hips, and she answers with a wiggle of hers, which of course only serves to harden my cock even more. Unable to resist holding her anymore, I bend down and lift her up into my arms. When her legs wrap around my waist, I start to walk towards the path – or at least where I think the path is. It's hard to see, given my eyes are closed as I kiss her deeply.

Ella is smart enough to break our kiss after a moment and moves her lips over to my ear. She whispers softly, "Take me home, Marcus."

I don't waste another second, spying the trail in the trees and striding purposely toward it. Once we're at the road, she wiggles, and I let her down reluctantly. But when she tucks close into my side, I smile. She's not getting far away from me ever again if I can help it. Does that make me sound like a caveman? Maybe. Do I care? Not at all.

We reach my car within minutes; one benefit to a small town, I suppose. If I'm being honest, this place is starting to charm me, and it's not just because of Ella. There's something nice about the slower pace, the friendliness of knowing your neighbors, and the quiet beauty of the island. I can see why Robert wants to build a development here and I think it could work. If it's done right.

But all thoughts of work, Robert, and the development disappear when I park in front of Ella's cottage. It's charming, with a front yard full of flowers, light blue shutters on the windows, and a cobblestone path leading to the front door. I notice these details this time, whereas earlier when I picked her up, I was so focused on seeing her again I was oblivious to anything around me. Now, even knowing what's about to happen between us, I'm so much more aware of everything. It's as if Ella has opened my eyes to how much I've been missing in life these last few years. I see clearly now; I know what I want and what I need, and she's standing beside me, unlocking the door to her house, and inviting me in. I just hope she's also inviting me into her heart.

Inside, Ella walks around, turning on some lamps to bathe the room in a soft glow. I take in the textures and feel of her house; it feels like her. Warm, happy, and peaceful. It's more than a house, it's a home. Books line almost every surface, making me smile. My girl obviously loves to read, so her library comment earlier makes a lot more sense now. She turns to me, and the light behind her gives a halo effect that makes her look like the angel I'm beginning to believe she really is.

"So..."

Her voice is an aching combination of lust and nerves. My sole purpose becomes wanting to erase her nerves and satisfy our lust.

I prowl over to her and place my hands on her hips.

"So."

She licks her lips and my restraint snaps. My hands tighten as my lips plunder hers. Her kiss is like a drug, and I need another hit, then another. Our tongues tangle together, and the fire between us explodes into an inferno. When I feel Ella's hands crawl under my shirt, I reach one hand behind my head to pull it off. The flare of desire in her eyes is incredible, and I force myself to hold back and let her explore my body with her hands and her eyes. Her featherlight touch drifts over the phoenix tattoo on my pec, then travels down the smattering of hair that leads to the top of my shorts. But when she goes to undo the button, I stop her.

"Not yet, Ella. I need to see you first."

My voice sounds hoarse, laden with arousal. I check her face, and when I see no sign of hesitation, I let my hands skim up the sides of her body, pulling her sweater off. My first glimpse of her luscious curves and I'm a goner. Her nipples are erect behind her bra, straining to be free, and I can feel my cock straining just as hard. My head bends down of its own volition and I tug her lace covered nipple between my teeth gently. When Ella moans, and her hands clutch at my hair, I continue licking, sucking, and lightly nipping at her breasts, alternating from one side to the other and using my hand to caress the one not being tormented by my mouth.

"Oh God, Marcus," she moans, then she surprises me by reaching behind her back and unsnapping her bra, letting it fall away. Her eyes are burning into mine like fire, as I quirk a smile at her.

"That was my job."

"You were taking too long."

With that, Ella jumps into my arms, my hands reaching instantly around her body to cup her to me. Her legs squeeze my hips tightly as I stumble backward, vaguely remembering there was a couch somewhere near by. When I feel it at the back of my legs, I sit down. Ella is still straddling my lap, grinding her hips into mine. My hands travel up the expanse of her bare legs, wanting to feel more of her, but still wanting her to choose the pace. My prayers are answered when she shifts slightly and runs her hands down to where our bodies meet. She deftly unbuttons my shorts and sneaks her hand in to graze my rigid cock.

"Fuck, baby," I moan, then flip her over so she's laying with her back on the couch. Her eyes are filled with a fire that I know is reflected in my own. My lips and hands trail down her tanned stomach until I reach the top of her shorts. With one quick look up at her face to make sure those nerves have disappeared, I unzip her shorts and slide them down her legs, taking the scrap of lace she's wearing underneath with them.

"Shit. You're gorgeous, Ella. Is all this for me?" I run my finger through her glistening folds, inhaling her scent like it's the most precious perfume.

"Yes..." she moans in response, as her hands clutch my shoulders.

I don't need anymore encouragement as I lower my head and let my tongue sweep along her sex. She's drenched for me and the taste of her fills my senses. Two more swipes and she's moaning and writhing underneath me. I hold her hips in place with my hands and lose myself in devouring her. Every lick, nibble, and suck is driving me crazy, and she's so responsive that when I slide a finger inside of her core, I can feel her throbbing around me already.

"Marcus, I'm going to...Oh God, Marcus!" She cries out as her release floods through her. I continue to worship her until every last drop is gone and her body has relaxed. Fuck, she's the most beautiful thing I've ever seen, but when she climaxes, I'm pretty sure the world stops turning.

I lift myself over her, propping onto my elbows on either side of her as I pepper kisses along her neck. Her eyes are closed, and her chest is still heaving from her orgasm. Eventually her arms drape across my back and her lips find mine. We kiss for a while and I can't deny it's fucking hot as hell she doesn't mind that her essence is still all over me. She's as lost to the passion between us as I am.

This time when her hands go to unbutton my shorts, I let her, and even help to ease them off my legs. Her small hand finds my rock-hard cock and gives it a stroke, which feels so goddamn good I drop my forehead to her shoulder and try to hold onto some self-control.

"You feel so fucking good, Ella," I groan.

She purrs in satisfaction as her hand continues to work me up and down. I have to pull away before too long, or I know I'll embarrass myself. Reaching down, I grab a condom out of the pocket of my shorts that are on the floor. When I rip open the packet, Ella sits up and takes it from me, eyeing me seductively as she rolls it down my length.

I close my eyes and just let my head drop back, trying to think of anything that will slow down my own orgasm that is thundering towards me way too quickly. I want this to last, I want it to be the best sex Ella's ever had, and my traitorous cock is trying to ruin that with how eager it is to hit the finish line.

But all hope is lost when Ella lays back down and guides my cock to her hot entrance. All I can do is stare into her eyes, into forever, as I slowly slide in. She's tight, squeezing my length, and it feels amazing. She tilts her head up for a kiss as I begin to move, slowly, in and out. Her legs are wrapped around my back, holding me close. For a moment, all I can hear is the rhythmic sound of our bodies coming together. It's a fucking symphony to my ears. Pun intended.

Ella meets me thrust for thrust, and our breaths mingle together. The feeling of being inside her and this intimate connection; it feels like I'm home. Like I'm right where I am meant to be. But my sentimental thoughts flee when I feel Ella start to hold me even tighter, her nails raking down my back. Her moans are getting higher in pitch, and I know instinctively she's close. My lips find her neck, her shoulder, and I let out a curse as I feel her pulse around me.

"Fly with me, baby," is all I have to say before she lets go with a keening cry, into the most spectacular orgasm I have ever seen. My own release hurtles toward me at light speed, and with one last grunt I thrust into her, letting go of everything I am. I just barely catch myself before I collapse on top of her. Instead I roll to the side, bringing her with me. She sighs and nuzzles into my chest.

"I've never felt like that before," she whispers quietly.

I press a kiss to the top of her head.

"Me neither."

"Can we do it again?"

And that goes down as the moment in time I realized I was head over heels in love with Ella Michaels.

7

Ella

I'm slowly transitioning from asleep to awake, wrapped in a blanket of muscular heat. Marcus's legs are tangled with mine, and I can feel his heart beat strongly beneath my ear, and the gentle in and out of his breath against my hair. I'm pretty sure he's still asleep, so I stay still and just enjoy feeling safe, protected and loved.

Wait. Love? Where the fudge did that come from? But it's true. Even with my limited experience I'm pretty sure what we did last night was more than just sex. It felt like we were making love. Just thinking about all the incredible ways he made me come has me squeezing my legs together in anticipation. Marcus made me feel like the sexiest woman on the planet. He responded to me and met my needs as if I were made for him. Four, or was it five, orgasms later, I am one happy lady. And tired. So tired. Who knew marathon sex was exhausting?! Oh, right, I guess anyone who has actually *had* marathon sex would know that. Silly me.

Marcus takes a deep breath, and starts to move, his arms tightening around me. I look up at him and even though his eyes are closed, I know he's awake because there's a smile creeping across his handsome face.

"Morning, beautiful," he rumbles, and good gravy, does this man ever have a delicious morning voice.

"Morning," I reply, and of course my voice is nothing more than a squeak.

Marcus doesn't seem to mind, however, as he twists his body, tugging me on top of him. My hair falls down around us like a messy curtain, and he reaches up his hands to push it away from my face. The look in his eyes when he gazes up at me is like a shot of adrenaline to my heart, making it race double time. If that's not a look of love, then I don't know what is. I feel breathless. This man has literally taken my breath away. He's so gorgeous, so sexy, so perfect. And he's mine.

Mine...

I climb off of him, secretly loving his groan of disappointment, and try to sway my hips seductively, although I'm pretty sure it just comes across looking ridiculous as I walk into the bathroom. From the doorway, I turn back, and I'm pretty sure my mouth falls open at the sight of Marcus sitting up in my bed, the blanket pooled around his hips. His hair is mussed from sleep, he's got a light stubble on his face, and he is without a doubt the most delicious man I have ever seen.

Something comes over me. That secret inner vixen I didn't know I had.

"I'm going to take a quick shower. Join me? You can wash my back..."

He shoots me a wolfish grin, then launches out of my bed, grabbing me around the waist, and carrying me into the bathroom.

Then he proceeds to make me feel oh so dirty before we finally get clean.

A girl could get used to this...

* * *

Our drive to the north end of the island is quiet, but it's a happy kind of quiet. The kind that happens when you're so comfortable with someone, there's no need to fill the silence. Marcus's hand is resting on my leg, his thumb gently moving back and forth. Even though his hand is down by my knee, the movement is still sending shivers down my spine, as I imagine him sliding his hand upward. The sexual chemistry between us is off the charts. I never dreamed this feeling could exist outside of a romance novel, but here I am, falling for a man who is a generous lover, sexy as sin, and apparently rich.

I direct him to park at a trailhead that will take us part way up the face of West Mountain (I know, we're so creative with our geography names on the island), and should give him a good view of the coastline and the property down there. It's land that the residents on the island have often talked about developing to try and bring more people here, but no one has the money or expertise to make that a reality.

Once we are on the trail, Marcus takes my hand, lacing our fingers together. On impulse I say, "Let's play twenty questions."

He looks at me quizzically. "Okay."

"I'll go first. What's your middle name?"

He chuckles and shakes his head before he answers, "Owen, after my grandfather. My turn. Have you ever thought about living somewhere other than the island?"

Okay then, I guess he's skipping the easy questions and going straight for the big ones.

"Not really, I love it here. It's my home. I lived on the mainland for college and hated how busy it was." I don't miss his wince when I say this and suddenly it dawns on me. He lives on the mainland. If I'm over here, and he's over there, what kind of future can we possibly have? My heart drops into my feet, and we are both silent for a moment.

Eventually, I try to bring things back to a happier frame of mind. "Are you a dog person or a cat person?"

"Dog, definitely dog. But only if it's a big one. Small dogs don't count."

I smile at that; I've always felt the same way. "Agreed. Someday I really want a Great Dane."

He squeezes my hand gently, and I see his lips quirk up.

"What's your favorite color?"

I giggle, "Couldn't you tell from my bedroom? Yellow."

He stops and turns to me, and there's a hunger in his eyes. "I wasn't paying attention to your bedroom décor when we were in there. I only saw you."

Wowza. Suddenly I'm hot, like burning hot on the inside. And it's not from the hike. Marcus turns to face forward and starts to walk again, and I stumble to catch up. He's muttering under his breath, but I can just make out what he's saying.

"...too goddamn sexy."

He's talking about me. He thinks the kindergarten teacher who replaces curse words with food names, and is addicted to reading, is sexy. Holy shiitake. I mean, he's made that fact abundantly clear with his actions, but it still blows my mind. I don't think I've ever been called sexy before and I certainly have never felt that way. Until Marcus.

"Favorite sexual position," I blurt out.

But instead of answering, Marcus growls and turns, pulling me into his body so I can feel the rigid length of his cock pressing against me.

"Woman, you're making this hike very uncomfortable."

Then he kisses me. No, he devours me. I'm lost to the desire pulsating between us and it's a real struggle to remember we're in the middle of a hiking trail where other people or wildlife could come across us at any moment. It's not the time or place to strip him down and have my way with him, no matter how much I want to.

We break apart, both breathing heavily. Marcus leans his forehead to rest against mine and says, "My favorite position is any that involves touching you."

I've got no sassy comeback to that; I'm too busy blushing and trying to tamp down my arousal. Thankfully, during the rest of the hike we both manage to keep the questions light and easy, not sexual or serious. But I know this is my chance to find out why he's here and what his plans are.

Once we're at the lookout, we drop down on the bench someone built there years ago. The view is spectacular; you can see the north side of the island all the way to the coastline and simply vast ocean beyond that. I love this view, it's so different from what you see down at the wharf in town.

After we've both had some water, I decide to take the plunge and ask the questions I've been holding inside all day.

"Why did you want to see this part of the island, Marcus? Why are you on Westmount Island?"

He stills, staring straight ahead to the ocean. I try not to fidget nervously as I wait for him to answer, but the suspense is killing me.

Eventually, he takes a deep breath and turns on the bench to face me.

"I own a venture capital firm. I invest in small companies or go into a financial partnership with other people on large projects. One of my partners, Robert, is a property developer, and he wants to build a community of luxury cottages on the island. He was meant to come this weekend and check it out, but couldn't, so I agreed to come instead."

I digest this information, trying to figure out what it is about what he said that doesn't feel right in my gut. I should be ecstatic about this; a property developer interested in the island is exactly what we want.

"So, you're super rich and you partner with people on their projects? And your partner wants to build on the island?" I realize how simplistic my questions sound as soon as I say them, but I'm struggling to understand why it was such a big deal to tell me this.

Marcus chuckles, but it sounds hollow to my ears, not like the warm laugh he normally gives me.

"Yeah, I'm super rich. And yes, I help other people. But, Ella, this project..." he trails off and turns to the ocean for a moment. "I'm not so sure it's going to make the locals happy. At least, not if it's done the way Robert wants to."

"Okay..." I say, my mind still spinning. "You're worried we won't want new people to move here and invest in our economy and build our community? Because I can tell you, that's exactly what we *do* want." I'm still missing something, I can tell. How is it a bad thing that his friend wants to invest in our island?

"Ella, the community Robert has envisioned doesn't exactly fit with the small-town vibe you've got going on here. The kind of people he wants to attract, they won't be interested in salmon burgers from Seas The Day or talking to Mr. Thompson on the sidewalk. They're more interested in privacy, gourmet grocery stores, five-star restaurants, and luxury amenities. What Robert wants to build would destroy everything that makes Westmount Island amazing."

"Oh."

I'm starting to see the problem. Marcus thinks the island is too quaint, which also means slow and quiet. Part of me worries he's not just thinking of the development when he says this, he also means it's too quiet for him.

Marcus hops off the bench and comes to crouch down between my legs. His beautiful blue eyes pierce my soul as he settles his hands on my legs.

"I mean it when I say the island is amazing, Ella. And I don't just think that because of you, although you are a big part of that." He smiles softly at me, and I can't help but smile back. "But Robert won't see it that way. I'm going to try and convince him to change his plan, but I don't know if I'll be able to. And I have to go back to the mainland in a few days to meet with him." His voice goes quiet at the end, and I get the sense he didn't want to bring that up.

He's leaving. I knew this was coming, but it still hits me like a ton of bricks. I lean down to run my fingers through his hair, trying to push away the feeling that I've lost him already. He's right here in front of me, yet it feels like he's already gone. The reality of how different we are, how different our lives are, comes crashing down around me.

Marcus must sense my mounting sadness because he rears up, sits down on the bench, and pulls me into his lap. He strokes my hair, and I fight back tears. We sit that way for several moments until Marcus finally speaks.

"I don't want to leave you, Ella. You're everything to me. I'll come back, I promise."

All I can do is nod into his chest as the tears finally spill down my cheeks.

8

Ella

The hike down the mountain is a lot more subdued than the hike up. And the drive back to my cottage isn't filled with the comfortable silence of this morning. No, what's between us now feels heavy.

Marcus parks in front of the inn, not my cottage, and my heart plummets even further. Is this it? Is this already the end?

"I didn't want to presume I could come over..." he starts, and I cut him off with a kiss. He clutches me close, as if he, too, is scared that whatever is between us is over.

"Please presume, please. I need you. For as long you're here, I need you." I don't care if it sounds like I'm begging. All I know is, I'm not ready to say goodbye to this man. I want him close to me for as much time as possible.

He looks at me with such burning desire, I think I may combust into flames. Then with a sharp nod, he puts his car back in gear and drives the short distance to my cottage. Once there, we both leap out of the car, leaving our backpacks from the hike behind. I hurry to unlock my cottage door, Marcus's hands already roaming my body as he stands against my back. Inside, it becomes a whirlwind of clothing coming off and our bodies coming together. Marcus sweeps me up into his arms and carries me to my bedroom, where he lays me down on the bed and settles himself beside me. For a moment, we lay there, hands exploring each other, eyes staring straight into each other's souls. But the stillness doesn't last long before Marcus growls and pulls me underneath him. I wrap my legs around him and reach my hand down to grab his cock, but he stops me.

"Let me love you, baby."

It's the first time either one of us has said the word love, and even though he isn't saying he loves *me*, I feel it just the same. I nod, and he strokes some hair out of my face before moving down my body, peppering my skin with gentle kisses. When he reaches my breasts, my arousal spikes as he teases my nipples with his hands and his mouth. I never knew it was possible to come so close to orgasm from a man playing with my breasts, but fudge, am I close. I need more, though, and Marcus must know this because he continues down, swirling his tongue around my belly button and over my hip bones. His hands travel down my legs and back up, lifting them over his shoulders as he goes. His big hands cup my ass and draw me to his mouth. My eyes flutter closed as he sucks my clit into his mouth, and I climb higher and higher toward what seems an impossible peak. The heat from his mouth, sealed over my sex is making me burn from the inside out and my hips start to move. I move my hands from grabbing the sheets to hold onto his shoulders, holding him right where I need him. All sense of reality disappears when Marcus slides two fingers inside of me. He twists and turns, before he curls them over to hit that perfect spot, and I fly.

As I slowly regain an awareness of my surroundings, the first thing I notice is that Marcus is lying beside me again, and his fingers are drawing patterns across my stomach. The next thing I notice is his rock-hard cock, poking me in the hip. I roll over onto my side to kiss him, trying to pour everything I'm feeling into that kiss. Then, without saying a word, I gently push him onto his back, and make my way down to grab his cock in my hands. I lean down, and swirl my tongue over the tip, eliciting a groan from Marcus. I glance up, to see him watching me, a fierce gleam in his eye. I maintain eye contact as I open my mouth and take him in as far as I can go.

"Fuck," he growls, as his head falls back against the pillow.

I take that as an invitation to continue and begin to work him up and down with my tongue and my hands. He's so big, I can't get all of him in my mouth. But I run my tongue up and down his length, loving the silky smooth texture of his skin. So much softness covering so much hardness. I want to make him feel as amazing as he made me feel, so even when he tries to lift me off, I just shake my head at him and carry on.

Moments later, I feel him grow even bigger in my mouth.

"God, fucking shit, Ella, I'm going to come."

Secretly I love the fact that he can't seem to form a sentence right now. And when he does let go, I swallow his release down, and continue to suck until every drop is gone and he's lying on the bed, arms flopped to the side, panting.

I prowl up the bed, licking my lips with satisfaction. That felt good. I've never felt such power in the bedroom before, but bringing him such pleasure has me feeling on top of the world.

It's my turn to run my fingers up and down the ridges of his abs, as he slowly comes down from the high of his orgasm. Eventually, he turns his head toward me.

"Ella. That was fucking spectacular."

I don't hold back my giggle at the awe in his voice. Which apparently turns him on, because Marcus gives me a wicked grin, before pulling me on top of him. He's hard again already, which astounds me since I always figured guys needed time to recover. But apparently not Marcus, given what I can feel between my legs. He reaches a hand over to my bedside table where I put the strip of condoms that I found in my bathroom this morning. He tears one off and hands it to me silently. I don't waste any time rolling it down his cock, lifting up my hips, and sinking down on top of him with a moan of satisfaction.

"Yes..." I sigh, as my hands travel over his torso. His muscles flex underneath me as he thrusts up into my throbbing core. Slowly we find our rhythm, rocking together. Every time his cock hits me deep inside, I feel it like he's branding himself on me. Marking me as his. I want this feeling to last forever, this completeness that comes only from being connected to him so intensely.

"Shit. Ella. Fuck me, baby." Marcus's dirty words make me gasp. My hips start to move faster, until I'm bouncing up and down on him. My hands fall down to his chest, and he grabs my ass, holding so tightly I'm sure I'll see the evidence of it in the morning. But I don't care. Let the bruises be one more memory of our passion.

Out of nowhere, I feel the blood rush to my clit, and I start to pant, knowing my orgasm is close.

"Marcus, fuck, Marcus!" I scream his name as I come, and his answering groan tells me he's right there with me.

It's not until later, after we've cleaned up and are spooning in my bed, that he speaks.

"You said fuck, Ella."

I giggle, which turns into a snort, and then full on laughter for both of us.

"What can I say, you must be a bad influence."

His laughter dies out and I hear Marcus breathe in and out deeply before he replies.

"You're the best influence on me."

* * *

ELLA

When I wake up the next morning, I know he's gone before I even open my eyes. I'm cold without his arms around me, and my bed holds only a faint whiff of his tantalizing scent. Even as I try to convince myself he must have just gone to the inn for fresh clothes or something, I know better. Somehow, I know he's left the island.

I climb out of bed and tie my robe around me, before making my way to the kitchen to turn on the kettle for some tea. Only then do I notice the piece of paper next to a mug already prepared with my favorite tea ready to be steeped.

Sweet Ella,

I hate that I'm leaving you with a note. It feels cruel and so much less than you deserve. But I couldn't bring myself to wake you last night.

I got a call from home, a work emergency I have to attend to immediately. My assistant chartered a plane for me and I had to leave before the sun was up. I'm so sorry babe.

I will come back, as soon as I can. I won't say when, because I refuse to make a promise I can't keep. But I will be back for you, Ella. That I <u>do</u> promise.

There's so much I want to say to you, but a note is not the right place.

Keep me with you, beautiful.

M

I don't realize I'm crying until the first tear drops onto the paper, blurring the M at the bottom. I quickly wipe my face, and put the note down, not wanting to make it worse. I have so many questions, but no way to get the answers. Then I realize Marcus also wrote his phone number. I want to call him right away, but don't. He's dealing with something urgent, or so his note says. I don't want to be the needy girl who interrupts him just to hear his voice, no matter how badly I want to hear it.

The whistling kettle pierces through the growing fog of sadness I can feel blanketing me. Was it really only thirty-six hours that I had with

Marcus? It felt like a lifetime. Or rather, it felt like he has always been a part of my life, just waiting in the wings for the right time to appear. And now he's gone, and I honestly don't know what to do. I thought we still had some time together, at least a few days, and we could have talked about what was happening and our plans to be together. Instead, I have a note and a promise that he'll be back eventually.

I pour my tea and wander out to my back porch. Even wrapped in a cozy quilt, sitting on my swing staring out at the view that normally fills me with joy, I'm sad. I miss him, more than I thought was possible to miss someone. It's different from the way I miss my parents; their death had such a finality to it that once I had moved through the acute grief of losing them, I settled into a place of acceptance. This loss, Marcus leaving, I can't accept it. I'm holding onto the thread of hope from his note that he'll be back. Won't he?

I can hear my phone beeping inside the cottage. I debate ignoring it, but curiosity wins out, and I go to retrieve it. There's a message from Tawny.

TAWNY: Hey little sister. Your guy checked out early this morning, are you okay?

Her sweet concern brings a fresh wave of tears to my eyes. Even my overprotective big sister has guessed that Marcus is important to me. I wish my twin was here, but I can't even get Kayla on the phone. She finished her job in Alaska and immediately took off to Africa for another assignment. I miss her and right now I wish she was here.

ELLA: Not really. He left me a note, it says he'll be back when he can. But I didn't even get a chance to say goodbye.

TAWNY: Oh, Ella. Want me to come over with muffins?

ELLA: No, I kind of want to be alone.

TAWNY: Okay, but I'm coming to check on you this afternoon.

I put my phone down and turn to go back outside, but it rings. Without looking at the screen, I answer, assuming it's Tawny.

ELLA

"You can check on me after lunch, T. Get back to work and leave me alone to wallow."

Instead of Tawny's voice, a rich chuckle fills my ear.

"Oh, beautiful. Don't wallow, please. Leaving you was the hardest thing I've ever done."

"Marcus," I breathe, and my heart speeds up again. I take the phone out onto the porch and climb back under my blanket.

"I miss you."

I hear his sigh of regret through the phone.

"Ella, I miss you, too. So much. Which is insane, since I just saw you a couple of hours ago. But I do, baby. I'm so sorry I had to leave like that, but shit hit the fan over here with one of my other investments and I need to fix things."

I settle into my chair and cup my hot tea in my hands. Hearing his voice is calming me already, but also making me miss him fiercely.

"I understand. I hate it, but I understand. I just wish we had more time together."

"Me too. Trust me, heads are gonna roll for this. I was meant to be on the island until at least tomorrow night. There's so much I want to say to you..." his voice trails off, but I can read between the lines.

"I know. Me too."

"Ella, I lo..."

"No," I interrupt. "Don't say it on the phone, please. If you're going to say what I hope you're going to say, I need you in front of me when you do. Wait until you come back to me. Because if I can't kiss you, I'll go crazy."

He lets out a huff, but doesn't finish those three words.

"Okay. But just because I'm not saying it doesn't mean I don't feel it. Trust me on that."

I smile, even though he can't see me. Already I can feel my sadness leaving. This man is crazy about me and I'll be darned if we let a little distance tear apart what we've started to build.

9

Marcus

It's been two days since I stole away from Ella in the early morning. Two days of jacking off to memories of her in the shower, texting her all day, and video calls whenever possible. Two days of mounting stress at work as I bust my ass to help one of the companies that I am invested in to figure out a massive security breach. Thank fuck for my connections, because we're able to stem the leak before they obtain anything too sensitive, but now we're dealing with scared shareholders and plummeting stock. Not ideal conditions for my return on investment.

All I want is to finish shit up here and get back to the island. I need to see Ella, to feel her in my arms, and to tell her how much I love her. Two days with her was not enough; forever will not be enough. I need an eternity with that woman, worshiping and loving her.

What really surprises me after being back on the mainland is how much I miss the peace and quiet of the island. The noise and fast pace never used to bother me, but Ella has opened my eyes to more than just love. I see how slowing down and enjoying life can make it worth living to the fullest. I miss the friendliness of Wharf Street; fuck, I even miss that damn salmon burger. But most of all, I miss her.

So, when I'm not working, or talking to Ella, I'm putting plans in place that will change everything about the way I live my life and conduct my business. I just hope Ella is open to it all, because without her, life means nothing. I meet with Robert and tell him my honest opinion – that what he wants to create will not work on the island. He surprises me by accepting my opinion, and even confides in me that he had his doubts about Westmount being the right location for his community. We agree to stay in touch as he goes back on the hunt for a different property. Meanwhile, I've got my own ideas brewing. Ideas that could revitalize Westmount Island in the best possible way. But I'll need an expert, a local islander who is passionate about their home to help me. Good thing I've fallen in love with someone who fits that description perfectly.

On our next video call, Ella is full of excitement about the upcoming school year. She really loves her job and it shows.

"It's just going to be such a small class, only fifteen this year. Every year my class gets smaller and smaller, but that means I can do some different projects with them, I suppose."

She's been telling me about her plans for her class the last few minutes, and I'm just enjoying the melodic sound of her voice.

"...back before school starts?" There's a hesitancy in her voice and I realize I've missed the first part of what she said. It doesn't take a genius to guess what she's asking, however, and I wince at the fact that I don't have an answer for her. She must see that on my face, because her pretty face falls.

"I wish I knew, beautiful. Things are still pretty shaky over here. I've got meetings the next couple of days, then after that we'll see. I hope I can get back to you soon. It's killing me not being able to touch you."

Ella sighs, and the look on her face kills me.

"Me too. Do you ever..." She stops and fidgets with her hands. Suddenly I'm really fucking nervous.

"Do I ever what, baby?"

Her eyes drop down to her lap, then back to me, and even through the screen I can see tears shining in them. Damn it, I wish I was there.

"Ella, talk to me. Please don't cry," I beg.

She sniffs, and I smile because it's fucking adorable. But what she whispers to me next breaks my heart.

"Do you ever wonder if those few days were just a dream? I mean obviously not a real dream, but like a fantasy dream. Of course it was real because we were both there, but now you're gone and it all feels like it was some perfect, amazing dream. But maybe I sound crazy; I feel fudging crazy right now."

She's rambling again. Shit. She told me she only rambles when she's nervous. I lean forward and try desperately to let my love come through in my words.

"It was a dream come true, beautiful. A perfect, amazing, out of this world couple of days that was the start of a lifetime full of dreams coming true."

"A dream come true," she murmurs, and there's a small smile on her face now.

"Yes. You are all of my dreams come true, Ella. And I'll prove it to you as soon as I get back there."

Her soft sigh sounds peaceful this time and I feel my shoulders sag in relief. I lean back against my chair. It's almost nine o'clock at night, I should be at home. No, I should be with Ella. I run my hands through my hair, so fucking pissed that I'm not with her.

"Hey, Marcus," she says softly and I sit up and look at her face through my computer screen. "Could we, I mean, I've never, but..." There's a different tone to her voice now. Her cheeks are flushed, and she bites her lip. She's nervous, but there's desire laced through it. Suddenly, I think I know what my beautiful girl is suggesting.

"What are you wearing, Ella?" I ask in a low voice, as I start to unbutton my shirt. I'm rewarded with a gasp from Ella and her cheeks flush.

"Just my pajamas," she replies, then pans her phone down so I can see the thin tank and panties she's wearing. I groan.

"Fuck, Ella. I'm hard just looking at you, baby."

"I want you so badly, Marcus," she whimpers.

"I'm right here," I growl. I push my chair back slightly before I unbutton my pants. As soon as my dick is free, I groan from the relief.

"Marcus..." she whispers, and I see her hand sliding down her body, and disappearing beneath her panties.

"Touch yourself, Ella. Imagine it's me touching you. It's my fingers playing with your clit, sliding through your folds."

My voice sounds hoarse to my own ears as my hand grasps my cock and begins to slide up and down. The friction is intense, there's nothing to use for lube in my office, but I don't care. My discomfort is the penance I have to pay for not being with Ella right now.

The sight of her, writhing on her bed in the low light, her hair spread beneath her, her eyes closed, just about has me losing control. But I refuse to come before she does.

"Pinch your clit baby, and slide a finger inside. Remember how high you fly when it's my mouth between your legs, when I claim you with my cock."

"Oh God, Marcus," she cries out. Damn, she's so responsive. I can feel the inferno building inside of me and judging by the way Ella is breathing heavily, she's almost there.

"Let me see you come, baby," I ground out the words as my body betrays me and my orgasm hits me like a freight train. My release is warm in my hands; it's been a while since I jacked off anywhere other than the shower and I forgot what a mess it can be. But that can wait, because I'm glued to my screen where Ella is crying out my name like a chant as her body detonates.

"Christ, that was beautiful," I moan, as she slowly blinks her eyes and smiles at me. "The only thing that would've made it better is if I was there with you, instead of miles away."

I regret the words as soon as I say them, because the bliss that was on her face falls away, to be replaced with a longing that I feel, too.

"I wish you knew when you were coming back," she says sorrowfully, and I want to hit something for making her sad again.

"I'm going to try and figure it out tomorrow, I promise." And I vow to myself that I will have an answer for her. I have to get back there before she decides what we have isn't worth the pain. I want to tell her that I'm trying to find a way to move there, but I also don't want to get her hopes up just yet. There are still a few pieces of business I have to tie up before I can make the move.

Ella sighs, then I watch her snuggle under her blanket. She's in her bed, and I'm still at my office. Our opposite locations are a stark reminder of how different our lives are and I have to struggle to push down the worry that she won't accept my lifestyle – even if I move to the island. She hates the city and I have to be here often. Socializing and making connections are part of my job, and I want her by my side. But she's a quiet, small-town kindergarten teacher. Will she be able to meet me halfway? An idea comes to me. A way to see Ella and find out if she can handle being in my world, too.

"Why don't you hop on the ferry and come over here for a couple of days? You can stay in my apartment while I'm at work, or do whatever, and then we would have the evenings together. I've got an event tomorrow night and I would love to have my beautiful girl with me." I hope I don't sound too eager, but it suddenly feels like there's a lot riding on her answer.

She chews her lip for a moment and I don't know if it's a good or bad thing that she isn't answering me right away. Eventually, she does and while it's not the answer I wanted, I can accept it.

"I would love to come and see you, and your life, but I can't this week. I'm sorry, there's just too much to do to get ready for school starting up."

I push back my disappointment and plaster on a smile. At least she would have been willing, I think.

"No worries, babe. It's not a good time, I get that. I just miss you."

Her smile softens, "I miss you, too. If I could come, I would. Please trust me on that."

I nod. "I believe you, Ella. Besides, without you here to distract me, maybe I can finish up my work faster and get back to you sooner."

Ella yawns, then smiles at me sleepily. "That sounds good. Really good."

Her eyes are fluttering closed and she's close to dozing off.

"Sweet dreams, baby. I hope you dream of us."

"Night, Marcus..."

My screen goes dark and I'm left sitting at my desk with my shirt and pants undone, my hands still sticky from the hottest phone sex ever and my heart aching for Ella.

10

Ella

Ten days. That's how long it's been since I saw Marcus. Every day that passes without knowing when he will come back makes the memory of the time we spent together blurrier. My body remembers his touch, my heart remembers the emotion he stirred up in me, but my gosh darn brain is starting to question it all. I mean, really, who falls in love in just a day and a half?

It's a good thing I'm so busy getting ready for school to start, or I would be one big mopey ball of crazy. As it is, Tawny has started popping up wherever I am. I know she's lying when she says it's coincidence. She's checking up on me, making sure I'm not completely losing it.

Marcus said he would never make a promise he couldn't keep and he promised me he would tell me when he was coming back. The look of regret on his face when he had to admit he still didn't have an answer for me was both reassuring and soul destroying. I could tell he truly hated that he couldn't say what his plans are, but a part of me was heartbroken that this is our reality – him on the mainland, buried in work, and me committed to the island and the life I have here. I've even started to question if I could handle living in the city if it meant being with Marcus. But the truth is, I'm not brave enough to uproot my life and go somewhere I know I'll be miserable, for a man I've only spent a day and a half with. I'm no longer confident enough in what we have to know without a doubt that moving for him would be worth it.

What if our connection was only meant to last those two days? What if that was my one chance to experience true love? Oh fudge, am I doomed to be a spinster with nothing but thirty cats for company the rest of my days? Oh man, this is not good. The full-on crazy that Tawny has been worried about is showing.

I head to my kitchen to whip up some cookie dough. Nothing beats the blues like cookie dough and I need to stress eat.

Later, bowl of dough in hand, I settle down on my couch. It's cold outside, unusually so for August on the island. But the weather matches my mood, dreary and depressing. I pick up the book I'm reading, a rom-com by one of my favorite authors, but even bad boy millionaires can't get me to smile. Not when I'm missing my own millionaire. Yep, I looked him up. Marcus and his business are worth over ten million dollars. Holy shiitake, am I right?

The obvious difference in our bank balances unnerves me slightly; it's one more way that Marcus feels like my opposite. But don't they always say opposites attract?

My mouth is full of sticky, sweet chocolate chip cookie dough when my phone rings. It's a video call from Marcus. I answer quickly, and belatedly realize I'm a hot mess with wild hair, sloppy clothes, and my next spoonful of dough in hand.

His smile turns into a quizzical frown when he sees me; he's still the most perfect man I've ever seen.

"Umm, hey beautiful, how are you doing?" he asks in that rumbly voice that makes me want to purr.

"Mmmfffggg," I mumble as I frantically try to swallow down the last bites of chocolatey goodness. Once my mouth is clear, I smile, hoping I don't look like a total weirdo. "I'm good. Hi."

ELLA

Now that sinful smile is back and I swear he shoots laser beams of lust from his eyes because I want him so badly right now.

"I've got news, Ella," he says, and the excitement in his voice has me sitting up straighter and my heart pounding faster.

He's grinning like a fool now and I can feel a smile stretch across my face in response.

"I'm coming back tomorrow," he says triumphantly.

I'm speechless. Legit, cannot formulate a response. And that's weird for me. Marcus knows this and he's starting to look worried at my silence.

"That's a good thing, right, baby? This time tomorrow I'll have you in my arms."

I clear my throat and finally regain the ability to speak.

"Of course, it's good. It's more than good. It's amazing. I can't, I just, I can't believe it. Ten days isn't long, but it feels like forever," I babble, and I'm pretty sure I sound totally bonkers.

"Every moment between us feels like forever, because what we have can't be measured with time. You and I, we are meant to be for eternity."

Cue swoon.

Marcus continues, telling me he'll be on the first ferry in the morning and he'll be able to stay for two weeks before he has to go back to the mainland again. I don't love the idea of him going back and forth; I wish he were here permanently. But even that wishful thinking can't dim how happy I am that I'll get to see him again. I need to feel his arms around me, reassuring me that the feelings we share are real and not just some fantastical memory.

Happy tears are forming behind my eyes, and I blink furiously, trying to hold them back. My snack is forgotten and that's saying something, because I love cookie dough. But my joy at knowing Marcus will be here tomorrow is even bigger than any joy that could come from a bowl of comfort cookie dough.

"Tomorrow," I whisper, and he nods.

"Tomorrow, my sweet Ella."

* * *

Naturally, I don't sleep very well that night. The excitement and nerves over seeing Marcus again keep me tossing and turning for hours. All of this means that in the morning, I've got dark circles under my eyes that rival a racoon. Not exactly the look I'm going for.

Still, here I am waiting at the ferry dock, wearing a yellow sundress and sandals. My hair is hanging down my back, and I'm grateful there's no wind today. I can't stop wringing my hands together as I wait for the boat to turn the corner into the harbor. *He's almost here.*

I've debated in my mind how to act when I see him. I know he's driving, so he'll have to park his car somewhere before meeting me on the pier like we planned. But do I run and jump into his arms like you see in the movies? Do I wait for him to make the first move? Will he kiss me? Wait, did I brush my teeth today?! I do the breath check and a subtle armpit sniff. Yep, personal hygiene is on point. The morning has been such a blur, I'm impressed I didn't forget anything.

Just then I see the ferry turning into the harbor. Even as my eyes strain to try and see Marcus, my brain laughs at my stupidity. He'll be in his car, waiting to drive off the boat by now. But then my phone vibrates in my purse.

MARCUS: I can see you, beautiful. I'm right at the front, and I'm going crazy knowing you're so close.

Oh...my...goodness...

ELLA: I wish I could see you. Which car are you?

MARCUS: The silver one.

ELLA: I SEE YOUR CAR!

ELLA

MARCUS: lol yep, that's me baby. I'm almost there.

The boat is pulling into the docks now, the process seeming to take way longer than it normally does. Doesn't the boat captain know he's got the man of my dreams on board?

"Hurry up, hurry up," I mutter under my breath, not caring who might hear me talking to myself like a weirdo.

Finally, the boat docks and I see Marcus's silver sports car zoom off the ramp. In a couple of minutes, he'll turn the corner onto Wharf Street and park. There's a spot right near the entrance to the pier and then a short walk to the end where I'm waiting. Thankfully, it isn't too busy today, because the butterflies in my stomach are doing acrobatics and I don't think I want a big audience for our reunion.

Like a vision from a dream, he appears. He parks his car expertly in the space at the front and then he's walking towards me as I stand frozen. No, Marcus isn't walking, he's running; then I'm in his arms and everything in my world rights itself.

"Ella, baby. Ella. I'm here." He's talking into my hair, because my face is buried in the crook of his neck to hide the tears that have suddenly started to stream down my face. He's holding me tightly, stroking my hair, and murmuring reassurances to me.

After a moment, he pulls back slightly to cup my face, and I get my first close look at him in what feels like an eternity.

"Hi, beautiful," he says as he wipes my tears away with his thumbs. Then he leans forward and presses a sweet kiss to my lips. But I need more than sweet. I need him to soothe my soul with his kiss. I press into him closely, crushing our bodies together as I deepen our embrace. He groans and when I feel his mouth open, my tongue tangles with his until I can no longer tell where he starts and I end. I can feel the hard ridges of his body crushed against mine. This is what I need. I'm home in his arms.

A cry from a seagull overhead breaks us apart and Marcus grins down at me. I lift my hands to trace his smile and his jaw, drifting down his neck to his shoulders and finally to his chest. He traps my hands there.

"If you keep going, things are going to get a little inappropriate for such a public setting. Every night since I left, I've been dreaming of having you again, and you're even sexier than in my wildest dreams."

I take his hand and give him what I hope is a sultry smile.

"Then let's go somewhere private."

11

Marcus

All of the stress and chaos in my mind disappeared the instant I saw Ella on the pier. And now, driving back to her cottage with her hand in mine, I know I've made the right decision. I still need to tell her how I feel and most importantly, what I've done. Briefly I wonder if I should do that before I make love to her again, but I don't know if I can wait a second longer than I have to. My body is craving her and having her so close, but not close enough, is driving me crazy in the best possible way.

Thank fuck this island is small, because it's only a short drive until we're at Ella's cottage. I jump out of my car, leaving my bag in the backseat. I open Ella's door and pull her out of the car, straight into my arms. When I lift her, she wraps her legs around my waist, and I have to hold back a shudder at how good it feels to be this close to her. She's wearing a short little dress, which is torture, and I can feel my cock pressing against my shorts, desperate to get inside of her.

I reluctantly set her down so she can find her keys and open her front door, but the entire time I keep myself pressed up against her sweet body, kissing her bare shoulders.

"Marcus, it's really hard to focus when you do that," she giggles.

"Good," I rumble into her skin with a smile, not stopping what I'm doing for a second.

Finally, she gets her door open and we rush inside. Ella turns to me and tugs impatiently at the bottom of my shirt. I pull it off and I swear to God the sigh she makes almost has me coming in my pants.

"This dress needs to go, baby," I growl, then I grab the hem and lift it slowly over her head. She's not wearing a bra, so Ella is standing before me in nothing but pale blue lace panties. The sheer need in her eyes is all I need to see before I scoop her up into my arms again and walk quickly to her bedroom. I lay Ella out on her bed, and she reaches up to pull me on top of her. Our kiss is slow this time, unhurried. It's as if our bodies have realized we have all the time in the world now. We're together again and I'll be damned if I let anything keep us apart.

I pull my lips away from hers and make my way down the slope of her neck, to where her breasts await my attention. Her rosy nipples are already perked and aroused, and when I suck one into my mouth, Ella moans with pleasure.

"You like that, beautiful? Did you miss my mouth?" I ask, greedily sucking and playing with her breasts.

"Yes, oh God yes, Marcus." she says breathily.

I need more. So, I work my way down her body, licking, kissing, and nipping everywhere I touch. Her skin is soft and warm under my touch; familiar, yet not. Like I'm exploring a favorite place for the first time in a long time. But before I get to the heat between her legs, I stop and lift myself back over top of her. I prop up on one elbow, and use my other hand to stroke down her face.

"Ella, I can't hold it in any longer. I love you. I think I've loved you since the moment you used "fudge" as a swear word on the ferry. You found a place in my heart when we ate salmon burgers on the beach. And I knew I wanted you forever the first time you came apart in my arms. I love you, beautiful girl, and I always will. That's a promise."

Ella's smile grew with every word I said, but where I expected her usual happy tears, there's nothing but sheer joy in her eyes.

"I love you, too, Marcus. You complete a part of me I didn't know I was missing. You're all of my dreams come true and more. Love me forever, and I'll promise to do the same."

I have no words, so I pour my love into her through a kiss. Somehow, I manage to remove my shorts and underwear, and then her panties, and finally we're naked together.

"I need you now, please, Marcus. I need you," Ella begs. I quickly lean over to grab a condom from my shorts on the floor. Her eager hands help roll it on, and then I'm sliding home into her hot, wet core.

"Oh, fudge," she breathes, and it's so perfectly Ella, I drop my head and chuckle. She starts to giggle as well and the movement causes her to tighten around my cock, changing my chuckle into a groan.

"This requires more than kindergarten-friendly swear words for me, baby. Fuck, you feel good." My voice is hoarse as I slowly begin to move my hips, sliding in and out of her slick folds. This is heaven.

Ella meets me thrust for thrust, lifting her hips in perfect synchronicity. It doesn't feel like it's only our second time together. No, she's a part of me in this and in everything. We're two souls entwined into one.

"God, I love you, Ella Michaels. I love you so fucking much."

My movements speed up and I can feel my orgasm barreling down on me. Ella's cries are becoming more and more sharp, and I can tell by the tightening around my cock that she's close as well.

"Yes! Marcus! Love....you...Marcus...YES!" With one final cry, her body convulses in pleasure, and I follow with one final grunt and thrust of my hips.

I almost collapse onto her, but manage to move to the side so I don't crush her. I'm drained, physically and emotionally. Confessing my love and being with her again has erased all of the tension that built up over the last ten days, leaving behind a peaceful exhaustion.

We lay there for a while, letting our heart rates return to normal. My hands can't stop exploring her body, mapping her curves and committing every single inch to memory. I find her ticklish spot below her ribs and the spot just above her hip bone that makes her gasp. She's staring into my eyes with a soft smile on her face and no more words are needed right now.

I love her.

She loves me.

That's all that matters.

* * *

Eventually, my stomach betrays me, so Ella and I get up to find some food in her kitchen. She's wearing my T-shirt over those lace panties and I've got nothing but my boxer briefs on. Ella's turned on some low music and the whole thing feels so domestic, so normal, and so completely unlike anything I've ever experienced with a woman. I guess that makes sense, since everything with Ella is different in the best possible way.

Once we have our plates loaded with sandwiches and fruit, we head out to her back porch. It's private enough that it doesn't matter we're barely dressed. Ella turns sideways on the cushioned bench and lifts her legs over mine. We eat in comfortable silence for a while, but I know I need to talk to her soon. I need to tell her my plans for her, for us, and for the island.

It's now or never.

"Ella, you know how I said I have to go back to the mainland in a couple of weeks or so to finish up some things," I start. Ella puts her sandwich down and looks at me worriedly. I smile and try to change the nervous tone to my voice. "I'll be coming back as quickly as I can and I was hoping that when I return you would be open to a roommate?"

Her mouth drops open and I laugh at her face. It takes a lot to render her speechless and I seem to have succeeded again.

"A...roommate? Does that mean you're staying? Wait. Why would you be my roommate? Oh my God, you want to live with me. But we're dating, aren't we? Shoot. I hope we're dating. Wait, we said "I love you" so of course we're—"

I cut her off mid-ramble with a deep kiss. She's nervous, which somehow makes me feel less so.

"Slow down, baby, and let me explain. Roommate was the wrong word to use. I love you and sometime soon I'm going to ask you to marry me. In the meantime, I want to romance you day and night, and I can't do that unless I'm with you day and night. I'm moving to the island and I very much want to live with you. As for the *are we dating* question, Ella, we're more than dating. I don't know how to label it and I don't care. But what we have is way more than just dating."

And there are the happy tears I'm starting to expect from the love of my life. Ella's smiling, even as her eyes fill up.

"If you're living on the island, it had better be with me," she whispers, then she puts both of our plates down on the ground before climbing into my lap and straddling my legs. "And for the record, when you ask me to marry you...I'll say yes."

I didn't think it was possible to love her even more, but with those words, I do.

"There's more."

Ella's about to kiss me, but when I speak, she pulls back and looks at me quizzically.

"It's about my job. I'll have to maintain my office and staff on the mainland, so I'm going to have to go back there probably once a month to check in on things. And there will be other work trips. But I want to be here as much as possible, so I'm looking into renting some office space in town for myself."

She smiles and this time I let her kiss me.

"I can handle the odd trip as long as you always promise to come home to me. But you don't need to rent space, we can make room here. Once the school year starts, I'm not home all day."

"You're right, baby, but for what I'll be working on, I'm going to need an actual office for me and for a team."

This is it. Now I get to reveal my other big plans. I just hope she approves.

"I've taken over the development of the north end of the island. Robert didn't want to change his vision, so he's changing his location. I bought the land instead and I'm going to build a family-friendly cottage community. Think Cape Cod, but West Coast style. Year-round homes and summer cottages, all mapped out around a central common area with a playground for the kids. Road access to Wharf Street is going in, so the new residents will bring more business to the locals, but we might have to think about expanding to include a few new amenities. Like, perhaps a library?"

Her squeal of excitement makes me laugh, and the passion behind her kiss makes me breathless. I will do anything to make her this happy every day for the rest of my life if she'll let me.

Suddenly, she pulls back slightly, a wondrous look to her face.

"How the heck did I get so lucky?" She shakes her head slightly, "All I wanted was a hair tie, and I ended up with the love of my life."

"And a library. Don't forget the library," I tease as I dip forward to capture her lips again.

"Of course, I won't forget the library. It's only the most romantic thing anyone has ever done for me," Ella teases right back. I scoop her up in my arms and begin to walk back inside. I'm going to love this woman and her perfectly quirky sense of humor for the rest of my life.

"If you think that's romantic, stick around for fifty years or so. I'll

show you more romance than you can handle."
   "Promise?"
   "Promise."

II

Falling Again

12

Kayla

After experiencing one of my greatest fears come to life and making it out alive, there's only one place to go. Home. Still, moving back to Westmount Island after promising myself I would only stay long enough to visit my sisters isn't an easy decision to accept.

Yet here I am, standing in the early morning light on the dock of the ferry carrying me back to the small-town life I had once hoped to escape. I haven't been back in months; not since my twin sister Ella married the man of her dreams, Marcus. I'm happy for them, he's a great guy and I've never seen my shy sister so happy. She loves Westmount Island and the quiet life she lives.

But not me. I've been itching to leave the island ever since I was a teenager and fell in love with photography. Traveling the world these past five years since I graduated from college has been a dream come true and there is no way I would be giving it up now if it weren't for what happened a couple of months ago. I just have to keep reminding myself this is temporary. I just need to come home for a while, to let the memories of what happened fade a bit before I go back out there.

My sisters don't know I'm coming back for more than just a short visit; I haven't been able to tell them what happened. After all, admitting that I was trapped in a cave because of a rockslide and it was almost a full day before they could get me and my co-worker out isn't exactly something you can do over email.

So here I am, heading home on the advice of the therapist I spoke to after my rescue. I have to admit, for all that I swore I would never come back to the island for longer than a week, I'm okay with the idea of spending a few months in a quiet, safe, small town. When you've been all around the world in some of the harshest environments, you start to see some benefit to the peace and quiet of home. But I already signed a contract to do a shoot in Asia for an adventure-seeker magazine in a few short months, so I don't have long to enjoy the quiet.

The trip from the mainland over to Westmount Island is just under an hour long. Which means I have approximately half an hour left before I have to face my sisters. I know Ella will realize something's wrong right away, call it twin intuition or something. But Tawny, my oldest sister, she's the worrier. Once she hears what happened, I wouldn't be surprised if she starts scheming to keep me on the island permanently.

I'm lost in thought, trying to figure out how to tell them about the cave-in, when something bumps into my legs.

"Ooops, sowwy."

I look down to see a head of curly hair, bright blue eyes, and a gap-toothed smile looking back at me. I can't help but smile back.

"All good, bud."

I glance up to see if I can figure out who's with the adorable little guy, but there's no one else out on the deck with me.

"Where's your grownup?" I ask, as I keep scanning to see if I can find his parents.

"Lookin' fo me," he says, and the fact that he can't seem to pronounce the letter 'r' makes my heart melt.

"Okay, ummm, are you playing a game?"

Now the little dude is looking sheepish. I'm pretty sure that face means he isn't supposed to be wandering around alone. Makes sense, a ferry isn't exactly a safe place for a small child to run around by themselves.

"I dunno," he replies with a shrug.

Just as I'm about to grab my bag and take the kid to find a crew member who could locate his parents, a deep voice calls out.

"Toby? Toby!" A tall man runs over, bends down and picks up the kid, and crushes him tightly to his chest, turning away from me. All I can see is wavy hair, the color of milk chocolate, peeking out from under a backwards baseball hat, and a muscular back with a grey T-shirt stretched over it. And woah. Even from behind, this guy's body is bangin'.

"Toby, you can't scare me like that, dude. You promised you would stay in your seat while I grabbed snacks. What were you thinking, walking outside by yourself?!"

Damn, that voice should be narrating romance novels or something. It's rich and sexy, and making me feel all shivery inside. Can a voice be sexy? I guess so, because his absolutely is. He still hasn't acknowledged me, and I'm starting to feel a bit weird just standing here.

"I was just about to take him inside to find a crew member," I say, haltingly. Not sure why, but I want him to know I was going to take care of the freaking-cute little kid.

Finally, he turns to me, adjusting Toby to sit on his hip, and I have to catch myself before I stumble. He is, without a doubt, the most gorgeous man I've ever seen. And I met the Hemsworth brothers when I was shooting in Australia two years ago.

"Thank you," he says gratefully, before he looks at Toby. "What do you say to this nice lady?"

Toby gives me another grin. "Thanks, nice lady."

The veritable god in front of me rolls his eyes affectionately, before holding out one of his hands to me.

"I'm Sam, and this monster is my son, Toby. Thanks again for your help."

I shake his hand, still dumbfounded by how smokin' hot this guy is.

"Kayla, and it was no problem. I barely did anything," I mumble. Good grief, this isn't me. Ella is the awkward one. I'm the confident, free spirit who isn't afraid of anything. At least I used to be.

"Well, Kayla, I really appreciate it." Sam smiles at me and I'm a goner. His teeth are perfect, he has dimples, and his eyes look like they're smiling, too. Suddenly, I'm self-conscious of the fact that my hair is a mess and I'm wearing leggings and a hoodie I picked up in Alaska a year ago. It's got the outline of a grizzly bear on it, and says "Caution, Wild Animal" on it.

"What brings you two to Westmount Island?" I ask, hoping that my voice sounds normal.

"We bought a house! But it isn't built yet," Toby says excitedly. "I might get to see a weal constwuction twuck."

Sam chuckles at his son before turning to me. The intensity from his delicious blue eyes warms me from the inside out. Hot damn, this man is turning me to mush and we just met.

"He's sort of right. We bought a place in the first wave of homes going in on the island, the Northgate Community. Our house won't be finished until the spring, but Toby is starting kindergarten in the fall and we wanted to have a couple of months to settle in before he starts school."

I smile at Toby, "My twin sister is the kindergarten teacher here. She looks just like me and she's a really awesome teacher. I think you'll have fun!"

Toby looks at me with wide eyes, "You have a twin? Cool!"

Sam is also looking at me, but there's a different kind of interest in his gaze. I shiver involuntarily.

"So, you're from the island?"

KAYLA

It's an innocent question, but I am simultaneously filled with dread and excitement. I know the dread is because, for so many years, I tried to distance myself from my small-town identity. But where the heck is the excitement coming from?

"Ummm, yeah, I was born here. I haven't lived on the island for a few years, though." Sam must not sense the hesitant way I answer, he just nods. I hate how meek I sound. This isn't me. I'm Kayla Michaels, award winning travel photographer. I've gone paragliding, I've snorkeled in cenotes, I've done things most people only dream of. But being trapped, not knowing how long it would take to be rescued, has turned me into a fearful, uncertain version of myself that I really don't like. Here's hoping I made the right call by coming home and I can somehow find myself again.

13

Sam

Toby wriggles out of my arms and I put him down on the deck. I'm held captive by Kayla's mesmerizing eyes, but still remember to call out to him to stay close. Then I'm drawn back to the beautiful woman in front of me. Her hair reaches down to her ass, she looks strong but feminine with curves I could get lost in. She's got clear blue eyes that seem to see me straight through to my soul, and a smile that promises mischief.

"I'm sorry again about Toby, he's a good kid, but really curious. I'm not surprised, actually, that he came outside. I should've known he wouldn't sit still when there's so many cool things to see." I shrug my shoulders sheepishly. It's been just me and Toby since the beginning, but I still feel like I'm screwing up every day. I guess that's just part of parenting.

Kayla laughs off my apology. "Don't worry about it, my sisters and I used to run around the ferry boats all the time. They're pretty safe and there's plenty of crew about. If I hadn't found him, someone else would have."

I smile at that. She's managed to reassure me without making me feel like a shit Dad for letting my kid run away. I glance over to him and am relieved to see he's just standing there, holding on to the railing,

SAM

looking at the water rushing by. We're still too far from the island to see anything exciting, so I know the view won't hold his attention for long. Which means I need to act fast, because there is no way I am leaving this boat without knowing more about Kayla.

I haven't been a monk since Toby's mom died giving birth to him five years ago, but I also haven't been in a relationship. When Sarah was pregnant and we were finally writing our wills, we talked about how if something happened, we'd always want each other to find love again. I never expected to actually be in that position of finding someone again, and needless to say, love has been the last thing on my mind. There were a couple of women who were fine with casual flings when my parents would babysit, but no one has really captured my interest since Sarah. Which makes my attraction to Kayla all the more intriguing. All I know is that I can't let her go just yet.

"So, Kayla from Westmount Island, are you going to be around for a while? I'd like to take you for lunch as a thank you for keeping an eye on Toby."

As soon as I say the words, I realize how ridiculously cheesy they sound. It's not like she saved his life or anything; all she did was stand with him until I found him. But it's the best I can do in the moment. To my relief, she smiles.

"I'd like that, but it's really not necessary to thank me," she says softly.

"Well, good, because I lied. I don't want to take you for lunch to thank you, Kayla, I want to take you for lunch so I can spend more time with you."

The truth spills out of me like a waterfall of words, but I wouldn't take them back even if I could. I'm always trying to teach Toby that honesty is the best policy, so why not practice it myself? I'm rewarded with a sweet chuckle from Kayla and an even bigger smile.

"Normally I wouldn't like the fact that you lied, but I guess I'll let it slide," she teases.

"I guess I should be relieved you forgive easily," I respond, enjoying the banter between us.

"Nah, it's just because I'm a sucker for a free lunch."

I can't hold back my laughter as Kayla shrugs her shoulders and flashes me an impish grin.

"A woman with her priorities straight. I admire that." I put my hands in my pockets, to stop myself from touching her. The desire to feel her skin against mine is fierce and unexpected. But since I don't want her to think I'm a fucking creep, I won't give in to it. Not yet, at least. "So, where do you suggest we go?"

"Seas the Day. It's the local diner and they make some killer seafood sandwiches. If you're going to be moving here, you better like fish," she answers readily and I'm glad she seems fully on board with us continuing to spend the day together.

"We love seafood." Then I turn toward my son. "Hey, Toby, you good with going to lunch with Miss Kayla?"

He runs back, yelling "Yeah!" as he goes. I love my kid's enthusiasm and from the look on Kayla's face, she appreciates it, too. But looking at Toby means I'm unprepared for when she leans in close and I get a whiff of strawberries when her hair brushes my shoulder. Her hand touches my arm and she whispers in my ear, "I lied, too. It's not just because I want a free lunch."

Holy. Hell.

If it weren't for my son grabbing my hand and yammering on about a boat he can see, I'm almost positive I would have kissed her. Her intoxicating scent, the feel of her hand on me, and those words are enough to have my cock stirring in my pants. Suddenly the desire to touch her has morphed into a desire to do something a lot dirtier. Fuck no, a *lot* of somethings.

Before Toby can pull me too far away from her, I grab Kayla's hand with my free one.

"Come and look at a boat with us?"

She nods and takes my hand, lacing our fingers together in a way that feels much more intimate than I would have expected from someone I just met. It's now that I'm realizing she might be feeling the same kind of intense attraction that I am, and my mind fills with thoughts on how I can get us some time alone. Not an easy feat as a single dad, but my parents are coming to visit next week, so I'll figure something out.

She drops my hand when we reach Toby and I have to admit I'm disappointed. So once we've oohed and aahed at the sailboat he spotted, I turn to lean against the railing, making damn sure my shoulder is touching hers.

"How long are you staying on the island?"

A voice inside my head starts chanting *forever...forever...forever...*and I shake my head to try and dispel that madness. I just met the woman and something inside of me is already planning our future together.

Kayla hesitates and a look of uncertainty moves across her face that has my protective instincts roaring.

"I don't know, really. I've got a job lined up in a few months, but..." she shrugs and lets her voice trail off. My Spidey-sense is tingling. There's something she isn't saying. But I know it's too soon for me to push, so I keep the conversation moving.

"Cool. Well, that's plenty of time for my kid to drive you nuts with his endless energy and non-stop questions."

She laughs and smiles affectionately at Toby before looking back to me with a sassy grin.

"First of all, you're assuming I'll be around your son enough for him to drive me nuts. My sister is the teacher, not me. Second of all, Toby is awesome. I don't believe he could drive anyone nuts."

I lean down—now it's my turn to whisper in her ear. And if my lips happen to brush against her skin, well, it can't be helped, now can it?

"You don't live with the kid. Trust me."

Right on cue, Toby comes back over from where he had moved for a better view of the sailboat, and starts asking questions.

"Dad, how do sailboats move? Do they have engines? What does *sail* mean? Can we get a sailboat? How 'bout a dog? I want a dog. Can we get a dog?"

Kayla starts giggling and I can hear her trying to contain her laughter, but her eyes are filled with mirth as she looks at me. I shake my head as if to say, *See? Told you so...*and her giggle turns into a snort, and then full-on laughter.

Poor Toby looks at her with concern. "Miss Kayla, what's so funny? Did you toot? Dad says tooting is nowmal and evewyone toots."

Now it's my turn to hold back my chuckles.

"Toby, dude, it's rude to ask someone if they...ahhh..." Damn it, I don't want to say the word in front of Kayla. She beats me to it, with laughter written all over her face and filling her voice.

"Tooted?"

Now we're all laughing, over something as ridiculous as a word. Somehow, Kayla has gone from a total stranger to a woman who seamlessly fits in with mine and Toby's sense of humor and general silliness. And that's alluring in a way I never would have expected.

"Alright, back to what's important. Lunch." Kayla reaches into her bag and pulls out her phone, then looks at me expectantly. I quickly pull mine out, hiding my elation that she's showing her interest so clearly. We exchange numbers and then confirm plans to meet at the diner later. Toby and I are renting an apartment in town until our house is ready, so Kayla tells us how we can easily walk to the diner from our temporary home. When I ask her where she'll be staying, her answer surprises me.

"My sister runs an inn just outside of town, I think I'll stay there."

"Not with your family?"

"No...my sisters can be overbearing. And I need some space."

She reveals nothing with her answer and yet I'm starting to get the feeling Kayla's return to Westmount Island might be about more than just seeing her family.

"I get it. Family can mean well, but when you need time to breathe, they don't always understand."

Kayla nods. "Exactly."

She's quiet for a moment, but I can see her eyes glancing over to me and then to Toby, and I'm pretty sure I know what's coming next. Before she has to ask the awkward question, I offer up the answer.

"His mom died giving birth to him. It's been just me and Toby for the last five years," I say quietly.

Her hand flutters down on top of mine and gives it a gentle squeeze. Her gaze is full of compassion.

"I'm so sorry, Sam."

I shrug. "Thanks. I won't lie and say I don't miss her, but it's been long enough that I've made peace with it. I tell Toby stories about her so that he can know her in a way. He's never seemed bothered by not having a mom, probably because my own mother has always been so involved." Thinking about my mom and her reaction to us moving, I let out a low chuckle. "Grandma's having a tough time accepting our move to the island. Not being able to pop over any time she wants is going to be hard on her, and on Toby, but personally I'm ready for a bit of space and, like I said, time to breathe."

"Yeah," Kayla says softly. "It's hard on family when you move away. But sometimes you just need a change. Something different. Something that lets you be yourself and not the person everyone expects you to be."

I turn to face her, careful to still have an eye on my son.

"Is that why you left?"

She nods. "My parents died when I was a teenager. Everyone on the island rallied around us and I'm grateful for their support, but I needed to go somewhere that I wasn't known as Kayla Michaels, the girl whose parents died. Or Kayla Michaels, the girl whose family founded Westmount Island. I just wanted to be Kayla Michaels."

I take both her hands in mine, and let my thumb slowly stroke across the back of her hand. After a moment, Kayla raises her eyes to look at me, and the sadness mixed with longing that I see there hits me.

"I see you, Kayla Michaels. Just you. And I really like what I see."

14

Kayla

Damn. This guy should come with a warning label — 'risk of swooning'. He's so easy to be around, I feel my confidence returning, making it easy to tease and flirt with him. I've never felt this depth of attraction to a guy before, and the irony of the fact that this is how my twin sister met her now husband — on a ferry boat — is not lost on me. Not that I'm hearing wedding bells or anything. I mean, Sam and Toby are moving to the very island I was always so desperate to get away from. Still, I can't deny the fact that my goals and priorities have begun to shift lately. As much as I love the freedom of being a nomad and traveling the world, I've started to want a home base. Living out of a backpack and sleeping on friends' couches gets old after a while, and I've found myself missing my sisters even more than usual.

But a part of me is quite certain that after a few weeks on the island I'll be itching to run away again. And that's why I probably shouldn't let myself get too attached to the handsome single dad and the adorable little boy who are currently looking picture perfect as they look over the railing at the island, which is just coming into sight. Acting on autopilot, I grab my camera out of the bag that is always with me and start snapping pictures. The lighting is perfect this morning, glinting off Toby's curls and giving him an angelic halo of light that I'm sure Sam will laugh at.

After a moment, Sam glances over and when he sees me with my camera, his quizzical look has me feeling a bit guilty, so I'm quick to explain.

"I'm a photographer, and you guys just looked so perfect. I would've asked if you were okay with it, but candid shots are the best kind. Here, look."

Sam walks over with Toby in his arms and together they lean down to look at the small screen on the back of my Canon. This brings Sam's head dangerously close to me and mere inches separate his face from mine. Somehow, I hold myself back from leaning in closer and sniffing him, or worse, kissing him. That would be insane.

When he stands back up, Sam is smiling.

"Those are amazing, Kayla. You've got such a good eye. Can I have a copy?"

I blush, which is so unlike me that I'm taken by surprise. "Of course. You can have them all."

"Daddy, look! The dock!" Toby's excited voice interrupts us. Sure enough, we're nearing the dock on the island, a fact that is confirmed by the voice coming over the loudspeaker telling us to return to our vehicles.

"So, lunch in an hour?" Sam stares at me, like he's not going to let me go until I confirm our plans. I nod swiftly.

"You bet." I reach over to ruffle Toby's hair. "See you soon, squirt."

"Bye, Miss Kayla," he says cheerfully. Sam just quirks a small smile at me, then turns to head toward the vehicle deck. I hold back, needing a second to regroup before I go to my car.

"What the fuck was that?" I whisper to myself as I watch them walk away.

I slowly make my way to my car, musing on the insane feelings swirling inside of me. Looks like I have even more to confess to my sisters. Maybe telling them I met a guy will soften the blow of telling them about being trapped.

Oh, who am I kidding. There's nothing that can soften that blow. Tawny's going to freak and Ella will probably start to cry. I know their reactions will come from their love for me, but I can't help but dread the moment I come clean about why I'm really home. I know they'll both start pushing for me to stay on the island. And if I so much as hint at the fact that I'm willing to consider the idea of at least making Westmount my home base and traveling less, they'll never give up. That kind of pressure is the last thing I need right now. Briefly, as I wait for my turn to disembark from the ferry, I debate not telling them right away. But I dismiss that idea almost instantly. My sisters know me too well; they'll see right through any façade I try to attempt.

Sam's reaction when I told him I wouldn't be staying with my family was pretty much what I expect from everyone. I've always stayed with one of my sisters when I visit, and sure, by being at the inn that Tawny runs, I'll see them lots. Especially since Ella and Marcus are still staying in her cottage, which is on the inn's property. But knowing I have a private room to which I can escape each evening is what made me email Carrie, the front desk manager at the inn, and ask her to keep a room free for me.

The drive to the inn is a short one from the ferry terminal. As I drive past the familiar landmarks, I feel a sense of calm wash over me. It's a feeling I've never had in the past when I come to visit, and I have to say, I like it. It's a peace I haven't felt in a long time. As I drive through the intersection that would take me down wharf street and to the diner where I'll be meeting Sam and Toby, I smile, thinking of them. I always figured I would settle down eventually and have a family. But the idea was always so nebulous in light of my constant traveling. Watching Sam and Toby stirred something in me, a desire to take a step back and look at my life and my goals with a new perspective. I've met single dads before, I've hung out with some pretty cute kids, but none of them have ever made me think or feel this way. I'd have to be completely clueless to not realize that my pull to Sam and his son isn't exactly normal. I just met them and I'm already eager to see them again. It's not just because Sam is bloody gorgeous, either. No, when I first saw him, it was as if my soul sighed in relief.

Before I can spend another minute trying to figure out what that means, I've arrived at the inn. Tawny and Ella knew I was on the early ferry, so I'm not surprised to see the two of them waiting outside for me, along with my new brother-in-law Marcus. Even if they don't know I'm staying at the inn, this is always my first stop, since it's almost always where they can be found.

As soon as I'm out of my car I'm surrounded by my sister's arms and something inside of me rights itself. *Home.*

"You look tired," Tawny comments, pulling back and examining me.

"Of course she does, she's probably been on a plane for the last two days," Ella interjects. She's smiling, but I can see a shadow of concern. We've always been able to communicate without words. Which means I can see in her eyes that she's asking me if I'm okay, and I try to shake off her concern by mouthing 'later'.

Tawny reaches into her pocket and moves to hand me her keys. "I'm guessing you'd rather stay with me than the lovebirds," she nods over at Ella and Marcus.

When I don't immediately reach out to take the keys, Tawny looks at me curiously.

"Actually, I was thinking I'd just stay at the inn this time," I blurt out.

"Why?" Ella asks, "You always stay with me or Tawny. And no matter what she says, Marcus and I would love to have you at the cottage."

"I know," I start to fidget with my hands. I really don't want to get into this out here; hell, I don't want to get into it at all. But certainly not now. I'm going to need a whole hell of a lot of booze before I dredge up the memories that I've been pushing down for so many weeks. "I just figured it would be nice to stay at the inn. Check out the new soaker tubs."

My excuse sounds feeble, even to my own ears. But thankfully my sisters don't push me any further. Not sure why, but I'll take the break.

"Well. Good to see you all. I'm going to go inside and unpack, then I'm meeting someone for lunch. I'm sure you guys have to get back to work anyway, so I'll see you for dinner later." I rush the words out, suddenly desperate to be alone and collect myself. It's harder seeing my sisters than I thought it would be.

"Okay, yeah, dinner at Tawny's house at seven," Ella says softly. Tawny is uncharacteristically silent. They know something's up, and the clock starts counting down toward the moment I have to tell my sisters the truth about why I'm here. But for now, I make my escape.

"Seven. Great. See you later." I hurry inside, stopping only briefly to grab my bag. I manage to get my room key from the front desk and go upstairs without having to talk to Tawny or Ella again. Once I'm inside my room, I flop down on the bed with a sigh.

Part of me feels guilty for the confusion and worry I'm sure I've caused my sisters. They mean well, but I just couldn't handle it. Not now, not with my emotions all confused by Sam and Toby. And not while seeing them brought up a longing for the safety and comfort of home, deeper than I've ever felt. I didn't know how adrift I was over the last few months until now.

A glance to the clock tells me I'm running short on time to get ready before I meet Sam and Toby for lunch, so I quickly get up and turn on the shower. Once it's steaming hot, I climb in and let the heat from the water wash away my stress. Or at least I pretend it does. Let's face it, no shower is going to completely erase my particular worries.

But the scent from the luxury body wash that Tawny stocks adds to the soothing experience of a hot shower. When you've traveled to the remote areas I've been to, you start to appreciate the simple things, like hot water, a lot more. Showers are my indulgence and my second favorite way to unwind. Unbidden, my mind goes to my favorite way to unwind. Orgasms. It's been a long time since I had sex, so any release I've had lately has been by my own hand. Don't get me wrong, I know what I need and I can do it well, but a man bringing me to climax is so much better. Suddenly I'm picturing Sam in the shower with me... his hands sliding down my body as he kneels down in front of me, his mouth covering the part of my body that is starting to throb with desire. *Damn...* I let my fingers drift down and lose myself in the fantasy. I come quickly, and the release definitely helps me to relax from the tension of seeing my sisters and keeping my secret from them.

Once I've rinsed off, I step out of the shower and dry off using one of the soft, fluffy, oversized towels that are in every guest room. I'm impressed by the quality of products Tawny's providing; clearly our guests are getting pampered at the inn. I'm so proud of her; running the inn can't be easy, but she seems to be doing a fantastic job. But I worry about her. Tawny has always been the ultimate big sister, protective and loving, to the expense of her own happiness. I've never heard of her dating anyone and the selection of available men on the island is limited, to say the least. She rarely leaves home, instead spending most of her time here, making sure this place runs perfectly.

But Tawny is not my concern right now. No, now I'm faced with the ultimate dilemma for all females. What to wear on a date. Wait, is this a date? I'm having lunch with a handsome man and his son. It's so totally not a date, no matter how much I want it to be. Time to stop overthinking this, Kayla Michaels.

I grab some jean shorts and a tee I got from Australia. It has the outline of a koala on the front and is a souvenir from one of my favorite memories — when I spent a day at an animal reserve, photographing their programs and learning about how they're working to conserve Australia's wildlife. Cuddling koalas and feeding kangaroos is high on my list of best experiences ever.

Once I'm dressed, I twist my long hair into a braid. I'll ask Ella to give me a trim later, she's got a good eye for that and it's getting ridiculously long. A swipe of mascara and lip gloss, and I'm good to go. Call me low maintenance if you want, but I've never been a girly girl. With my room key and cellphone in my back pocket, I head out. There's no need for a wallet; partly because Sam implied that he was treating me for lunch, but even if that wasn't the case, any local can eat at the diner and just put it on their tab.

I duck out the front door of the inn, managing to avoid Tawny. I don't know why they let me get away with staying here so easily, and I know I'll have to explain everything at dinner tonight, but for now I'm grateful for the space. It's a short walk to Wharf Street where the diner is, so I can leave my car here. It feels good to stretch my legs. Ella was right when she said I was probably tired from traveling. It was a long journey from France, where I arrived from Germany, to here — our tiny island off the West Coast of Washington. France helped to calm me; I stayed with a friend, a fellow photographer who heard what happened through the grapevine. She hooked me up with an ex-pat who lives nearby and happens to be a psychologist. Doctor Dave helped me begin to process my experience, and he was the one who suggested I take some time and head home. We made plans to check in via video calls once every couple of weeks, but other than that, I'm on my own, trying to move on from everything.

15

Kayla

When I get to Seas the Day, it's not that full inside. That's a relief; I don't need all the prying eyes of the locals who've known me since birth watching me with Sam and Toby. The gossip and rumors that would start...oh man. Let's just say, the paparazzi could learn a thing or two from some of our residents.

Moments after I've slid into a booth, the door opens and I can hear Toby before I even see him. He's chattering away to his dad about a rabbit they saw on the walk here and I smile. The kid is going to love it here; there's all kinds of wildlife to see. Sam spots me and gives a wave before directing his son over to where I'm seated.

"Well, hey there, fancy meeting you two handsome boys here."

Toby fixes me with a look that clearly says *duh*. "Miss Kayla, did you fowget we was comin' fow lunch?"

I grin at him as Sam chuckles. "Nah dude, she didn't forget. Miss Kayla is just being funny."

"And Miss Kayla doesn't mind if you just call me Kayla, Toby. The 'Miss' part makes me feel old."

I waggle my eyebrows when I say the word old, and Toby giggles. He's such a cute kid, and clearly used to being respectful and polite toward others. The fact that Sam is an amazing dad is evident, even in the short time I've been around him.

"Okay, Kayla, what's good here?" Sam asks as he pulls a menu over to look at it. He places it in front of both himself and Toby, and I love how Toby's tongue sticks out as he looks closely at the words.

"Dad! I see cheese! Ch-eeeeeeee-sssssss. Is that gwilled cheese? Can I have that?"

"Mmmm good choice, buddy. The grilled cheese here is awesome. And if you like tomato soup to dip it in, that's even better." I rub my hands on my belly for emphasis. "In fact, I think that might be what I get!"

Toby's eyes grow big. "You like gwilled cheese? It's my favowite!"

Sam is watching his son with love in his eyes and when he turns that gaze on me, I feel a rush of heat go down my spine. Good grief, that look is potent.

"Yeah, I love grilled cheese," I stammer out my reply to Toby, hoping my lust isn't showing to the five-year-old sitting across from me.

Now Sam's eyes are filled with laughter and heat, as if he knows how he's affecting me.

"Grilled cheese for three it is."

When the waitress comes over, Sam places the order, adding a chocolate milk to Toby's joy, and water for him and I. The waitress, Terry, is the daughter of Lois and Charlie, who own the diner and her eyes are moving in a circle from Sam and Toby, then over to me so quickly I'm surprised she isn't dizzy.

Let the gossip games begin.

After scarfing down his lunch in record time, Toby shows that he is, in fact, a regular kid by starting to whine about wanting to go outside. Sam handles it well and informs his son that if he can sit nicely while he and I finish eating, then he'll take him to the playground they walked past on their way here. When he glances up at me, I see the unspoken question and nod. Of course I'm going with them. There's no way I want to leave these two yet. I feel happy, and calm, and complete.

To appease Toby, I quickly finish my soup and sandwich, and we head out after Sam pays the bill. Toby asks if he can run on ahead and after a reminder about traffic safety and not turning any corners without us, Sam lets him go. The energy that kid has is amazing.

Without Toby hovering around us, the energy changes. I drift closer to Sam as we walk down the sidewalk and our fingers brush together. After the second time, Sam reaches one finger out to grasp mine. I take the invitation and entwine our hands together. It feels so natural to be walking with him like this.

When we reach the park, Toby is already climbing all over the wooden structure like a monkey. Sam leads me over to a bench and we sit down close enough that our legs are touching and our hands are still clasped together between us.

"I want you to know, I haven't been in a relationship with a woman in a while. And never around Toby."

Sam's voice is low, full of heat, and also holds a thread of hope. I squeeze his hand in response as I think about what to say.

"It's been a while for me, too. But if I understand what you're trying to say, then that means you feel it, too. The pull between us. I don't want to make things awkward for you with Toby, so you're in charge. All I know is I want to spend more time with you. With both of you."

I've always been up front and honest with my feelings; that's part of what's bothering me so much with my sisters not knowing what happened. Keeping secrets is very unlike me. But putting myself and my attraction to Sam out there so boldly is nerve-racking, nonetheless. The piercing stare he sends my way and the sensual perusal of his eyes up and down my body does more than melt away my nerves. It obliterates them in a tidal wave of pure lust.

"Oh, I feel it, Kayla. I love my son to the ends of the earth, but right now it's killing me that you and I aren't alone so I can properly show you just how attracted I am to you. Holding your hand is both heaven and hell. Feeling the heat of your leg against mine and not being able to touch that soft skin is the most extreme torture. I don't want to sound too forward, because I truly am a respectful guy, but ever since I saw you on that ferry boat, I've wanted to see you naked and spread out beneath me, mine to worship."

Holy. Shit. Did he just say that? I'm speechless. But in a good way. In an incredibly turned on, squirming to ease the ache between my legs, kind of way. Suddenly that shower fantasy I had earlier seems like it could become a reality. There's something powerful about knowing he wants me just as much as I want him, but there's Toby to consider. I've never dated a guy with a kid, so I have no idea how this can even work.

But when I look back into Sam's eyes and see the fire burning there, I suddenly know what the saying *where there's a will, there's a way* means. We will be together. Soon. Or I may spontaneously combust from pure arousal.

16

Sam

I grin at that. Kayla's forward and honest, and that's a massive turn on. She's not afraid to say what she wants and I admire that. But she's right, we need a babysitter. It's not that easy when you've just moved to a new place, however. The only solution for now is to wait a week until my parents arrive.

"That problem will be solved soon. My parents are coming to visit and I know they'd love to hang out with Toby for an evening. What about your sister, the teacher? Would that be weird for her to hang out with Toby outside of class?"

Kayla laughs and I realize just how eager I must sound. I shrug, not embarrassed in the slightest. She makes me feel bold enough to go after what I want as well.

"What? I don't want to wait over a week to get you to myself."

"Slow your roll, lover boy. My sister doesn't even know about you yet, so I can't exactly ask her to babysit." A shadow comes over her face.

"What's that look for?"

She shakes her head. "Nothing. I just have a lot I need to discuss with my sisters. Including an explanation of you and whatever this is." She gestures between us.

"This is me being insanely attracted to you and wanting to spend time with you, without my minion present. This is me wanting to date you. It's that simple."

"Well, when you put it that way." Kayla's face softens, and the look she gives me is filled with wonder.

I can't stop myself from leaning down to kiss her, but before my lips can reach her skin, a sweaty little boy throws himself onto my lap.

"Daddy! Are you gonna kiss Kayla?" Toby's voice is jarringly loud.

I huff out a sigh and Kayla giggles under her breath. Reluctantly I let go of her hand so I can hold on to my wriggling son.

"So what if I was?" I ask Toby and I'm curious as to what he'll say. He simply shrugs, then climbs down and grabs Kayla's hand.

"Kayla, come push me on the swings, please?"

She looks at me to make sure it's okay, but of course it is. I'm a little stunned, actually, at how quickly Toby has connected with her. In the back of my mind is a warning that I need to be careful. If my son gets too attached and then she leaves, it'll be hell. But that's not something I want to worry about right now. We stand up and walk to the swing set. Kayla goes over and starts pushing Toby, and he launches into another story about his favorite cartoon. I stand back a bit and every so often Kayla glances over at me with a smile. It's such a normal, domestic situation; a couple with a child at a park. Yet it's unlike anything Toby and I have ever experienced. He's never been to a playground with me and a woman because there's never been a woman important enough for me to warrant her being in his life. Kayla may have come into our lives in an unconventional way, but it already feels like she was meant to be here with us all along.

And that is both terrifying and exhilarating.

Eventually, Toby tires and we turn to walk home. Kayla's got plans to have dinner with her sisters and I really should spend some time with my son at home, settling in. But when we get to our apartment building, I'm seized by irrational panic. I don't want today to end. But my kid is getting restless and cranky, and I can see in Kayla's face that she might need a moment to process. Even if we haven't done anything more than hold hands and exchange some heated whispers, I know she feels the intensity the same way I do.

We're standing just outside the door and Toby is verging on meltdown status. Guess it's been a big day for him, too.

"Can I call you tonight?" I run my hand through my hair, hoping that I don't come across as overeager again.

Kayla nods eagerly. "I'd like that."

I grin. "Perfect. I'll call you later."

She smiles back at me and it sends a punch of warmth to my heart. Then she squats down to Toby's level and offers her hand for a high five.

"Hey little dude, I'm really glad you ran into me on the ferry. It made for a super fun day."

Toby throws himself into her arms, foregoing the high five for a hug, and even if it isn't manly of me to admit, I melt. He's an affectionate kid, but there's something about him easily going to the woman I'm interested in that feels really fucking good.

"Bye Kayla, thanks fow pushin' me on the swing."

When she stands up, I grab Toby's hand, and with my other arm I reach out and pull her in for a brief hug. I can't help myself, so I press a gentle kiss to her cheek. Her answering blush is sexy as hell and I feel my cock stirring in my pants. Thankfully, it isn't noticeable.

"Okay, guys, I'll see you around soon." She gives us a wave, then heads off down the road toward the inn.

Once she's out of sight, Toby starts tugging me to the front door. "C'mon Dad, I'm hungwy, I need a snack."

Dad duty calls. And that douses the arousal that had spiked from the contact of my lips on her cheek, like a bucket of water on a campfire.

17

Kayla

A few hours later, I drive over to Tawny's house for dinner. Ella texted me earlier to say Marcus wouldn't be joining us — something about an overseas work call he has to deal with. Part of me wishes he would be there as a buffer with my sisters, but at the same time, I don't really know him that well yet. Maybe it's best he doesn't see the breakdown I'm certain is coming.

Tawny still lives in the house we grew up in after our parents died. She was nineteen at the time and on the mainland for college; Ella and I were seventeen and just finishing high school. My grandmother moved in with us so that Tawny could finish her associate's degree in hotel management, then she moved back to the island and back into this house. Grandma moved out and now spends half the year in Arizona as a snowbird. When she's on the island, she stays at the inn.

Ella and I both wanted out of this house as soon as possible. Too many sad memories in it. But Tawny declared she wouldn't part with it. To be fair, since she came back after college, she's done a lot of updating and remodeling. With different paint and furniture, it isn't all that similar to our childhood home anymore.

When I walk in the door, I can smell the scent of Tawny's famous garlic chicken. Well, it's famous in our family at least. It's an old recipe of my mom's and my absolute favorite dish. I start to salivate just thinking about it, it's been so long since I tasted it.

My sisters are in the kitchen and I notice a bottle of wine on the counter with three glasses.

"Three glasses?" I ask, looking at Ella. I know she and Marcus have talked about starting a family soon.

My twin shrugs her shoulders, not meeting my eyes. "Nope. Not yet." She seems sad about that fact and I make a mental note to come back to that topic. But right now, I can feel their energy shift to focus on me, so I quickly pour the wine and drink half of my glass.

"Okay, if the inquisition is about to begin, can we at least get comfortable?" I walk into the living room and sit down in one of the cozy chairs Tawny has in here. There's a blanket on the back and even though I'm not cold, I pull it over my legs, tucking my feet underneath me, just for comfort.

Once my sisters are sitting down on the couch opposite me, Tawny starts.

"It's not an inquisition, Kayla, but we know something's up. Why are you back, why are you staying at the inn, and why do you seem so jumpy and distant?"

"We're worried about you," Ella chimes in softly.

This is it. The moment I come clean. I know they're going to freak out, but before I can overthink it, a picture of Sam leaning close comes into my mind. It's like a soothing wave of peace washes over me. It's bizarre that a man I just met can have such an affect on me, but I'm grateful for the strength that fills me just from picturing his face. He's been through a traumatic loss and he's still standing and thriving. I can do the same.

"Alright, I'll tell you everything, but let me just start by reminding you that I am here, I am safe, and I am physically fine."

They exchange worried glances with each other and sit up straighter. I take a deep breath and dive in.

"Remember last month when you didn't get an email from me for about a week? I was in Germany, shooting for that company that sells rock climbing gear. On the second day of our shoot, we were inside a cave. There was a rockslide and the entrance got blocked. I was trapped with one of the reps from the company for a while before they dug us out."

The cries and gasps of shock from my sisters are making my eyes mist over and I'm struggling against the onslaught of memories. I can hear the rumble as the rocks begin to fall and see the light disappear as the entrance was blocked. Once again, unbidden, I think of Sam and Toby. And once again, it calms me just enough that I can continue.

"The rescue team got us out as fast as possible, but it was a long time to be trapped. I went to France, stayed with Amalie to get my bearings. I've spoken with a psychologist and he suggested I take a break from work and come home, so here I am. As for staying at the inn, I just wanted to be able to have a little space. I love you guys, but I need some time alone to figure my shit out. I hope you understand."

When I finish, the room is silent except for the quiet sounds of crying coming from Ella. My twin is the more sensitive one of us, so I'm not surprised by this. Tawny is frozen, her eyes boring into me. The quiet doesn't last, however. Within moments they're both crowding me on the chair. Ella has climbed into my lap and Tawny is on the arm of the chair, wrapping her body around both me and Ella. They start to speak at the same time, and between that and the sobs coming from Ella, it's hard to make out what they're saying.

"...can't believe you didn't tell..."

"...holy fudge, we could've lost you..."

I let go of the tension I've been carrying ever since we were rescued. It feels overwhelmingly good to have my sisters with me, to feel their love and concern for me. I don't know why I was so worried about telling them. Hearing Ella's food versions of cursing and Tawny's gentle chiding over me keeping it a secret just reinforces that Doctor Dave was right. I needed to come home.

Eventually, our tears dry up and we go into the kitchen for more wine and dinner. They ask me a few questions, but both of my sisters seem satisfied with the answers I give about how long I'm staying — I don't know, but for a while; and about what support I need — not much, I've still got my therapist.

Over dinner, we shift the conversation to Marcus's development on the north end of the island. Ella's eyes light up when she talks about her husband. Their story is a crazy one, meeting on a ferry and instantly falling in love, but I can't help but draw a parallel to Sam. We met on a ferry, and while it's not love, I certainly do feel a strong pull towards him. When I mention Sam and Toby and the fact that they're moving into one of the homes, Ella leans forward eagerly.

"Oh my gosh, you know who he is, right Kayla? Sam is a super famous mystery author. He writes under the name S. Thomas. His books have hit all kinds of bestseller lists! Marcus told me he's super keen on moving here with his son. I can't believe they're here already. The house won't be done until spring." She frowns at that, and I'm quick to fill in the gap.

"He is here with his son, Toby, who will be in your kindergarten class this fall. He wanted Toby to have time to settle in and start the school year here, instead of having to move mid year. They've rented an apartment in town."

"It certainly sounds like you know a lot about our newest resident..." Tawny drawls, and I can feel the blush covering my cheeks.

"Well, I, umm, we went for lunch today. He wanted to thank me for helping with his kid on the ferry ride. Toby had wandered away and he was with me when Sam found us."

KAYLA

"Is his kid as cute as he is?" This is from Ella, who is now looking positively giddy. I know she's already picturing wedding bells for Sam and I in her head. The girl reads too many romance novels and is now living one out herself. Of course she wants to see both Tawny and I as happily in love as she is.

I roll my eyes at her, even though on the inside, I'm nodding wildly. "Yeah, Toby is an awesome kid. Sam seems like a great dad and a great guy."

"So you're going to see him again?" Tawny asks, a satisfied smile on her face. Suddenly, I get it. They're both excited because they think Sam and Toby might be enough enticement for me to stay here forever. I can't tell them they're wrong, because who knows what I'm going to do, but I also don't want them to get their hopes up too high.

"I mean, I guess so. But he's a single dad. He's not going to be interested in anything serious, he's got a kid to worry about."

My efforts to downplay things with Sam go unnoticed.

"This is so great. We'll have to invite them over for dinner soon, on a night when Marcus is free. Oh, Tawny, maybe we could do a big dinner at the inn?" Ella is chattering on excitedly. Thankfully, Tawny must sense my growing panic because my big sister puts a hand on Ella before turning to me.

"Kayla, we're just really glad you're home. No matter how long you stay. And if Sam and his son are going to be a part of your life while you're here, no matter how small, I would love to meet them."

Her calm and accepting words are exactly what I need to hear. Ella, on the other hand, seems put out.

"Excuse me, Tawny Michaels, where the heck was this understanding when I fell for Marcus? You were insane with your overprotective act!"

I stifle a giggle at how indignant Ella sounds. I heard from Tawny that when she first met Marcus, she didn't trust him with Ella. She thought he would take her away from the island and she knew how miserable that would make Ella. Obviously, she loves her brother-in-law now, but I understand why Tawny gave Marcus a hard time.

"Whatever, Ella. I love Marcus, you know that. I just needed to make sure he was here for the right reasons and wasn't just looking for a vacation fling with you." Tawny tosses her long hair over her shoulder and moves to the fridge to pull out my favorite dessert — pecan pie. She dishes up a slice for each of us, adds some whipped cream, and carries the plates back to where we're sitting.

This is what I needed. Time with my sisters, teasing each other, but more importantly, loving each other. It's time to fill my soul with the love and comfort that can only come from family and home.

18

Sam

Is it normal to miss someone you just met, when it's only been a few hours since you last saw them? I sure as shit hope so, or I'm going insane.

Once Toby is fed, bathed, and tucked into bed, I sit down on the tiny couch that's in the living room of the apartment we've rented. It's a small place, but good enough for the next few months. Part of me wonders if moving here so early, before our house was ready, was really the right choice, but I had to get out of the city. Everyone has bought the idea that we moved so Toby can settle in at school, but that's not the whole truth.

The thing is, I'm a writer. I should be able to do my job anywhere, right? Wrong. Lately, my creative muse has disappeared. And I know why. The hectic pace of the city, the constant juggle of single parenting and working, the constant feeling of being on guard, worrying about Toby's safety, it's all exhausting and I'm burnt the fuck out.

Toby's mom and I always dreamed of raising our kids in the country. When she was pregnant, we would talk about buying a farm somewhere and letting our kids run wild and get dirty. That dream disappeared when she died, but over the last year or so, the idea of finding somewhere with a slower pace to raise Toby set root in my mind. When someone at a networking event for my publisher mentioned the new development being built on Westmount Island, I was intrigued. Fast forward six months and here I am, with my furniture and belongings in storage, living in a two-bedroom apartment with my son. It's far from ideal, but I can already feel the stress leaving my body in the day that we've been here. Although I must admit, the beautiful surprise that is Kayla is probably contributing to my relaxed state. Not all of me is relaxed however, as my cock has stayed uncomfortably hard since this afternoon when I kissed her cheek. I want more of her, which could prove to be difficult given my living situation and kid situation. But I'm nothing if not determined and horny.

It's after nine and I figure she should be done having dinner with her sisters, but just in case I'm interrupting, I send her a text instead of calling right away.

SAM: Are you done with your sisters?

The '…' that tells me she's writing a reply shows up immediately and I sink back against the couch with a grin of anticipation.

KAYLA: Yup. Just got back to my room. Gimme a few minutes?
SAM: You bet.

I hop up and grab a beer from the fridge, opening it and taking a drink just as my phone vibrates with an incoming call.

"That was fast."

Kayla's warm chuckle fills my ear.

"Yeah, well, it doesn't take that long to change into something more comfortable."

"Fuck, Kayla, you don't want to know where my mind just went," I groan.

"Maybe I do," is her throaty response.

I reach into my pants to adjust myself; her voice alone is enough to cause a reaction from my cock, but throw in this unexpected — but not unwelcome — flirtatious dirty talk and my semi turns into a full erection in no time.

"Kayla, Kayla, Kayla. Were you holding out on me today?" I tease.

"Well, your son was with us. It's not like I could just jam my tongue down your throat in front of him, even if that is what I wanted to do at the park."

I huff out a sound that comes out as part groan, part laugh. "Shit, I love my son, but I might have to leave him at home next time."

She laughs and I can hear blankets rustling on the other end of the phone before she replies. Her voice is sleepy, but still filled with anticipation and desire.

"Don't do that, I like Toby. But if we *could* find a way to have a moment to ourselves..."

"I'll figure it out, sweetheart, I promise." Resolve is strong in my voice and my words. I'm not waiting a week for my parents to get here. Somehow, I need to see Kayla without Toby being a cockblocker. "But for now, tell me something. Are you in bed?"

She giggles quietly. "Yep."

"Are you naked?"

Her intake of breath is barely audible. "No, but I could be."

"Don't. I need to feel you in real life before we go any further. I'm not gonna lie, I'll be using that mental image of you in bed to relieve some pressure tonight."

"Sam..." she moans softly.

"I'm gonna let you go now. Not because I don't want to talk to you more, but because if I keep you on the phone, I can't guarantee I'll be able to control myself."

Kayla lets out a small sigh. "Control is overrated."

I laugh at that. She's got a smart-ass attitude that I enjoy. "True, Kayla. True. But patience and anticipation can be our friend in this situation. Trust me, I'll figure out a way to get you to myself as soon as possible. Then I'll show you what I've been wanting to do since I first laid eyes on you this morning."

She makes a sound of satisfaction that sends a jolt through my already throbbing cock.

"Can I see you tomorrow?"

"Count on it."

* * *

"Dad! Can we hang out with Kayla today?"

Toby's small body bounces on my chest, making me grunt as I wake up fully from the fuzzy end of the dream I was having. Thankfully, it wasn't like the dream I woke up from in the middle of the night. The one that required a cold shower and my hand before I could fall back asleep.

"Sure, little man." My voice is gravelly, I'm still only half awake, and yet my mind instantly wanders to Kayla. Is she awake yet? A glance at the clock tells me Toby has gifted me with another ridiculously early start to my day. Kids are the worst at sleeping in, or at least mine is. It's barely seven a.m. I need coffee, preferably mainlined into my body, if I'm going to function today.

"Is it pancake day today? I love pancakes. I think I want apple pancakes today, Dad. We have apples, right?"

"No, Toby, remember —we didn't make it to the grocery store yesterday," I explain patiently. Normally Toby is a pretty accepting kid and handles it well when things don't go his way. Today he seems to be headed in that direction as well, until a surprisingly sneaky look comes over his face.

"I wonder if Kayla has apples," he says, innocently enough. But I can read between the not-so-subtle lines. Is my five-year-old trying to be

SAM

a matchmaker? I chuckle.

"Nah, sorry dude, she's staying at a hotel, so she probably doesn't have any apples." But that does give me an idea. A quick internet search confirms that the restaurant at the inn where Kayla is staying serves breakfast starting at eight.

"Tell you what, Tobes, let's get dressed and go for a walk. We can surprise Kayla and take her out for breakfast. Deal?"

"Deal!" With one final bounce, Toby is off my bed and running into his room. I climb out of bed and head into the en suite bathroom to turn on the shower. The one I had last night was more about cooling off and hiding the evidence of my desperate jerk off session than getting clean. While I wait for the water to warm up, I'm brushing my teeth and debating if I need to shave. I'm scruffy, but it's not too bad, and if I'm not mistaken, Kayla shivered when my chin brushed the sensitive skin by her ear yesterday. I'll leave it.

Just as I'm about to climb in the shower, my phone beeps with a message. I could ignore it, but what if it's her...

Sure enough, it's from Kayla, and it's all I can do to not rub my hands together in glee at her message.

KAYLA: It's stupid early, and I'm awake instead of happily sleeping because of time zones. My body doesn't know where I live anymore. You've got a small child so I'm assuming you are also awake. Misery loves company dontcha know.

SAM: It's true. Not the misery part, but the kid waking me up part.

SAM: How do you feel about breakfast... Toby wants pancakes.

KAYLA: He's got good taste. And it just so happens that the chef at my sister's inn makes great pancakes.

SAM: Apple?

KAYLA: Apple what

SAM: Apple pancakes. That's what he wants.

KAYLA: Oh. I'm sure they can handle that.

SAM: Great. See you in half an hour.

KAYLA: Crap. That means I have to get dressed.

SAM: I mean... I wouldn't mind if you didn't, but the rest of the inn's visitors might

KAYLA: Ha. Ha. Ha. It's too early for flirting, Sam. Besides. You might not be so excited once you find out that both of my sisters will likely be here too.

SAM: Bring it on.

KAYLA: Okay then, just remember you said that when you're facing the interrogators. See you soon.

SAM: Can't wait.

I put my phone down and step in the shower, still smiling. Toby wanders into my bedroom and starts jumping on my bed.

"Dad, awe you gonna kiss Kayla today?" His voice is clear despite the water pounding down on my head and I freeze. Not exactly an ideal moment to have a conversation with your kid about dating, but I guess I don't have a choice.

"How would you feel about it if I did?" I call out as I quickly rinse the shampoo out of my hair and reach for the soap.

Toby takes a minute to answer and when he does, his messed up 'r' sounds are hilarious as usual. "Giwuls are bo-wing. But Kayla's fun." Then he jumps off my bed and runs into the living room. I hear the television turn on and I guess that's the end of the conversation.

Fifteen minutes later, we're out the door and headed to the Westmount Inn. According to the directions I found online, it should only be a ten-minute walk. But that clearly doesn't account for a hungry five-year-old. Just as my frustration starts to hit the point of no return, we're saved by an angel.

"Hey you two, I wondered if you got lost so I thought I'd walk to meet you. I brought snacks."

Kayla is all smiles as she winks at me, then bends down to Toby's level. She waves a banana and a donut in her two hands.

"What do you think, Toby. Should we give your dad the banana or the donut?"

He's looking at her like she's Santa Claus and the Easter Bunny all wrapped in one and I cringe. Guess I really should've given him a snack before we left.

"Can I have the donut?"

"Toby, manners," I remind him gently.

"Please Kayla, can I have the donut?"

She glances up at me to make sure it's okay and when I nod, she hands it over to my son, who demolishes it in two seconds flat. Then Toby takes her hand and looks up at her with a very serious expression on his face.

"That was good, but I'm still hungwy. Awe you gonna have pancakes with us?"

"You bet I am; I'm hungry, too. Want to race to the inn? It's just up that lane." She points to the driveway that we had almost reached and I let out an internal sigh of relief. My usually good-spirited kid was getting a serious case of hangry that would not have left a good impression on her sisters.

"Yeah!"

Toby takes off and Kayla goes to jog after him. Before she gets too far, she turns back to me with a smirk. "You coming?"

"Nah, I prefer the view at the back of the pack," I reply casually, then toss her a wink of my own. She lets out a laugh that sounds free and relaxed before she turns and runs after my son.

19

Kayla

I'm glad to get away from Sam for a minute. I can't believe how unprepared I was for seeing him again. It's like each time I see his face, he's more handsome than the last. Running after Toby gives me a moment to get my pounding heart under control and gives me a better excuse for the flush on my cheeks that I know my sisters will notice.

Toby and I are sitting on the steps of the inn waiting for Sam, who's strolling up the drive, when Ella and Marcus come around the corner from their cottage. Ella's eyes light up when she sees me with Toby and I know she's guessed who he is.

"Kayla! You brought a friend to breakfast," she says cheerily as they come to a stop in front of us. Toby looks up at her in awe, then turns to look at me, then back to Ella. His head bounces back and forth between us, as if he can't believe he's seeing double. I nudge him with my shoulder, then whisper loudly.

"Remember I told you I have a twin sister? This is her."

Just then, Sam reaches our group, so I stand up and make introductions. He and Marcus shake hands with some familiarity and I realize they must have met already since Sam is buying in Marcus's development.

KAYLA

Once we're inside, breakfast is served quickly, and I take the opportunity to watch my sisters interact with Sam and Toby. So far, Tawny hasn't scared him off with her pointed questions about his move to the island. Ella has Toby captivated and I know he's going to love having her as his teacher in the fall.

It's a little overwhelming how easily they fit in with my family. What will happen when I leave again? Will my sisters still be friendly? Will they have meals together, without me there? That thought sends a swift pang to my heart.

I'm snapped out of my thoughts by chairs being pushed back. Breakfast is over and I spent half of it in a brain fog.

"I've got to go deal with some invoices. Nice to meet you Sam, Toby," Tawny says as she turns with a wave to head to her office.

"Hey Toby, would you like to come with Marcus and I to see the chickens?" Ella asks, reaching for Toby's hand.

Toby looks up at his dad pleadingly. "Can I Dad? Please?"

"Sure," Sam shrugs. I'm still frozen in my seat until Sam sits back down beside me. I feel his arm stretch along the back of my chair and then his breath tickles my ear.

"We're alone, Kayla," he whispers heatedly. Like a shot, I'm up, pushing my chair back loudly. I grab his hand and pull him through the dining room, towards the staircase that leads up to the second floor and my room.

I try not to run up the stairs, but then again, Sam's tight grip on my hand and long stride tell me he's just as eager as I am. Thankfully, the keycard swipes green on the first try, and then we're inside.

As soon as the door closes, Sam's hands are on my face, cupping my cheeks, and he's kissing me. Our mouths meld together and there's no awkward moments that usually come with first kisses. No fumbling as you figure out where to position your head. Not this time; our lips find each other instantly as if they were designed for just this.

Sam has taken control of our kiss and turned the spark between us into an inferno. My hands are holding his shoulders tightly as he walks me backward toward the bed. When I stop at the edge of it, he spins us around, then he sits down, pulling me down to straddle his legs. I groan when I feel his rock-hard length pushing through the fabric between us, teasing me. Sam captures my lower lip in his teeth, tugging me back in for another deliriously hot kiss.

Eventually, he pulls back slightly and starts to pepper kisses over my face and down my neck. When he reaches the juncture of my shoulder and neck, he stays there, licking, nipping, and kissing his way over my collarbone to the other side before traveling back up my neck to my face. He returns to my lips briefly.

"You taste even better than I could have dreamed," he murmurs in between kisses.

I moan when his tongue traces the outline of my jaw. The scruff on his cheeks is probably making my skin red, but I don't care. It feels incredible, the friction heightening every sensation.

I grind my hips in small circles on his lap and he groans as his hands tighten on my hips.

"How long will it take to look at chickens?" he growls.

"Depends on if they're awake or not, but probably not long," is my breathy reply as his hands travel up my sides, under my shirt. Then, as if an alarm went off somewhere, through my open window, we can hear Toby's voice chattering away to Ella. Of course. How could I forget, my window faces the same direction as the chicken coop. Sam freezes and drops his head to my shoulder.

"Damn it."

I slowly climb off his lap and straighten my shirt. When Sam flops back on my bed with a disgruntled sound, I giggle before I climb on the bed beside him. He opens his eyes and frowns at me before pulling me down so that my head rests on his chest. I can hear his heart beating quickly underneath his shirt and I place my hand there to feel his heat.

"What have you done to me, Kayla?" he mutters softly as his hand begins to slowly run up and down my back.

"Same thing you've done to me, I suspect," I answer.

"I can't get enough of you."

"Same."

Once we've straightened up as best we can, we head back downstairs to find the others. Just before we push the door of the stairwell open, Sam pulls me into his arms and presses a hard kiss to my lips, thrusting his tongue inside my mouth in a way that leaves no doubt as to what he would rather be doing.

"We're going to continue this, soon, Kayla," he rumbles in my ear.

Unfortunately life, and Toby, have different plans.

* * *

Five days later and Sam and I still haven't managed to find any time to be alone. Don't get me wrong, I've hung out with him and Toby every day this week, showing them around the island. I have loved spending time with them, in spite of not even having a single minute alone with Sam, thanks to one adorable child. My lips are going into some serious withdrawal from missing Sam's kisses.

And it's not for lack of trying, either. Ella had to leave the island with Marcus for a few days, so she couldn't watch Toby, and Tawny has been run off her feet with issues at the inn. She's been so busy I've been helping her out in the afternoons and having dinner with her each evening just to make sure she takes a break. Thankfully, Sam says his parents are arriving in a few days and we should be able to get some time to ourselves then.

Finally, an opportunity presents itself that I gladly take. Tawny has to work the dinner shift in the restaurant because her hostess is off sick, so I won't be eating with her. A quick text to Sam and I'm picking up a pizza from the joint in town and heading over to their apartment. I put on some sexy lingerie and make sure to shave everywhere, because the one thing I do know about kids is that they go to bed early.

Toby insists on sitting between the two of us while we watch a movie with dinner, and I can't say I mind that at all. Sam's arm is stretched along the back of the couch and his fingers are playing with my hair. When I feel a small weight leaning against me and look down to see Toby cuddled into my side, a part of my heart that I didn't know existed kicks in. This feels good, like, *happy family* good.

When the movie ends, Toby's asleep with his head falling into my lap. Sam looks at me with unbridled lust in his eyes, then stands slowly. He scoops Toby into his arms and walks down the hall to Toby's room. I can hear his low voice soothing Toby, who must have woken up slightly. I need to move, so I stand up and clear away the dishes and pizza box, then busy myself tidying up his already neat kitchen. I know what I want to happen tonight, but at the same time I feel weird about our first time being when Toby is around — even if he is asleep. How do single parents manage to have a sex life, anyway?

Strong arms wrap around my waist, startling me. Then warm lips descend on my neck as hands brush my hair over one shoulder.

"Do you have any idea how fucking awesome it is to watch you with my son?" Sam says gruffly.

I turn in his arms and the look I see in Sam's eyes shocks me. That's not just lust. That's something much more powerful and it scares me. Sam obviously doesn't notice my discomfort, so I work to push it aside and just enjoy the moment. Even still, it takes me a second to realize he's still talking.

"...so right having you here with us. And now I've finally got you to myself." Suddenly his hands are under my ass and he's lifting me up onto the kitchen counter.

I gasp at his firm touch pushing my legs apart so he can stand between them, pulling us close. My hands automatically go to the bottom of his shirt and I pull it up and over his head, then let out a moan. I've felt his body through his shirt, but seeing it revealed is something else. He's pure muscle, but lean — not beefy. There's a tattoo on his ribs and I realize it says 'Toby' in a beautiful script. My fingertips trace the outline of it as my thoughts spiral in every direction except the one Sam obviously wants tonight to go.

"Sam..." I start, then stop, completely uncertain how to put words to the turmoil I'm experiencing. He lifts his head from my neck and when he looks at me, I see the moment he registers my uncertainty.

"What's wrong?"

"Nothing," I answer quickly, then bite my lip before I continue. "Actually, that's not true. The truth is, I don't know what's wrong, maybe nothing, maybe something." A frown flits across his face and I quickly lift my hands up to cup his face reassuringly. "It's all me, not you, Sam. You, Toby, what's between us feels so good. So, so, so good. And it's unexpected, I guess."

He nods, his hands rubbing the top of my legs soothingly, gesturing for me to keep going.

"I came back here for a break after my job in Germany and it was meant to be just that — a break. I figured I'd be back out there, shooting in the wild before long. But you're making me want different things. And that's...I don't know, overwhelming."

Sam doesn't say anything and I worry that maybe I've screwed this up before it even truly began. When he does speak, it's not the question I expected.

"What happened in Germany?"

I let out a sound of surprise, because I'm startled to realize he doesn't know. I suddenly remember that, even though I feel as if Sam has been in my life for so long and we know everything about each other, our situation couldn't be farther from the truth. He has no idea what my life was like off the island and he has no clue about what sent me running home.

I push him away and hop down off the counter, handing him his shirt. Opening his fridge, I pull out two beers and hand him one before I walk over to the couch.

"This is going to require alcohol."

He sits down beside me, but instead of taking a drink himself, he just watches me take a long pull from the bottle, then pulls me into his side so I'm cuddled against him, just like Toby was with me during the movie.

"Tell me, Kayla." His voice is soft and comforting, but there's a steel behind his words. He's not moving until he knows everything.

So I tell him everything. I tell him about Germany, the cave-in, and my fear of being trapped. I tell him about my therapist and how he was the one to suggest I come home for a while. I tell him that I worry about my sisters hovering over me and pushing me to move back to the island, and I tell him about my career. How important it is to me, how it fills my soul, and ignites a passion inside of me that I've never found with anything else. What I don't tell him is that being with him and Toby stirs a different kind of passion.

When I finish, Sam is silent. His arm that's wrapped around me has tightened noticeably, gradually pulling me closer and closer to his body as my story unfolded. But now his grip loosens and his hand begins to move rhythmically up and down my arm. The movement is comforting in a simple way. And I appreciate the fact that he's not freaking out or pushing me away. He's calm and steady, and it's in this moment that I realize I need something — or someone — calm and steady right now. That's why Doctor Dave recommended I come home, to find something that grounds me. I guess I just never thought of the possibility that it would be a person.

"Kayla."

His voice is low, somewhere between a whisper and a rumble. It's filled with emotion; desire mixed with pain. I wait for him to say something more than my name, but he doesn't. At least, not with words.

Suddenly he's on the floor, kneeling between my legs. He's tall enough that our faces are almost at the same level, so it's easy for him to gently hold my face with his hands and pull me forward slightly so he can kiss me.

20

Sam

Kayla's confession ripped me apart and her strength is slowly putting me back together. But she doesn't seem to see her own strength, which kills me all over again. I want to wrap her in my arms and make her forget the memories that I forced her to dredge up. Fuck, she's been through so much these last few months and I just made her relive it all. The only positive to this is that I now understand. I get why she might hesitate, why she might struggle with the intensity and speed with which things between us are growing. But if Kayla wants a home base, then that's what I want to be for her. Toby and I can be the anchor that keeps her safe when she's out exploring the world. I want that more than I want anything else right now.

I stand up, bringing her with me and lifting her straight into my arms. When her strong legs wrap around my waist, I groan into our kiss. I can feel her lips curve up in a smile and she wiggles her hips slightly. I turn around and sit on the couch with her in my lap. She stills, and I know she can feel my cock pressing into her. Part of me wants to push things further, to strip her naked and lose myself inside her body. But that's not the plan.

Instead, I bring my hands up to cover hers, drawing her fingers to my

SAM

lips so I can kiss them.

"I won't say I understand how you must be feeling right now, because I don't, and I can't. I'll just say this — you're in control, Kayla. Take from me what you need and what you want. I'll be here, waiting for you to figure out what is best for you. I hope that Toby and I are a part of that, but if all you need is right now, then that's okay, too."

I'm not lying, I truly will be here for whatever she needs. At the same time, the thought of this only being a short-term fling feels like an ice pick being jammed into my heart. It hurts, it's cold, and I may not survive. She has come to mean more to me in just a couple of days than I would have ever thought possible. Still, if that's what she wants, I'll accept it for now. Doesn't mean I won't fight for more, but it does mean I'll give her what she needs. Kayla looks at me for a moment and I can't read her expression. I find myself holding my breath, waiting for her to say something.

When she leans in close to me, my heart speeds up. And when she places her mouth next to my ear, my hands find their way to her hips and hold on tight.

"I need more than right now. I need you."

Before I can respond, she leans back and pulls her tank top over her head, revealing mouthwatering breasts covered in black satin and lace. My breath comes out in a whoosh that she captures with her lips. Her tongue pushes into my mouth and her hands reach down between us to the hem of my T-shirt. I pull it off for the second time tonight and the instant I feel her pressed against my chest, my baser instincts take over. My hands crush her body to mine and her answering moan makes my cock press against my pants so firmly it's starting to ache. I draw back slightly just to make sure Kayla is truly on the same page.

"Is this what you want?" I press my hips into hers to emphasize the question and the blissed out, sultry smile that covers her face is all the answer I need.

"God, yes."

In the back of my mind a voice tries to tell me that our first time shouldn't be on a couch in my rental apartment with my son asleep just a few feet away. That spurs me to stand up, still with Kayla wrapped around me, like a monkey clinging to a tree. I walk quickly down the short hall to my bedroom, where I have the sense to lock the door behind us. Then all logic and reason are gone when Kayla slides out of my arms and down onto the floor in front of me. She opens my pants, sliding them over my cock, taking my boxers down at the same time until my dick springs free. She makes a satisfied sound that makes me grow even harder as her hand wraps around my length.

"Jesus. Fuck. Kayla, I want to — "

"I don't care, Sam. You said I could take what I need, and I need you," she interrupts me and there's a fire in her eyes that shuts me up. At least until the moment her hot mouth wraps around my cock. Then I can't hold back my groan, which is ridiculously loud even muffled behind my arm that I raise to cover my mouth. God, if Toby were to wake up right now... nope. That's a thought I'm not going to complete. *Dad* Sam has left the room and *Man* Sam is up to bat.

Kayla's licking me like I'm her favorite goddamn popsicle and it's making me lose my mind. Then she reaches one hand out to cup my balls and the other reaches down her own pants to start playing with herself, and I'm fucking done.

"Holy fuck," I groan, letting her carry on for a moment longer because shit, that's one hell of a view. Then I'm hauling her up to her feet and pushing her backwards until she falls onto my bed. I pull her leggings down and after taking just a second to appreciate the matching black panties covering the part of her that I really want, I pull them down, too. Kayla lifts her chest just enough to open her bra and let it drop to the floor, and suddenly I don't know where to look. Her perfect breasts are there, begging for my hands, but her sex is glistening with her arousal and I need to taste her more than I need air to breathe.

I drop down into a squat and lift her long legs over my shoulders. Thank God I can still reach her tits from here, which gives me the best of both worlds. One hand goes up to fondle a breast, feeling its heavy weight, playing with her nipple until it's like a pebble under my fingers, and the other hand goes between her legs to gently hold her open to my mouth. I don't waste any time, leaning in with a swipe of my tongue up her slit. Her hips lift up to meet me as she gasps and grabs at the blankets on my bed. Kayla's responsive as hell and it's the sexiest thing I've ever seen. She's writhing under my touch, but my hand on her breast is holding her in place as my tongue thrusts in and out of her core. The sounds of pleasure coming from her, my name falling from her lips in frantic whispers, it's building us towards something that is going to be monumental.

When her legs clamp around my head and her hands let go of the death grip on the blankets to thread into my hair, I know she's close. I bring both hands down to her sex, one hand holding her open so that I can slide my fingers inside, curving them upwards and stroking her until her whispered shouts hit a fevered pitch. She sounds hoarse and a part of me admires her restraint and ability to keep quiet, even as another part of me longs to hear her let loose with her passion. When I find that spot, my mouth moves to her clit, and I suck, gently. She goes still for just a second, then Kayla's body lets go in wave after wave of spectacular release. I ride her through it, sucking, licking, and teasing her with my mouth and fingers until her shudders stop and her body goes limp. Then I kiss my way up her body to where her chest is rising and falling, and I lick the light sheen of sweat that covers the skin between her breasts.

"Still with me, babe?" I ask with a grin, because her eyes are closed, and one arm is thrown across her face. It's the look of a woman well fucked and we haven't even hit the main event.

Kayla lowers her arm and lifts her head. "I'm with you. Just. Gimme a minute." Her head flops back down on the pillow and I drop my head down onto her stomach, not even trying to hold back my laughter. My body rolls off of her and I make my way to the head of my bed before pulling her up and into my arms. She comes willingly and my laughter dies down when I see the look in her eyes.

"Condom?" she asks, and when I gesture to my side table she stretches across my body, her nipples grazing my chest. On her way back, Kayla goes on all fours before she turns to look over her shoulder at me.

"Still with me?" she asks, echoing my earlier question and I jump into action. Her ass is sticking up in the air, enticing me, pulling me toward her like a magnet. The condom is rolled on and my hands are gripping her hips within seconds, but before I slide in for the first time, I lean forward and kiss a line down her spine.

"I'm with you."

One smooth thrust into her tight heat and I groan way louder than I should with Toby sleeping across the hall. But I don't think about that, all I can think about is how good she feels, how perfect our bodies have come together, and how the fuck I'm going to manage not to blow my load in seconds like a teenage boy.

Kayla's making these little noises every time I hit her deep inside, part moan, part sigh, all hot.

"So good, babe. So good," I mutter out, in between thrusts. I'm trying to hold onto a thread of control, determined to make her come again before I do. When her noises take on a keening quality, I know she's close. I wrap my hands around her stomach and pull her upright so that her back is pressed to my front. It forces my cock to rub against her front wall and I know instantly that it's *the* position for her, because she gasps and her hands grab my hair, pulling hard enough to make me lower my head to her shoulder. I nip at her skin gently, then suck over the bite, not hard enough to leave a mark, but enough that she knows I could. Then as my legs start to burn with the exertion of holding her upright and thrusting into her, my hand goes around to rub her clit and it's game over for both of us.

Kayla drops forward, moaning *oh God oh God oh God* over and over, and I drape over her as I lose myself to one, two, three more thrusts before filling the condom with the evidence of my orgasm. When I'm finally done, I somehow manage to maneuver us to be laying on our sides, spooning together, with my softening dick still inside. I know I need to slide out and deal with the condom, but honestly, I'm so fucking blown away by the intensity of what we just did, I can't quite bring myself to pull apart from her yet. Somehow, Kayla Michaels has inserted herself into my heart and soul. Now I just have to figure out how to convince her to stay with me.

21

Kayla

I've read about mind blowing, life altering sex, but I never imagined I'd experience it here, in an apartment on Westmount Island, with a single dad no less. But that's what just happened. The earth moved and I'm pretty sure I heard angels singing when I was coming. That was the kind of sex a woman dreams about. Sam is the kind of *man* a woman dreams about. And he's here, on the island I've been considering calling home once more. If this is what fate looks like, consider me a fan.

Sam pulls away from me and deals with the condom. Me, I still can't move, even though I know I should. I need to get up, get dressed, and go back to the inn. I absolutely, positively, must not fall asleep. But two back-to-back orgasms, preceded by an emotionally draining confession, really is exhausting. And when Sam slides back onto the bed and pulls a blanket up to cover us, I'm helpless to the pull to snuggle into his big spoon embrace and let my eyes blink shut.

The next thing I'm aware of is the sound of someone trying to turn a door handle and then a small voice saying, "Daddy?" in a tearful voice.

Sam shoots upright and is out of bed before I can even open my eyes. I stay frozen in bed, suddenly aware that we haven't talked about how to tell Toby that we're dating, and him finding me in bed, naked, is probably not the best idea right now. But then I register that we never closed the curtains last night and it's still dark outside. The time it takes for my half asleep brain to figure this out is the same amount of time it takes for Sam to deal with Toby and come back to sit on the edge of the bed beside me. He gives me a soft smile as he strokes my hair and we stay like that for a moment in this blissful quiet.

"I'm sorry I fell asleep," I whisper.

"I'm not," he replies. Then he sighs. "But Toby had a nightmare and when he has one, he often has another and needs to sleep in here with me. I got him settled for now and as much as I don't want you to, I think you should go."

I can tell he doesn't want to say that, so I don't feel any anger or hurt toward him essentially kicking me out. To try and soothe his discomfort, I sit up, letting the sheet fall away so my breasts are bare. Heat flares in his eyes and I can see the indecision warring there. I smirk, then when he sees my teasing grin, he chuckles.

"Don't worry about it. You're a dad first and a boyfriend second. This isn't the best way to tell Toby that we're together."

Sam leans in and kisses me. "Boyfriend. I like that. Text me when you get back to the hotel, okay?"

I nod, then climb out of his bed and get dressed. It's a good thing I drove to pick up the pizza tonight, so I've got my car here, since it's now a lot later than I thought. I don't get back to the inn until nearly two a.m. Thankfully, the front desk is unmanned so I can sneak upstairs without anyone seeing me. Once I'm in my room, I send a quick text to Sam, but he must be dealing with Toby or asleep, because he doesn't reply.

That's okay by me since I'm still exhausted. After brushing my teeth and putting on pajamas, I crawl beneath my sheets and I'm asleep in minutes, the word *boyfriend* bouncing around my head.

* * *

The next morning, I'm drinking a cup of coffee in my room, scrolling through the news headlines when a reminder pops up on my calendar. I've got a session with Doctor Dave starting in fifteen minutes. I'm caught off guard, but in a good way, because I forgot about therapy. This week is the first one in a long time that I haven't felt the need to talk to him; haven't felt the pull of fear, or anger, or grief over what happened and the uncertainty of my future. I feel good and it's because of a man and his son.

Still, it can't hurt to check in, so I get dressed and pull my hair into a messy bun before opening my computer and loading the video conferencing program. Shortly, my screen fills with the face of the man who pulled me out of a dark place.

"Hey, Doc," I say with a smile, and his weathered face crinkles into a grin in return.

"You look well, Kayla," he observes.

I nod, and take a sip of my coffee as I try to think of how much to tell him.

"I am well. At least I think I am. You were right, coming back here was a good choice. Seeing my sisters has been wonderful and the slow, peaceful pace feels nice."

Doctor Dave looks at me expectantly; he knows me well enough to recognize when I'm holding back. I take a deep breath and plunge in.

"And I met someone on the ferry. Two someone's, actually," I giggle at the shocked look on his face. "Get your mind out of the gutter, Doc, I mean a guy and his son. Sam and Toby. We've been spending a lot of time together and it's been good to be busy." I shrug, not sure how to explain the intense feelings that are growing between Sam and I. Part of me wants to keep it a secret, but I also know that Doctor Dave could help me process things a lot quicker than if I try to do it on my own.

"Busy is good, so long as you're not ignoring the work you have to do. Remember, part of the plan for your visit to the island was to think about your future and how to establish balance in your life, balance that allows for your career aspirations as well as your personal ones. After we finished our initial work of helping you to process the cave-in, you told me you wanted to find a way to continue to do the photography that you love, and make time for family. Have you reached any decisions on that?"

I think about his question for a few minutes. The immediate answer is no, I haven't done the tasks he suggested in terms of journaling and thinking about what I want in the future. I don't have pro and con lists, or journal entries, but I do have a gut feeling that is growing stronger and stronger. And that feeling is telling me to stay on the island and be with Sam. The problem is, I can't base my decision on a man I just met, can I?

"I'm going to make Westmount Island my home," I state and saying it aloud feels right. "I'm going to scale back on how many jobs I take on a year and try to focus more on North America for a while." That also feels like the right decision and I realize that I've had the answers in my heart all along, I just needed the push to voice them.

"And what about this man, Sam? How does he fit into your plans?"

Good ol' Doc, always hard hitting with the questions.

"I...want him to fit in, but I need to make my decision be about me and not him. Right?"

"Are you asking, or are you telling?"

That's one of Doc's favorite tricks. Not letting me try to get him to tell me what to do.

"I have to decide for me."

"How do you feel about Sam and his son?"

I pause. A small voice inside of me is whispering a four-letter word that I've never said about a man before. A louder voice is saying that's crazy and there's no way it's possible to love someone after just meeting them a few days ago, but then, look at Ella. She fell in love with Marcus almost immediately, even if they didn't say the words to each other right away.

"I care about them." Even I can hear the hesitation in my voice and Doc just raises and eyebrow at me. "Okay, I more than care about them. When we're together, even if we're just taking his son to the park or having lunch, it's as if everything in my life makes sense. I can't imagine life without them and it's hard to remember what it was like before them. At the same time, I feel crazy having these feelings for someone I've only known a week."

Doctor Dave is nodding slowly and even through a computer screen I can see the acceptance and compassion on his face.

"Kayla, do you trust yourself?"

I shrug. "Yeah, I guess so."

"Yes or no? Do you trust yourself? Has your gut or your heart ever led you astray?"

I consider that for a moment. I think back to the day of the rockslide. My gut had told me something was off that morning; that's part of what I had to work through with Doc. I was so angry that I hadn't listened to myself and suggested a change in the shooting location.

"I do trust myself."

"Then why do you think your feelings for Sam are crazy?"

I lean back in my chair, baffled by the simplicity of that observation. Suddenly I can see, with absolute clarity, what my vision is for my life.

"I love him, Doc. I love both of them and I want them to be my home."

He nods and there's a satisfied look on his face that I've come to recognize as his *now she gets it* face.

"Then make that happen."

22

Sam

As much as I hated making Kayla leave in the middle of the night, it's a good thing I did. Just as I predicted, Toby was in my bed about half an hour after she left. I love my kid, and he comes first, but I also loved having Kayla fall asleep beside me. With Toby snuggled up to me instead of her, I lay awake for another hour imagining what it would be like if she were still here. Would Toby cuddle up to her instead when he has a bad dream? Would she soothe him from his bad dreams?

Now it's morning and Toby is bouncing around, full of energy, clearly not affected by his nightmares. I, on the other hand, am dragging ass, drinking my third cup of coffee and trying to clear the cobwebs from my first sleepless night in a while. I reached a conclusion last night; I need to talk to Kayla, tell her how I feel, and ask her to consider making her life here on Westmount with us. Obviously, I know it's not going to be that simple, but I know in my heart I have to make it happen.

The other problem with this plan is that my parents arrive tomorrow and I'm not sure where things stand with Kayla in terms of our relationship. We talked about her meeting my parents, but things are different now. I want her in my life, preferably forever, and that means I'm not introducing her as a friend but as my lover, my girlfriend, my partner. I hope. The small nugget of doubt that rests in my heart is eating away at me, making me wonder if I'm insane, if I'm making a huge mistake assuming she is falling for me the way I'm falling for her. The fact remains that ever since Toby was born, I've had to adopt an attitude of *suck it up and do it* when it comes to the things I'm nervous about, whether it's cleaning up vomit after Toby had the stomach flu, dropping him off at daycare for the first time, or telling the woman of my dreams that I'm falling in love with her. I need to just do it, no matter how anxious I am.

Before I lose the nerve I've built up, I send her a text with a photo of Toby sprawled over top of me last night.

SAM: Hey beautiful, hope you slept better than I did...

KAYLA: Awwww. Poor guy.

KAYLA: Guess it's a good thing I left

SAM: I wouldn't say that. I'd rather sleep with you on top of me than him.

KAYLA: Sam...

I take a deep breath, tuning out the cartoons that Toby's turned on in the background. I can't do this over text, I need to see her face, so I quickly hit the video call button. Her face fills my screen and instantly I am reassured. She is everything I've ever wanted in a woman. This is right.

"Miss me that much, huh?" Her voice is teasing, but I can see the happiness on her face.

I don't even try to deny it. "Sure did. Falling asleep with you in my arms, even if we didn't mean to, was incredible."

Her face softens into a warm smile. "It was pretty great."

"We should do it again soon."

Kayla opens her mouth to say something, but my call waiting pops up and it's my editor.

"Crap, I'm sorry Kayla, I have to take this call, it's my editor, probably calling to yell at me for falling behind deadline again." I wince, knowing Shelley will have every right to yell. I've been so distracted with our move and then with Kayla that I'm behind by a few chapters. "But I want to see you today so we can talk. Could you come over later? I'll let Toby watch a movie and we can sit on the patio or something." Damn, having a kid and no babysitter is making this tricky. Thankfully, I seem to have fallen for an incredibly understanding woman because Kayla nods and I smile gratefully as I switch to the call with Shelley.

**

Once I've placated Shelley with promises of a few chapters by the end of the week, I get Toby dressed and we head down to Wharf Street for some groceries. I'm distracted by thoughts of Kayla and my son must realize this because before we even hit the store, he's stopped and is looking at me with his arms crossed over his stomach.

"Daddy. You didn't listen to my stowy, did you," he says accusingly.

"Shoot. Sorry bud, I missed it." I stop and go to a nearby bench to sit down. "Can you tell me again?"

"Why didn't you listen?"

I've got a decision to make. On the one hand, this could be the perfect moment to talk to Toby about me dating Kayla; on the other hand, I haven't yet been able to find out how she feels, so it could also be risky. I go with my gut, which is telling me she's in this as deep as I am and take this opportunity as it is.

"I was thinking about Kayla," I reply. Toby comes to sit beside me and his little legs swing in the air, reminding me of how young he is, despite the maturity he's showing with this conversation.

"Do you like Kayla, buddy?"

"Yup. Do you?"

How to answer that one stumps me for a minute, but I decide to proceed honestly.

"I think I more than like her, Toby. I think I love her."

"Does that mean you want to hold hands?"

I chuckle. "Yeah, it does. And I might kiss her, and she might have a sleepover at our house sometimes. Would that be okay with you?"

He seems to think about this for a while and I hold my breath nervously. This is the first time I've talked to him about my being with a woman and his approval is crucial.

"Yeah, that's okay. Can I sleep with you guys at the sleepovuh too?"

My heart feels like it might burst as I pull my son into my side and press a kiss to his head. He tries to get away but I don't let him, needing to show him my love, even if he doesn't recognize it as that.

"Maybe, little man. Maybe."

Toby hops off the bench, the conversation clearly over in his mind, and I stand up with a wide grin.

Sleepovers with Kayla are officially on the table. Now I just have to talk to her about that.

But first I have to corral a five-year-old around the grocery store and try not to let him fill the cart with too much junk food. Don't get me wrong, I like sugary cereal and chips as much as the next guy, but as a dad, it's my job to balance that with fruit and vegetables.

Once we're home and the food is all unpacked and put away, I reach for my phone to firm up plans with Kayla. It's then I see a missed message from my mom that changes everything.

MOM: Hi honey, SURPRISE! Your father was able to rearrange his schedule, so we're coming to see you today! Our ferry gets in at two and I've got ingredients for Nana's special lasagna with me for my favorite grandson.

Shit. As excited as I am to see my parents and show them Westmount Island, this means I won't be able to talk to Kayla today. I sigh as I open a text window to her.

SAM: Hey beautiful, I hate that I have to do this but I need to cancel our plans. My parents surprised us and are coming in early, so I need

SAM

to clean up and then get them from the ferry later on.

KAYLA: Bummer, but yay for your parents coming? (is it a yay?)

SAM: lol yeah, it's a yay. Toby really misses them, and with them here, I can get away and take you on a real date. After I tell them about you, that is.

SAM: Speaking of telling people.... I talked with Toby about us. He wants to have a sleepover with you. Didn't realize I'd be competing with my son for your attention.

KAYLA: What can I say, I'm a popular sleeping buddy. Also. Wow. So, this is like, serious now.

I can feel her nerves ramping up even over text messages, so I dial her number.

"Yes, it's serious, babe. Didn't you get that message the other night?" I tease and am rewarded by her throaty chuckle. Maybe she's not as panicked as I thought.

"I did, don't worry."

"Are you upset I talked to Toby without you? I wanted to talk to you first, but the timing was just right and he is totally fine with it, or at least he's fine with whatever he understands about us dating." I'm rambling and I need to stop.

"Sam. It's fine. He's your kid, you *should* be the one to tell him. But I hope we can talk soon, too, I...want to tell you something." Now I know I'm not mistaking the nerves in her voice, but she sounds hopeful as well and my heart starts to race.

* * *

The reunion between Toby and my mom makes it seem as if we haven't seen her in months instead of a matter of two weeks. I love their relationship and how close they are, but my dad and I also can't help but roll our eyes at how excited they are.

I take Mom and Dad on a quick driving tour of the island, pointing out where the new house will be and a few other landmarks. They ooh and ahh appropriately, and I can tell how relieved my mother is to finally see the place we are calling home. As we head back toward the main part of town and my apartment, we pass the driveway for the inn.

"Oh, that's where your father and I are staying, why don't we drop off our bags now," my mom exclaims.

"You're not staying with us?" Toby asks, and I realize I hadn't thought that through, either. We don't have a lot of space at the apartment and my parents must have realized that. Still, them staying at the same inn as Kayla feels like a little bit of destiny.

We pull up to the inn just as the front door opens and Kayla and Tawny come walking out. Toby immediately starts to climb out, calling her name as he runs up and wraps his arms around Kayla's leg, causing my mom to look at me with a rather pointed stare.

"Who's that lovely woman, Samuel?" she asks under her breath, but before I can answer, Toby is dragging a blushing Kayla over to our group.

"Nana, this is Kayla, she's going to have sleepovers with me and Daddy!"

My dad laughs, my mom's jaw drops open, and Kayla looks like she wants to run and hide. Thinking quickly, I realize yet again that honesty is the best way forward, so I go to Kayla and wrap my arm around her, squeezing her comfortingly.

"Mom, Dad, this is my girlfriend, Kayla Michaels. Kayla, meet my parents, Rob and Maryanne."

Dad shakes her hand, saying how nice it is to meet her, and then Tawny is taking him and Toby inside to get my parents checked in. Mom is still recovering from the news, but once she does, she's pulling Kayla in for a hug that I think does more to shock Kayla than Toby's announcement.

"Well now, I see my boys are making friends quickly," my mom quips, but I see only curiosity in her eyes, not judgement. "You must come for dinner tonight, Kayla, so we can get to know you better. I'm making lasagna, it's Toby's favorite."

"I, oh, well I mean, I don't..." Kayla's floundering and looks to me desperately for help. Without thinking twice, I lean in and kiss the side of her head.

"Come for dinner, babe."

She smiles at me and I see a hint of the confident woman who was in my bed last night. Then she turns to my mother and replies, "Okay, I'd love to."

"Excellent. I'm going to just pop inside and freshen up, then we'll head back so I can start dinner."

I nod at my mother without looking at her; I'm too busy watching Kayla. I hear mom chuckle, then walk away. Once I look around to make sure no one is in sight, I lean in and kiss her the way I wanted to when I first saw her.

"Surprise," I whisper to her softly, and she groans and drops her head to my chest.

"Oh my God, Sam! Dinner with your parents?"

"They'll love you, just like I do."

I freeze. But Kayla caught my confession and is looking at me with wondrous eyes. She goes to open her mouth and I lightly cover it with my hand.

"Pretend you didn't hear that." Her face falls and I quickly go on. "Not because I don't mean it, but because this is not how I planned on telling you. You deserve roses and candlelight, not a moment that could be interrupted by my kid or my parents."

Now Kayla's eyes are dancing and I uncover her mouth to hear what she was going to say.

"I think this is the perfect moment, Sam. Because there will always be a risk of a kid interrupting, or your parents, or my sisters, or your editor, or my work. And I don't care, because I love you, too."

She goes up on her toes to kiss me sweetly. I instantly take it deeper, needing to pour my love into her. After a moment, she pulls back and wiggles her eyebrows at me. "And I love lasagna."

23

Kayla

Any of my earlier fears about meeting Sam's parents so soon have disappeared. Knowing that he loves me and confessing that I love him has made me feel stronger than I have in weeks. Deep down I know we've still got a lot to figure out, but he is my new beginning.

I let Sam take Toby and his parents back to his house for a while, because I know I've got to face the sister inquisition that is waiting for me in Ella's cottage. I saw Tawny head over there a couple of minutes ago and there was no mistaking the pointed look she gave me that couldn't mean anything other than *explain*.

I'm grinning like a fool when I push open Ella's front door and plop down on the couch beside my twin sister.

"Somebody's a little love-drunk," Tawny says drily.

Ella giggles and wraps her arm around my shoulder. "I think it's adorable. Kayla's in looooooove."

I can't help but roll my eyes at how she strings out the word, but it's true. I am. Sitting up, I look over at them. "Wait, how do you guys know that? You weren't outside when we said the words."

"I knew it!" Ella cries.

"You're right, we didn't know for sure, so thanks for confirming it,"

Tawny laughs, then comes over and joins us on the couch, making a sister sandwich with me in the middle.

"Seriously? Was I that obvious?" I ask.

"To us, yes. And we might have been spying on you guys when Sam's parents came inside. The look on your faces and then that kiss, well... that gave it away."

I ponder that for a moment and a warm feeling comes over me.

"I think I'm done traveling so much for work," I blurt out. I expect my sisters to freak out about this news; instead they're just nodding their heads as if they already knew this fact.

"Of course you are. You've got a man and a kid to come home to now," Ella says seriously.

My eyes blink slowly as I look at her. Somehow, the fact that loving Sam meant the possibility of being Toby's stepmom didn't quite hit me until now.

"A kid," I breathe. Motherhood hadn't really been on my radar, but suddenly I can see it. Taking Toby to school, having him cuddled between us in bed, and who knows, maybe another child someday. I stand up abruptly, this train of thought giving me a desperate desire to see Sam and Toby.

"Gotta go, I'll talk to you guys tomorrow. Love you, bye."

I'm out the door before they can even stand up, but I hear their laughter behind me. My grin is so wide, my cheeks are starting to hurt. I love him. I love them. And I need to be with my boys.

After a quick stop at my room to grab a sweater and some lip gloss, I'm out the door. The walk over to Sam's apartment will hopefully give me enough time to get rid of some of this energy coursing through my body. I feel like I'm vibrating with excitement, lust, love, and just pure joy.

Halfway there, my phone vibrates. I pull it out and the message I see makes my heart sing.

SAM: Hurry up and get here so I can tell you I love you again.
KAYLA: Five minutes.

I send a heart emoji and pick up my pace so I can see the man of my dreams.

* * *

Dinner with Sam, Toby, and Sam's parents is remarkably easy. It's been so long since I had a proper family dinner, with kids and grandparents and chaos. I forgot how loud and full of life and love they can be. Toby hasn't stopped talking since I arrived, telling his grandmother all about the things we've done. Sam's mom, Maryanne, keeps smiling at me, and I think that must mean she's happy Sam and I are together.

After a delicious meal of lasagna and salad, Maryanne announces that she wants to spend some time with Toby. Sam and I are ushered out of the apartment with instructions not to hurry back.

Standing outside of his apartment building, we look at each other for a minute, grinning like fools. Then he draws me into his body, tucking my head under his chin and wrapping his arms tightly around me. I feel safe, warm, loved, and at home.

"I love you, Kayla Michaels," he whispers softly before pressing a kiss to the top of my head.

I tip my head back so that his lips land on mine. It's a kiss full of promises for the future and for right now.

"Come back to the inn with me."

Sam senses it isn't a question and we head over to his car, climb in, and drive to the inn. Somehow, we manage to sneak past the front desk without Tawny seeing us and I wonder briefly if she's still at Ella's, discussing my love life.

But any thoughts of my darling sisters disappear when Sam closes the door to my room. The click of the lock pierces the silence. I look over my shoulder at him leaning there against the door. He's watching me with hunger in his eyes and it makes me bold. I pull my shirt over my head and quickly take off my shorts until I'm in nothing more than my bra and panties. Then I turn and sit on my bed before I crook my finger at him, beckoning him closer.

Sam prowls toward me but stops just out of reach.

"Lie back, babe." His voice is a rumble and I feel his words vibrate through my core. I scoot backwards and use my feet to push the blankets down to the bottom of the bed. The cool sheets feel amazing on my heated skin and I know things are only going to get hotter.

Sam slowly peels off his shirt, unbuttons his shorts, and steps out of them along with his underwear. Now his cock is free and my mouth waters at the sight of his rigid length. He climbs up on the bed and crawls over until he's on top of me.

"I want to make love to you and watch when you let go while wrapped tight around me."

I nod, furiously, because I need him inside of me, now. But before Sam can slide into my throbbing heat, he drops his head to my shoulder with a groan.

"Shit, I don't have a condom with me."

I reach down between us and run my hand up and down his cock before positioning it at my entrance. Only then do I wrap my other hand around his head and tug his ear down to my mouth.

"I don't care."

And I don't. Yes, I'm on birth control and yes, I'm clean. More importantly, I trust this man and I love this man. I want to give him something I have never given another guy.

Sam searches my eyes and he must see my certainty because he leans down and kisses me just as he thrusts into me.

"Jesus, *fuck*," he growls. I can't form words, so I let my body do the talking as my hips rise to meet his movements. He presses kisses to my face, my neck, anywhere his lips can touch.

When Sam reaches down and lifts my leg up and over his shoulder, I gasp at the change in sensation. Suddenly, he's deep. So deep he's stroking my soul with every pass of his cock. I'm spiraling into bliss, and the sounds coming out of my mouth are almost animalistic. It's raw, it's passionate, it's better than any sex I've ever had, because it's not just sex. We're making love.

I no longer know where I end and Sam begins. We are one, tangled together, letting our love fuel our actions higher and higher. The sheer intensity of my orgasm catches me by surprise and it seems as if I lose all awareness of my surroundings for a moment. When I eventually drift back to reality, Sam is laying on his side, his leg over top of mine, and his hand lazily tracing over my body.

"Hi," I say with a satisfied sigh. He grins down at me, then presses a sweet and gentle kiss to my lips.

"What would you say if I told you my mom texted and told me not to come home tonight?"

A delicious shudder goes through my body at the very thought of spending the night with Sam.

"I would say that sounds like heaven and while I'm grateful to her, I'm a little embarrassed that your mom is interfering in our love life."

He chuckles before dropping his head down on my shoulder.

"Babe, I know. Welcome to my life. My interfering mother means well, but I'm not gonna lie. Having some distance between us is a good thing. She's been bugging me to start dating for the last couple of years, so I think meeting you has her already hearing wedding bells and planning on more grandchildren."

Sam has raised his head and is looking at me closely. It doesn't take a genius to realize he might be looking for my reaction to what he just said about marriage and kids. The thing is, that idea doesn't freak me out at all. In fact, I can see our future together in much the same way. Toby will make an excellent big brother some day and I'd be lying if I didn't say I could happily marry Sam and be with him for the rest of my life.

He must see how I feel in my eyes, because he nods before covering my body with his and rocking his hips into mine. My eyes widen when I feel his hardening cock rubbing against me.

"Already?"

"With you, I'm always ready for more."

A fact that he proves to me all night long.

24

Sam

6 months later...

If you had asked me a year ago where I saw my life heading, I probably would've rambled on about my next book release, Toby starting kindergarten in the city, and some sort of half-assed plan to relocate to the country. I could have never predicted that I would be living in an eco-friendly, custom designed home on an island that has brought a sense of peace and balance to my life in a way only nature can. I *certainly* would not have known that moving to this island would also bring me the love of my life, the only woman I can see being a mother figure in Toby's life, and the one woman who completes me in a way that I thought was impossible to ever have again.

Toby and I finally convinced Kayla to move in with us last month, just in time for Thanksgiving. We had dinner at Ella and Marcus's home, which is conveniently just down the street from us. The girls are actively working on getting Tawny to move here, too, but I don't see that happening; she's too attached to their childhood home.

I've just finished the latest round of edits on my manuscript and am hitting send to throw it back to my editor when a key turning the lock on my front door makes me look up in surprise. Kayla walks through the door and surprise turns to lust. She's been away for a week in Thailand for a photoshoot and despite our best efforts, I wasn't able to join her. So seeing her home, ahead of schedule, is pretty much the best thing ever.

"Honey, I'm home," she teases in a singsong voice, a grin stretching across her beautiful face.

I'm out of my chair and halfway across the room before the words are out of her mouth and my lips land on hers just in time with her laugh.

Only when I've satisfied my hunger for her kiss do I pull back and stroke her hair, staring at her, getting my fill of her beauty. Kayla loves her job and with the support of me and her sisters, she's worked it out so that she only does one international assignment every other month. The rest of the time she's shooting in North America and most recently, she started freelance writing articles for one of the magazines that buys her photos. She also has plans to open a studio here on the island. All of it keeps her busy enough and keeps her home a lot more, which makes both of us happy.

"Babe, I thought I was getting you from the ferry with Toby after school?" My tone is chiding, but my body says differently. There's no doubt she can feel my burgeoning erection pushing into her hips; I want her. Need her.

Kayla smiles at me and runs her fingers through my hair. "I wanted to surprise you." Then she backs away from me. Before I can protest, she's lifting her sweater over her head and dropping it to the floor. "Besides, I wanted a few hours with you to myself before the little man is here and I have to be quiet when you ravish me." She waggles her eyebrows and a throaty chuckle escapes me.

I stride forward, grab her by the hips, and toss her over my shoulder. She shrieks and I slap her ass gently as I carry her down the hall to our bedroom. Once there, I drop her on the bed before immediately climbing over top her. Kayla wraps her arms around my waist and pulls me down on top of her. I nuzzle her neck, pressing kisses up until I reach her ear, where I whisper, "I love my surprise."

Then I lift myself off of her and make quick work of removing my clothes. Kayla senses the change in energy, the urgency that has filled the air, and removes her bra and panties. A fleeting desire to do that myself crosses my mind, but I know I can do it next time. Right now, I need to be inside her, joining us together in the deepest way possible.

The reality of being apart for a week acts as foreplay for both of us, because by the time I'm naked, my cock is rock hard, and Kayla is rubbing herself shamelessly. When she lifts her fingers away from her clit, I pull them into my mouth and suck.

"Fuck. You're soaked for me," I growl. The taste of her arousal drives me wild and I flip over onto my back, pulling her on top. She lines up with my dick and lowers herself without hesitation.

We don't need anymore words, we let our bodies do the talking. The rhythm is fast and frantic, as it always is the first time we're together after being apart. Kayla rides me with her hands on my chest and I grab her ass to guide her. When her moans turn to gasps and she starts calling out my name, I know she's close. Thank fuck for that, because I'm ready to blow.

Kayla comes with a moan and the tightening of her heat around my cock is exactly what I need to explode into my own orgasm. I spill into her, her sex milking my dick for every last drop. When she collapses onto my chest, I wrap my arms around her and hold her close. Our heartbeats are racing together. It's one more way that we are connected.

* * *

Sex with Kayla is better than anything. But feeling her warm body next to mine as we lay there, tangled together, open and connected, is perfection. My hand lazily traces up and down her spine, and Kayla is drawing spirals on my chest with her fingers.

"I was thinking of taking next year off from international trips."

I tilt my head so I can look down at Kayla. Her statement takes me by surprise; I thought she loved the balance of still doing a few bigger trips each year. Don't get me wrong, I miss her like crazy every time, and selfishly I want her here all the time. But I would never stand in the way of her career.

"Are you sure? I thought we were doing okay with your work schedule," I say.

She lifts herself up on one elbow so she can look down at me and I see an odd mixture of excitement and trepidation on her face.

"We were, we are, but I miss you and Toby so much when I go. And with Ella's baby coming in the spring, I don't want to be away from my family."

Her eyes drop to where her fingers have started drawing faster shapes on my chest and I can sense the nerves growing.

"You and Toby, you're my family, just as much as my sisters are. Right?"

"Of course we are."

"So, you wouldn't be opposed to making that official?"

Now it's my turn to lift myself up so I can look her in the eye. If she's saying what I think she's saying, I don't know whether to laugh or cry.

"Not opposed at all," I say slowly.

Kayla's eyes rise to meet mine and they're shining with tears.

"Will you marry me, Sam?"

My heart is bursting, but I can't answer her right away. I climb out of bed and walk over to the dresser. Reaching into the back of the top drawer, I pull out a small box, walk back over to the bed, and drop to one knee beside Kayla. She's sitting up now and has never looked more beautiful, with her hair all mussed, the sheet pooled around her waist, a joyous smile on her face.

"I'll marry you, if you'll marry me. And be Toby's mom."

I open the box and Kayla gasps at the oval cut amethyst and diamond ring inside. I had it designed last month and Toby helped. We wanted something unique and this is it. He's going to be bummed he wasn't here for this; we had planned to ask her together. But this moment is perfect. There's just one more word that I need, and it could be the most important word of all.

"Yes."

III

Falling Forever

25

Mac

Growing up on a small island has its perks. And its downfalls. And then there are the things that are a mixture of the two.

Tawny Michaels is just that. She is the best and the worst memory I have from growing up on Westmount Island.

My childhood best friend, my secret high school girlfriend, and the reason I've stayed far away from the small island in the Pacific Northwest that I used to call home.

I've kept my distance over the years, only returning to visit my family briefly on holidays. There's always a reason not to linger and that's helped me avoid the awkward pain that flares when I think of Tawny. Seeing her might destroy me.

Which makes my temporary return to the island a truly bad idea. I know this, but here I am, sitting in my truck on the vehicle deck of the ferry that is carrying me toward the place I used to call home, but now is nothing more than a place filled with heartbreaking memories. Coming back to Westmount Island was the right choice. I know this, but I'm still worried. I'll be here for at least a month, the longest I've ever been back since I left for college eleven years ago. Avoiding Tawny for that long will be impossible, which means I have to figure out a way to handle seeing the woman I once thought was my soul mate. A ring from my back pocket startles me from my ruminating. Caller ID says it's my dad and my heart jumps into my throat.

"Dad, hey. Is everything okay? I'm on the ferry." I can't hide the panic in my voice. It's been there ever since the day the call came through that my mother was ill.

"Everything's fine, son. As fine as it could be, I suppose."

He sounds calm, much calmer than I sound, I'm sure. And it's a relief because that's normal — Dad has always been the steady one of my parents. When he called me from the hospital two weeks ago to tell me that Mom had a stroke, the worry and fear I could hear radiating from him terrified me more than the news itself. If it scared him that much, I knew it had to be bad. And that's why I'm coming home.

"I just wanted to ask if you could stop at Pete's and pick up some more wood for the railings. He's got it set aside for us, but I don't want to leave your mother."

I exhale. An errand. Something I can handle. Somehow, I've got to get control of my anxiety, I can't keep running on stress like this. Hopefully once I lay eyes on Mom and see for myself that she's okay, I'll be able to breathe normally again.

"Yeah, of course I can, Dad."

"Thanks, Son. See you soon."

Conversations with my father are always short and to the point. Mom is the one who always liked to chat for hours and when the realization hits me that I might never get to do that with her again, I feel angry at myself for all the times I cut her off or screened her call. I guess it's true, you don't know what you have until it's gone. I'll never cut my conversations with my mother short again.

***

The sun is getting low in the autumn sky when I pull into my parents' driveway. The quick stop at the hardware store didn't lead to any Tawny sightings, so it looks like I'll get through today without my heart being ripped apart. Thank fuck for that.

I unload the lumber and supplies into the garage, which my dad left open for me. Just as I'm carrying in the last load, the door opens and my father steps out. I know he won't want me to mention the relief I can see etched on his face, so I just flash him a quick smile as I head back to my truck to grab my bags.

"Hey Dad," I say casually. He stays in the doorway, his hands in his pockets as he nods back at me. Not one for showing emotion, my dad is steady, strong, and unruffled.

"Son. Glad you're here."

And that'll be all he'll say about it, you can bet on that.

We head inside and the first thing I notice is that it doesn't smell like home anymore. My mom is, or was, always baking. Bread, muffins, cookies, pies — you name it, she baked it. Most of it she gave away to neighbors or to the church to distribute with food baskets, but the kitchen always had delicious aromas wafting from it. Not today. The air feels heavy, almost stale.

"Where's Mom?" my voice echoes down the empty hallway. It's not just the lack of baking that makes this place feel like a shell of what it should be. There's no noise, no life. No TV on in the background with a sports game, no footsteps, no sound of my mother humming under her breath.

"Upstairs. Resting. I was going to figure out some dinner soon, I just want to build that railing out front first. Your mother, she needs it."

We're stopped in the kitchen and I take a close look at my father for the first time. The lines on his face seem deeper and his entire body sags with fatigue or stress. Probably both.

"Dad. I'm here now, let me help," I say quietly. This is why I put my business on hold for a month and came home. Because even though he's a man of few words, I could read between the lines. He's running on fumes and struggling to keep it all together now that Mom is out of the hospital.

He nods and sits down on one of the stools at the kitchen island.

"Thank you, Shawn."

My parents and my business partners are the only ones who still call me Shawn. I'm named after my father, so a nickname felt like a necessity when I was younger. My company might be called 'Shawn Macdonald Contracting', but to everyone I'm Mac.

As I turn my attention to the fridge to see what I can make for a quick dinner, there's a knock at the door. My dad goes to stand up, but I stop him with a hand on his shoulder, and slide a bottle of beer in front of him instead.

"Let me get it."

I walk swiftly to the front door and pull it open, intent on dealing with whoever this is quickly so I can get back to my Dad. But when I see the person standing there, having a beer with my father is the farthest thing from my mind.

26

Tawny

It takes all of my self-control not to drop the casserole dish in my hand and run. Mac's here, in front of me, and judging by the shock on his face, he's not exactly happy to see me.

"Ummm, hi. Sorry. I didn't know you were here. I just..." my voice trails off and my eyes drop to the pan of chicken and wild rice casserole in my hands.

I thrust the dish into his hands, turn and walk swiftly back to my car, ignoring the burn of tears pooling in my eyes. After all this time, why am I crying over this man?

Because he's the only person to hold my heart and he's the only person to crush it into dust.

**

Eleven years ago, late August

My heart skips a beat when I see Mac, just like it always does. He's dreamy, there's no other way to say it. Tall, even as a teenager, muscles hardened and skin tanned by weekly football practices and a summer of working various construction jobs with his dad. Green eyes that seem like they're lit from within, with a fire that burns just for me, and that smile. My smile. I shiver when he does that, because that smile means he's picturing me naked.

Mac was the first boy to touch me and I want him to be the last. It's Wednesday, so we're meeting at the base of West Mountain like we do every Wednesday. Our parents think we go for a hike and if they suspect there's anything more to our relationship than just friendship, they don't bring it up. The truth is, Mac is more than my secret boyfriend. He's my everything and I can't imagine life without him in it. And on Wednesday's, we do hike sometimes, but mostly we just drive to the North end of the island and find a private place to park Mac's truck. Today we're hiking and Mac said he wanted to talk to me. I'm excited, because part of me thinks he might ask me to marry him. We haven't talked about our future and I know we're young, just eighteen, but I love him. And I always will.

"Hey, Tawny," he grins as he takes my hand. I look at him with an answering smile. We walk in silence for a little while and I'm content to just be here with him. But after a while, my curiosity gets the best of me.

"What did you want to talk about?" I try to adopt a casual tone.

Mac doesn't answer right away, but I can sense him stiffen. That confuses me. He pulls me over to a log on the side of the path that is on its side, making a convenient bench. Once we sit down, he lets go of my hand and clasps his together in front of him. This isn't good, I can feel my heart sinking, even though I can't begin to imagine why.

"Mac...what's wrong? You're scaring me," I whisper. When he turns to me, the anguish in his eyes makes me gasp.

"T, I'm sorry. I don't know how to tell you this, it fucking sucks, and it's also amazing at the same time." He jumps up and starts pacing in front of me, taking his ball cap off and putting it back on over and over, a sure sign he's nervous. "And we'll be okay, I know we will. But still, to not be with you every day is gonna be so hard."

"What are you talking about?" I interrupt, confused and worried about what I think he's going to tell me.

"I got accepted to Texas State on a football scholarship."

My heart stops beating for a minute. A football scholarship is what Mac has hoped for, but Texas is so far away.

"That's great, Mac. I know this is what you've dreamt of," I say quietly.

"I thought we'd be closer together." His voice is taut with worry, and I smile to try and soothe him.

"I did, too. But we'll be okay."

* * *

And that, as they say, was the beginning of our end. Long distance is hard enough, but when your relationship is also a secret from your family and friends, it's damn near impossible. We tried, but only communicating through emails and phone calls suck. Still, I think we could have survived it and moved ahead with our plan to move in together once we both finished college if it weren't for *the picture*.

I can't blame our mutual friend Sara for showing it to me. Her cousin Riley was at school with Mac and must have sent Sara some photos of their time at college and she figured I would want to see my friend. She had no idea that seeing a picture of Mac smiling with his arm around some other girl at a party would rip me in two, but it did. And when you put that photo in context of our already struggling relationship, well, it felt like the ultimate betrayal. It was the final wedge between us.

The next week, before we had even had a chance to talk about things, the unthinkable happened. My parents both died in a car accident on the mainland. Mac tried to call me, but I couldn't handle it, not then. So, I ignored his calls and messages. And when Rory Montgomery put his arm around me at the funeral, I let myself be comforted by him, even though Mac was standing at the edge of the crowd, looking at me with such pain and anger in his eyes.

I wasn't given a moment alone that week and my anguish over my parents and childish hurt over Mac's actions led me to block his number on my phone and avoid him in every situation. If my actions seemed strange to anyone, they chalked it up to grief and left me alone. After all, they had no idea we were anything more than friends. In my mind it was clear, we were over.

What followed was the most difficult year of my life. I was grieving the death of my parents and the loss of my most precious relationship. No one knew the truth about why losing Mac had hit me so hard. And when my sisters would ask why I wasn't talking to him, I made up an insignificant lie about friends drifting apart. Maybe I should have come clean and admitted that we had been dating, but we were young and stupid. We didn't want the pressure of the town knowing we were together. Looking back, I don't blame us for deciding to keep things a secret, but I could have used the support of my two younger sisters.

My coping mechanism became work. I buried myself in learning how to run the Westmount Inn, eventually taking over as manager from my grandmother so she could retire. And over time, the sharp pain of losing Mac and our young love faded into a dull ache.

It has been just over ten years since I last saw Mac standing across from me at my parents' funeral. We've somehow managed to avoid each other since then. I've grown up a lot in that time and maturity has helped me realize how rash I had been. I know that I screwed up the best relationship of my life, but I can't bring myself to talk to him.

Seeing him tonight sent me into a panic. A mixture of longing, grief, and confusion flooded my brain and any words I might have wanted to say were stuck in my throat.

He looked the same, only better. I knew from his mother that he finished college with a business degree and opened his own contracting business on the mainland. He relocated to the West Coast, but refused to come back to the island, no matter how hard his mom tried to convince him to come home. She missed him terribly and I had to hide my guilt, knowing that I was likely the reason Mac wouldn't move home.

But he's here now, brought home by her stroke. Mary Macdonald is a wonderful woman and I can't imagine not seeing her around town, tasting the amazing muffins that she would drop off at the inn, or hearing her cheerful laugh when she would come in for dinner with her husband. Shawn Senior told me that she was home, but tonight was the first chance I had to come over for a visit. I hadn't expected to run into Mac.

The question is, can Mac and I handle being in the same town again? Or are things about to get really awkward?

27

Mac

Tawny. She's still so beautiful, with her wavy hair around her shoulders, shining under the porch lights. She still has a smattering of freckles across her nose, and her eyes still tell me exactly how she's feeling. But her body has matured into a curvy, sexy woman's body. And she holds herself with a new confidence. She's the same, but not.

Somehow, I manage to bury my shock at seeing her and have a somewhat normal evening with my dad. The casserole she brought over is delicious and when Dad mentions it's Mom's favorite, I hide my surprise at the news that they eat at her inn often enough to have a favorite dish. Apparently while I was nursing a broken heart all this time, they were acting friendly and welcoming to the one woman who successfully destroyed my ability to believe in love.

That's a lie.

I believe in love; I believe I loved Tawny Michaels and I believe a small, masochistic part of my heart will always love her.

And I guess I can't really blame my parents. They had no idea what happened between Tawny and I. They didn't know the sharp pain I felt when her communication with me suddenly stopped, my emails went unanswered and my phone calls were ignored. They had no clue that seeing her with Rory's arms around her at her parents' funeral gutted me.

I should have been the one comforting her, holding her, kissing her. Not him. But I couldn't even make a sound of protest because of our stupid decision to keep our relationship a secret. It made sense back then; in a small town, dating can be tricky with so many eyes on you. The downside of it was that when everything fell apart, I had no one there to witness my heartache and help me through it.

The next morning, I help my dad build the ramp and railing down the two steps at the front of their house so that Mom can get her walker up and down. It's a simple project and since my father was the one who instilled a love of carpentry and construction in me, it's fun to work with him again. We work together well, the peaceful silence only broken when one of us needs a tool. Once the job is done, we sit on the front porch with a beer.

"How long are you back?"

I knew this question was coming, but I'm still unsure how to answer. The answer isn't a simple one. I want to be here as long as my parents need me, but at the same time I'm itching to get away from the discomfort that comes from being close to Tawny and not being able to have her. She's a drug and I'm an addict who's still in recovery.

"Don't know."

Dad nods and seems to accept my noncommittal response. At least I think he does until he fires off the next question.

"What did you say to Tawny last night that sent her running off without a hello?"

"I, nothing," I sputter, trying to recover from the accusation in his words.

"Don't lie. That young woman has been a part of our lives since you two were knee high. I know she wouldn't leave without checking in on your mother unless you said something to scare her off."

For a man of little words, my dad sure does have a lot to say about Tawny.

"It's nothing, Dad. She had to go. That's all."

"Bullshit." He turns to me and his blue eyes pierce into me with the ultimate stare down. "Something happened between you two when you went off to college. You went from best friends to strangers. Now, your mother and I never pushed you for an explanation, we figured you'd sort it out eventually. But you haven't. And don't think for a second that we haven't figured out the fact that she's the reason you won't come home. Last night, she was coming over to drop off dinner and visit your mother. Instead, she didn't even make it in the front door. So, I'll ask you again. What did you say to her?"

I'm speechless. Did my parents know all this time and never said a word? Perhaps we weren't as subtle as we thought. With a sigh, I find myself telling him everything, from our secret relationship, to her disappearing act. When I mention Rory, he raises an eyebrow at the obvious jealousy in my voice. And when I'm done, he lets out a small sound of understanding. I expected him to be surprised by my confession, but he certainly doesn't seem to be.

We go back to silence, but I can't stop fidgeting, waiting for him to say something.

"Do you still love her?" he asks casually, as if he were asking if I still liked Mom's smoked ribs.

My heart flips over once, twice, then starts to beat again, stronger than it has in a while. Getting everything out in the open has made me realize something. It's not all Tawny's fault. I walked away and didn't push her for an explanation. I avoided her all these years, building a wall of hurt feelings between us that is now so high, she can't stand to be in my presence for more than a minute.

As I sit there, for the first time in a decade, and think as objectively as I can about how things ended between us, I realize something. Tawny must have had a good reason for cutting off all contact with me. And I was an idiot for never finding out why.

"Yeah, I do."

"Then you need to fix this."

* * *

It would seem that my father is determined to hold me to that. The next day, he's up early and tells me that he needs my help on a job he promised to do for someone. He's arranged for one of Mom's friends to come and sit with her for a few hours so that we can go work on this urgent job he says absolutely cannot wait.

I should've known something was up when we pulled into the parking lot of the Westmount Inn and again when he left me on the ladder, repairing the shingles on the roof, under the pretense of going to the store for more supplies.

I was so focused on getting the job done and getting out of there that I didn't hear someone walk up behind me as I climbed down the ladder to get some more nails. Next thing I know, I turn around and bump into a wall of soft skin.

"Shoot!" Was all I heard before ice-cold liquid seeped through my shirt.

"Damn, that's cold." I jumped back, lifting my shirt away from my skin just as the realization dawned on me that Tawny is standing so close, I can smell her perfume.

We both freeze. I can see her chest rising and falling with each breath, and it feels like she's so near me I could count her eyelashes. Inches are all that remain between me and the woman I once thought would be my wife someday, and I couldn't bring myself to move if I tried. Her hair is longer than I remember and falls in soft brown waves down her back. I can see the freckles that lightly dot her cheeks and I'm consumed by a memory of laying naked beside her, counting them.

Her pupils dilate, she licks her lips, and fuck, do I ever want to kiss her. The memory of her soft lips on mine is imprinted on my soul. I haven't been a monk all these years, but no woman has ever come close to making me feel the same level of visceral, physical need that Tawny Michaels does.

"Sorry," she whispers. "I thought you might need a drink."

I take a step back, because hearing her soft voice is threatening what little control I still have.

28

Tawny

Oh my God. *Oh. My. God.* Mac is so close I could lean forward and lick him. And neither one of us is running away. This close, it's hard to remember exactly why I have spent so many years avoiding him. His familiar, woodsy scent is overlayed with the tang of the lemonade I just spilled on him, but he still smells like Mac. Like home.

When he takes a step back, my breath comes out in a whoosh.

"I really am sorry about your shirt," I say as my eyes travel to his chest where the lemonade has made his white T-shirt almost see-through.

Mac just shrugs. "I've got a spare in my truck." He turns away from me and pulls his shirt off, making my jaw drop. When did I start finding back muscles sexy? Now. Right now. Every muscle is clearly defined and glistening slightly in the sun. Even as he's walking away from me, I'm helplessly drawn to him. It's not like I ever stopped finding him attractive, but over the years of just seeing him in the odd photo his mother would share with me, I managed to convince myself he couldn't possibly be that handsome in real life. Boy, was I wrong.

He saunters back over and pulls the clean shirt on. He must see the desire on my face because he shoots me a grin and winks at me.

"Like what you see, Tawny?"

"I, umm, what? No. I just. Here. Drink this." I thrust the other glass of lemonade at him, flustered. Mac takes a long swallow of the beverage and I watch his throat, fascinated by the sight of his Adam's apple bobbing up and down. He even makes drinking sexy. I'm in trouble. It would be so easy to fall for Mac again. Heck, I never stopped loving him, despite the pain he caused me. And I don't have anyone to tell me not to make the same mistake twice.

He finishes the glass and hands it back to me. I set both cups down on the steps beside me, not quite ready to leave. Now that I'm near him again, the pull between us is as strong as ever.

Mac watches me carefully, then lifts his ball cap off and on, his signature move when he's stressed.

"Look, Tawny, I'll be here for a while helping my parents. We're going to have to see each other, maybe even have another conversation. So, can we just clear the air now and move on?"

"Clear the air?" I say, surprised. Clear the air from what? Of him cheating on me, breaking my heart, ruining me for any other man? I'm not exactly sure I want to hear this.

"Yeah, I mean, I don't know why you disappeared back then, but I guess you had a reason. Let's just talk about it so things can stop being so awkward between us."

"Why I disappeared?" I realize I'm parroting him, but I'm just so confused. When it dawns on me, I can hardly believe it. Does he honestly think our breakup was all my fault?

"Jesus, Tawny, why are you so surprised? I just want to make things easier for us while I'm here," he says sharply, glaring at me like I'm being unreasonable.

I put my hands on my hips, furious at him. "What the hell, Mac? You can't just come here, looking like that, act all flirty, then confuse the heck out of me by asking why I stopped talking to you when you were in Texas, and not expect me to be surprised. Why do you *think* I stopped?!"

My voice has risen to a yell by the end my tirade and I can feel the heat rising on my face.

Now I know he's really upset because he pulls his cap off and tosses it on the ground.

"I don't *know*, Tawny, that's why I'm asking. Why did you suddenly start to ignore my calls, why the fuck was Rory Montgomery holding you at your parents' funeral, and why the fuck did you *break my heart*?"

My jaw drops and so do I, straight down onto a stair. My legs can't hold me up anymore, I'm so shocked by his outburst. I broke *his* heart? He shattered mine. But an ugly thread of doubt that I've ignored for ten years is weaving through me, growing stronger by the second. I've thought about that photo many times over the years. What if I made a big deal out of nothing? Did I ruin us? I'm not sure I want to find out, but I have to.

I take a deep breath. "Sara Hawthorne from high school showed me a picture of you at a party in October, after you left for college. You'd only been gone a couple of months, but it felt like an eternity. You were with a girl. It looked cozy." I look up at him, and I'm sure my pain is in my eyes, just as his are filled with bewilderment. "It was so hard being away from you. I had no one I could talk to about it and I was already feeling so scared about our future with you being so far away."

"So, you assumed I cheated on you." His voice is flat and I wince. It's becoming increasingly clear to me that I was wrong. That maybe *I* am to blame for a decade of pain.

"Yes," I whisper, as my eyes fill with tears. He walks over and sits on the step beside me with a sigh.

"Was the girl a redhead?" he asks quietly.

I look over at him, he's blurry through my tears, but I know the answer. Hell, I memorized that photo instantly.

"Yeah."

"She's my cousin. She was going to another school in Texas and came up for the party with some friends. I hadn't seen her in years. My cousin, Tawny. Not some girl I was hooking up with, my fucking cousin. You threw us away for nothing." His voice cracks on that last sentence and he drops his head into his hands.

My tears are falling freely now as the weight of what I've done comes crashing down.

"I'm sorry." I don't know what else to say. My heart is breaking all over again as I realize what I've lost.

"Me too."

A foolish part of me wants Mac to pull me into his arms and tell me it's all okay, that we will be okay. I want him to forgive me. But he doesn't. Instead, after a moment he just stands up, grabs his hat off the ground and heads back up the ladder without another word.

So much for making things less awkward between us; I'm pretty sure I just made it a thousand times worse. I head back inside, keeping my head low as I hurry into my office. Minutes after I've closed the door, it bangs open again and one of my twin sisters, Kayla, comes in.

"Holy shit, is that Mac I see out there? He looks *hot!*"

I look up from my desk and Kayla takes one look at me and hurries over to crouch beside me. She grabs my hands and holds them tightly.

"Tawny, what's wrong? What happened?" Worry is evident in her words and it makes my tears start to fall all over again.

"Mac. He...we..." I can't say it.

"Hang on. We need Ella." Kayla stands up, keeping one hand holding mine as she types out a message to our sister with the other. Ella must have been at her cottage next to the inn, because it's not long before she comes hurrying in as well.

"What's going on? Tawny?" Ella's face is etched with worry and I can't take it anymore. The tears are pouring down my face and I'm sobbing.

Somehow my sisters get me over to the couch that lines one wall. We pile onto it, me in the middle and my younger twin sisters flanking me on either side. They hold me and let me cry for a while, and when I can finally take a breath without making an embarrassing sobbing noise, I tell them my secret.

I was in love with my best friend and I ruined it.

Neither one of them seems shocked by my revelation and Ella even admits she suspected Mac and I were dating in high school. But when I get to the part with the photograph and the ensuing fallout, Kayla flings herself back on the couch muttering "Oh my God." Ella shakes her head and squeezes my hand sympathetically.

"I know. I was a fool. A total idiot and a chicken for not talking to him about it. But I was scared, I was scared that we were drifting apart with him in Texas and me here, and seeing him with another girl just felt like my fears were coming true. I panicked." I drop back against the couch and cover my face with my hands. "And now I don't know if he'll ever forgive me. I ruined everything." A fresh round of tears threaten to fall and when Ella hears my sniffle, she hands me a tissue.

"Tawny, this isn't completely your fault. Mac could have tried harder to talk to you, he could have called one of us, or tried to see you when he came home," she says hesitantly.

I sit up and take a deep breath in and out, then I tell them the rest.

"No. He couldn't. Because the next month was Mom and Dad's funeral, and I let Rory Montgomery hug me. Mac saw that and he assumed I had cheated on *him*, and that Rory was the reason I stopped answering his calls. So he stopped calling and now ten years later I know the truth. I screwed up."

"Oh." This comes from Kayla, who has sat up and is leaning her head on my shoulder. "You weren't just grieving Mom and Dad dying, you were grieving losing Mac, too. And you had to do it alone."

All I can do is nod.

Ella wraps her arms around me and Kayla layers hers on top. And we just sit there, huddled together, as my sisters, my best friends, let me fall apart once again. At least this time, I'm not alone.

29

Mac

I finish fixing the shingles on the inn's roof in record time, clean up, and get in my truck and drive away from Tawny as fast as I can. I didn't miss her sisters rushing into the inn and I wonder if she's going to tell them what happened between us.

Fuck, I still can't believe it. One goddamn picture of me and my cousin Holly was all it took to destroy a relationship that I thought was headed towards marriage.

I'm angry, and hurt, and insulted, and...weirdly hopeful. Tawny hadn't disappeared because she stopped loving me. But how the hell could she ever think I would cheat on her?

Without thinking, I've driven to the base of West Mountain. This is where we used to get away from everyone and just be together. I've climbed this trail with Tawny countless times, we've made out at the viewpoints; hell, we had sex at the summit one summer night before I left for Texas. This is the most important place on the entire island for me and Tawny and I haven't been back since I left for college.

I grab a water bottle from my backseat and lock my truck before starting to hike a trail that's as familiar to me as the road that leads to my parents' house. As I walk, memories come flooding back of the years Tawny and I spent together, first as friends, then as boyfriend and girlfriend. This is where I kissed her for the first time, this is where we talked about our future, this is where we fell in love.

She made a mistake when she saw that picture of me at the party. But I suppose I can see why she did so. We had been drifting apart and that was my fault. I'm the one who took the scholarship out of state and I'm the one who had the insane schedule that interfered with our phone calls. There were letters I didn't answer right away, phone dates that I missed, and even though it was only a couple of months that we were apart, it was enough to drive a wedge between us. Do I wish she'd given me a chance to explain? Hell yeah. It could have saved a lot of pain. But at the same time, do I honestly think we could have survived four years of distance?

That question fills my head for the rest of my climb to the summit. The truth is, I don't know that we would have.

By the time I've hiked back down the mountain, my anger is gone, and all that's left is a burning need to see her, and actually feel her again. I drive back to the inn, speeding recklessly and not caring. All I can think about is Tawny.

It's dusk by the time I get there, and I take a moment to sit in my truck and find some self-control. I can't burst in there and tear her clothes off, no matter how much I want to. My physical desire for Tawny is just as powerful as ever, but more importantly, I miss *her*. I miss her heart, the conversations we would have, the way we knew each other better than we knew ourselves. I know we need to talk about the last decade and about what we both want *now*. Hell, for all I know she could be in a relationship and I might make a complete fucking fool of myself. But I have to try. She's worth it.

Armed with that resolve, I get out of my truck and walk into the inn. I bypass reception and go straight to the office where I suspect I'll find Tawny. She isn't there, nor is she in the kitchen or the dining room.

"Damn it," I mutter to myself as I fix my hat on my head.

"Looking for my sister?"

I turn to see one of the twins — Ella, I think — standing in the hallway with her arms crossed and a smirk on her face. Yeah, she knows what's going on.

"Yup. Where is she?" comes my short reply. Ella's grin widens.

"If I tell you, what are you going to do?"

"Find her. Apologize. Then hopefully kiss her."

Ella claps her hands and I won't lie, I'm relieved that she seems to approve of my plan. It dawns on me that she should be surprised that I want to kiss her, but obviously Tawny has probably explained our past to her sisters by now.

"She's at home. We sent her there for the afternoon when it was clear she couldn't function properly after your conversation earlier." Ella cocks her hip at me and I know she's not letting Tawny take all the blame. "I haven't seen my sister that upset since our parents died. Fix it, Mac."

I nod, soberly. "I will. If she'll let me."

* * *

I pull into the driveway of what used to be Tawny's parents' home. I knew she had stayed there even after their death, but she's made some subtle changes. The contractor in me notices a few things that need to be done, like the front step that needs replacing and the corner of the garage where the paint needs a touch-up. *I could do that for her...*

I ring the doorbell and wait anxiously for her to answer the door. Nothing prepares me for what I see when she does.

"Babe." The endearment slips out and I pull her into my arms before I can even register what I'm doing. As soon as I saw her red eyes, evidence that she's been crying, and her wearing my college football sweatshirt, I knew she was hurting just as much as I was. And I wanted to be the one to take away that pain.

Tawny folds into my arms with a sob and all the years of heartache are instantly erased. Not completely, because there is a slight twinge in my heart that tells me I should be mad that I've missed out on so much with her. But right now, all that matters is stopping her tears.

I don't bother saying anything else, I simply lift Tawny into my arms, secretly thrilling at the feel of her arms around me once again. I walk into the house, closing the door behind me with my foot. I kick off my shoes and then carry her into the living room to sit on the couch.

Tawny stays curled into my arms, but I can feel her body relaxing and her tears slowing down. Eventually, they stop, and she lifts her head to look at me. I pass her a tissue from the box on the table beside the couch with a small smile.

"Thanks," she says quietly. She goes to move off of my lap and my hands tighten around her waist, holding her in place.

"Don't, please. Having you in my arms is the best feeling I've had in years."

The confession pours out of me and I feel Tawny freeze in my arms.

"Mac..." she starts, and I lift a finger up to cover her lips.

"Hold on. I need to say something." She nods and settles back. It's now or never as I take a deep breath and launch into the speech I prepared on my hike.

"I'm sorry I didn't try harder to talk to you back then, to figure out what was wrong. You're right, we were drifting apart and that was my fault. If I had tried harder to talk to you, or write to you, maybe you wouldn't have jumped to conclusions. I'm sorry that I avoided you all these years, instead of manning up and facing you. But I'm here now, T. I'm here, asking if it's not too late for a second chance."

When I finish, it's so quiet in the room I swear I can hear both of our hearts beating.

The silence is broken by Tawny whispering my name again. Only this time, it doesn't sound apologetic. It sounds reverent.

"Mac."

Then she kisses me.

Something inside of me settles at the feel of her lips against mine. My soul breathes a sigh of relief at finally being back where I belong.

It isn't long before my baser instincts kick in and my need for her roars to the surface. I guide her body over me until she's straddling my legs, bringing her center right over top of my hardening cock.

"Fuck," I groan, as she settles her hips down onto me. "Tawny. T. You...this...God."

"I know, Mac. I know." Her hand flutters down my face and she cups my jaw. I pull back just enough so I can look at her and the relief I see in her eyes tells me this moment means as much to her as it does to me.

"I never stopped loving you."

The words are whispered, so low I almost miss them. But I can't miss the hopeful smile that is stretching across her breathtakingly beautiful face.

"Me neither," I rumble in response before pulling her back to me, desperate to feel her kiss again. This one is different. This isn't a reunion between our souls, this is a celebration between our hearts. A re-affirmation that everything is as it should be — I am hers and she is mine.

30

Tawny

Oh my God. Oh my God. Oh my God. I'm kissing Mac. He's kissing me. He just said he still loves me. Is this real? I've dreamt about Mac and I being together again so many times that part of me is certain this must just be another fantasy. But he feels real. His arms are wrapped around me, his lips gently caressing mine. It's new and familiar at the same time. I know the contours of his body, how to set him alight with passion, but at the same time he's different now. Stronger, more dominant, and gentler at the same time. He knows what he's doing as he plunders my mouth, gently tugging on my lip with his teeth until I open to accept his tongue.

My hands are trapped between us, but I manage to snake one up to reach around his neck. Our kiss turns needy, desperate; we're both aching for more. My other hand finds its way under his shirt and flattens against his stomach, feeling the ridges of his abs ripple under my touch. He groans into my mouth and his hands move down to my ass, gripping it tightly.

"Tawny, I..." Mac's hands are at the bottom of my sweatshirt, his sweatshirt I suppose, and he's looking at me questioningly. I nod, and he lifts it up and over my head so that I'm left in just my bra.

"God, you're so beautiful," he says on a sigh as his eyes and hands travel my body. I'm comfortable with him, more comfortable than I have been with any other partner. He knows me and I know him.

"Touch me, Mac, please, make me feel good." My voice sounds needy, and I am. My desire is pulsating inside of me, desperate to be quenched.

"T," he breathes in deeply, "I want to. So much, but we have to talk about this. About us."

"Talk later."

I grab at his shirt twisting and pulling it until he helps me get it off of him. Then I slide down onto the floor in between his legs and unbutton his pants, tugging at his briefs until I can free his now rigid length.

"Tawny. Fuck." Just the barest of touches and I've reduced him to growls. I like this. Some wanton part of me takes over and I bend down to take him in my mouth. But I only get a few pumps of my hands and lips before I'm lifted into his arms. He kicks off his pants as he walks down the hall, unerringly finding my old bedroom, where I still sleep.

"I'm not taking you on a couch our first time after reuniting. You deserve better than that." The words are ground out, as if he's barely holding back, his restraint slipping. But the way Mac lays me down on the bed is with care and reverence, and when he stretches over top of me, his gaze is full of wonder.

"I don't know how we got back here, babe, but I'm not taking one minute of it for granted. If this is all we get, I want to make it amazing."

I don't have time to think about what he means by that statement before he's pulled my leggings down and is settling between my legs.

His fingers are slick when he slides them up my seam. I know my arousal is intense and when Mac leans down and nuzzles me, his groan is full of lust and need. His tongue begins to move and I gasp. He's always been able to tell what I like and what I don't, and he's using that knowledge now to drive me wild. The pressure and the heat from his mouth, coupled with the slight burn from the stubble on his cheeks, is a combination of sensations almost too intense for me to handle. When he sucks my clit into his mouth, his name comes out of me in a hoarse cry. He slides two fingers inside of my tight heat and I swear I feel like I could orgasm from that alone.

"Jesus, T, you're squeezing my fingers so tightly, babe," he growls as he lifts his head to look at me. His lips are glistening with my essence and I can't help it, the sight turns me on like nothing else.

"It's been a while," I gasp in reply.

"How long?" He cocks his head as his fingers continue to thrust in and out of me, curling upwards slightly to rub against my sweet spot.

"Years."

I don't tell him the truth. That I haven't let another man go down on me since the last time he did it. Sure, I've had sex a couple of times, even I'm not strong enough to be celibate for over ten years. But oral sex has always felt too intimate to me and I couldn't bring myself to let another man get close enough.

Mac returns to what he was doing and whips me into a frenzy. I don't have control over my own body anymore, my hips are lifting and writhing against his face and I couldn't stop it if I tried. He's got one arm holding me in place while the other brings me to the height of my arousal. Just when I think I can't take it and I'm screaming out his name, he presses up on me from the inside and it's like he launched a rocket inside of me. My orgasm shatters me, breaks me apart into a million pieces, but he's there holding me, loving me as I slowly come back down from the highest of highs.

When I finally float back to reality, Mac has his arms wrapped around me and I'm tucked against his naked body. His cock is rock hard, laying against his stomach. I lift myself up and over his legs to straddle him, taking him in my hands as I line him up with my entrance.

"I have an IUD. Are you clean?" I hate that I have to ask. I hate that eleven years has gone by and I don't know if Mac is safe.

He just nods and I slowly lower my body onto him, taking him inside of me inch by inch. Our groans intermingle in the silence as my body stretches to accommodate him in a way that it hasn't for a very long time.

Mac doesn't move at first, he lets me take control. I've always loved that about him; he has an alpha side, but he also has a sensitive side that enjoys letting me be in charge of our pleasure. The give and take in our lovemaking hasn't changed, and it's my turn now to make sure Mac gets exactly what he needs.

I start to rock my hips, using my hands on his chest to brace myself. Mac reaches up to tangle his fingers in my hair, a soft smile on his face as he watches me move. Slowly I pick up speed, then bring it back down. It's a dance, a seductive tango between our bodies that I'm leading.

I'm already primed from my first orgasm, so I can feel another one building quickly. It's always been this way with Mac, I thought it was normal to come twice or even three times in one session. I realized just how wrong I was when I struggled to reach even one orgasm with anyone else.

I want Mac to come with me this time, so I lean back, and grind down onto him, thrusting my breasts up to the sky. He's always loved my breasts and sure enough, he lets out a feral growl when he sees them on display and his hands come around to cup them. His thumbs work over my nipples and it becomes increasingly harder for me to hold back on my own release.

Thankfully I don't have to wait long. I can feel him growing impossibly harder inside of me and if there was ever any question that he was about to lose control, what he says to me next eradicates any doubt.

"Fuck, Tawny, I'm gonna come babe, you feel like heaven and I'm gonna come so hard." His voice is taut with tension and his hips lift to meet mine as he moves with me.

"Mac, Mac, Mac, now please Mac, oh God Mac, now!" I gasp and plead with him. He grabs my hips and takes over, thrusting up into me with such passion, such power, that my cries echo around the room as I explode. His name the only thing I can say over and over again. Then he's coming, and I can feel him filling me, I can hear his groan of release, and the way he just keeps saying *Jesus, T. Fuck. Tawny.* Until we collapse onto each other, a tangled mess of sweaty limbs.

Lying there in the afterglow should feel amazing, shouldn't it? This is normally a time of intimacy and connection after two people have come together. But something's off, like there's still a small wall between us.

He was right earlier, we should have talked before having sex and figured out what we both want. It's not enough to just admit our mistakes and that we still love each other. There are too many years of heartache between us. I need to get away from it, from him, and figure out what this means, what's happening. I climb out of bed, not looking at Mac. Grabbing the first pieces of clothing I can find, I stumble into the bathroom and turn on the shower.

I should have known better than to expect Mac to give me space. He's always been in tune with my emotions and can tell when I'm upset from a mile away. I'm really not surprised when the shower door opens and he steps inside, his hands coming to rest gently on my hips. I turn around under the spray and look up at him to see vulnerability and uncertainty etched on his face.

I lift up on my toes, unable to stop myself from kissing him. His grip on me tightens and he pulls me in close. The hot water pours down over both of us and it would be so easy to get lost in this moment, in him again. But I can't let myself go there once more, so I take a step back, placing my hand on his chest.

"We should talk. You were right."

Mac looks at me and then nods quickly. He doesn't say another word, just grabs my shampoo and begins to wash my hair, his strong hands massaging my scalp. He's taking care of me, reinforcing his love and our connection with every touch. When we're done, I step out first and pass him a towel. We dry ourselves in silence, then Mac walks into my bedroom and pulls on his jeans. Only his jeans. Sweet baby jesus he's going commando and with that happy trail of chest hair leading down to the bulge in his pants, I'm suddenly salivating.

No, Tawny. Talk first. I silently reprimand myself. You can't erase a decade of pain with sex.

Once I'm dressed, I take his hand and lead him into my kitchen. I pour us both a glass of water and the silence between us continues. Maybe it should be awkward, but its not. It's comfortable, and easy, like our souls know that we don't need words right now. It's enough to just be together.

Eventually, we make it to the couch and sit down at opposite ends. But even still, Mac needs to be touching me. He grabs my feet and swings my legs up so that I'm stretched out on the couch and my feet are in his lap. He flashes me a smile and I suddenly remember a time when we were sitting in this very room as teenagers, watching a movie, and he did that same move. My feet in his lap was as affectionate as we ever got in front of my family and I can recall the thrill of having his hands on my body.

"So..." he begins. I take a sip of water and try to calm my nerves. This conversation is crucial for us if we want to move forward.

"Clearly, we haven't lost our chemistry," he shoots me a wry grin. "And I for one can't wait to do *that* again. But there needs to be more than just great sex between us, Tawny. I love you and somehow you still love me. I don't take that for granted and I sure as shit don't want to mess this up again."

I smile, my heart warming to hear him say he loves me. Those words I never thought I'd hear again.

"Same. I don't know how we got so lucky as to get a second chance, but I don't want to lose you again," I say, and the truth of that rings in my ears.

"That means you have to trust me, T. And talk to me if you're worried or confused. You can't shut me out." Mac's voice hardens slightly, letting me know that there's still pain lingering under the surface between us.

I instinctively sit up straighter and go to pull my legs off his lap to create space between us. But his hand traps them there.

"Don't pull away from me, not now, please," he asks softly, and I relax again.

"Sorry," I whisper. "I don't want to. And I know I shouldn't have back then. It wasn't fair of me not to give you a chance to explain and I don't know how I'll ever forgive myself for that."

Tears are building behind my eyes again. Damn it. I thought I was done crying about this. Mac senses my emotions and in one smooth motion he's pulled my body onto his lap and is cradling me close.

"Tawny, babe, it's not your fault. Not entirely. Don't take this on your shoulders without sharing it with me, okay? We both screwed up. And now we can both fix it and move on. That's what I want, is that what you want?" His eyes are searching mine and I can see his love shining there. It's enough to calm my heart.

"I know it's not all my fault, Mac. And of course, I want to fix it and move forward with you, I just hate that we missed out on so much." I bite my lip before taking a deep breath and asking the question that has been plaguing me since he showed up on my doorstep earlier. "Our lives are so different now. You live on the mainland and I'm here. How can this even work?"

Mac nods his head slowly. "I don't have that answer, T. I just know I want to try."

"So do I."

He presses a kiss to my head and his arms, which are already wrapped around me, squeeze a little tighter, almost as if he's worried if he doesn't keep me close I might disappear. I know the feeling; I'm scared I might wake up and find this was all just a dream.

"I'm here for at least a month helping Mom and Dad. Can you give me that month? Give us that time to be together and figure this out?"

His voice is gently pleading and I can tell he's serious about wanting to make it work. As much as it scares me to think of him leaving in a month and my heart breaking all over again, I have to try. I owe it to him and I owe it to myself.

"Okay," I say softly.

A smile stretches across his face and it's as if the clouds parted and the sun is shining down on us; it fills me with such warmth.

He leans down and presses a chaste but loving kiss to my lips, his hands cup my face, his thumbs sweep over my cheeks. When he pulls back, he's still grinning.

"It's going to be so amazing being able to take you out on real dates this time," he says excitedly, and my heart plummets. If everyone knows we're together, then everyone will know if things don't work out when he leaves. I don't know if I can handle the pity, having everyone around me know I'm hurting.

"Can we keep it a secret for just a little while?" I blurt out, and wince when I see his face fall. "At least at first while we figure this out," I stammer.

"Why?"

I don't want to tell him. I don't want to admit that I'm already thinking about the possibility of us ending. Heck, I wish I *wasn't* thinking about this not working out, but I have to be practical. I've got to protect myself somehow.

"Well, you know, everyone expects us to still hate each other and avoid each other. Wouldn't it be weird if all of a sudden, we're holding hands and kissing in public? Let's just take it slow." My reason sounds feeble even to my ears and I know Mac doesn't like it based on the frown on his face.

"Tawny..." he starts, then he lets out a sigh. "I don't like it. I want the world to know you're mine and I'm yours." Mac pauses again, his head tipped back as he examines the ceiling, looking for an answer. He must find it, because his voice has a resigned acceptance in it when he continues.

"But if that's the way you want it, then I'll go along with it. For now." He shifts to look at me and his eyes are penetrating. "Are you going to tell your sisters?"

"They already know. I mean, they know about our past. But not about us now. They don't know about today. Obviously. It's not like I texted them mid-orgasm." I try to laugh but it comes out forced. "I guess I could tell them we're trying. It'll be hard to hide it from them. But no one else, please?"

Mac sighs. I hate that I've already upset him and part of me wonders if I'm making a mistake wanting to keep us a secret for now. It doesn't mean I don't love him, it just means I'm trying to protect myself if things go wrong. That's not unreasonable, is it?

31

Mac

"Fine, we'll keep it quiet."

My voice sounds hollow and to be honest, that's how I feel. The high of being back together with Tawny is tarnished by her stupid need to keep it secret. I know why she's doing it; she's scared. Something tells me that no matter how much I want to push her to go public, this is not the time. We're too fragile. Which means that if she needs the safety net of keeping our relationship a secret, I'll let her have it. For now.

She looks relieved. My heart bounces like a goddamn tennis ball, from frustration, to hurt, right back to excitement and joy. Tawny's here, in my arms, and other parts of my body are noticing the way her hips are nestled in my lap.

She quirks her brow at me. "Oh really?"

I shrug my shoulders and give her the smile that she used to say made her melt. When she turns her body to straddle me, I figure it's safe to assume it still works. I lean in and gently bite her neck before soothing it with my tongue.

"Really."

And with just that one word, Tawny's wildcat side comes out. She may seem cool, calm, and collected to most people, but I know her passionate side. Her crazy, sensual, adventurous side. And that's the Tawny that's here now. She whips her shirt off over her head and presses her upper body to my bare chest before capturing my lips in a kiss that is pure fire. I know that when she gets like this, things get...energetic, shall we say. I stand up with her in my hands, intent on heading back into the bedroom. But Tawny has a different idea. She wriggles out of my hands and turns around to lean over the couch, her pert ass right in front of me.

"Take me, Mac."

Three words shouldn't hold so much power, but I'll be damned, do they ever. Our pants are off in an instant and I'm sliding home with a groan.

"Yes, T," I ground out as she rotates her hips around me in a slow, sensual pattern. She might be thinking that she's in control this time, but she's wrong. It's my turn to show her just how fucking fantastic we are together. My hands dig into her side so tightly, I'm pretty sure I might leave a bruise, so I ease back slightly as I pull my cock almost all the way out of her tight heat, before slamming it back in. Over and over, with the slow pull back and fast thrust in. We hover the line between pleasure and pain, always on the exquisite edge where that little bit of aggression feels so goddamn amazing. In all the years we've been apart, I've never had a sexual partner who comes even remotely close to getting me and my desires the way Tawny does. We were made for each other. We know each other's bodies and needs better than we know our own. When to go soft and slow and when to go hard and heavy. I want to fuck every doubt out of her heart, brand her as mine, and never let her go.

I can't hold on for long, not in this position and definitely not with the sexy moans she's making and the way she keeps saying my name. I reach down with one hand and rub her clit in tiny circles and when her voice changes, I know she's close.

Seconds later we're both shouting out our release and Tawny's sagging into my arms, which shake with the power of my orgasm. I pull out, then guide Tawny to stand up, her back against my front.

"Looks like we might need another shower," I mumble into her neck as I kiss her sweet skin. She makes a sound of agreement and one of her arms drifts up and around the back of my neck to hold my head where it is. As if I would move my lips right now.

* * *

Surprisingly enough, we manage to keep our hands off each other while we shower. It's dark out and my stomach has let out more than one embarrassing rumble of hunger.

Which brings me to this moment, sitting at Tawny's kitchen counter in a pair of sweatpants I had in my truck and nothing else, watching the love of my life dish up pizza, wearing nothing but some sleep shorts and a thin tank top. If I were to look up domestic bliss in the dictionary, I'm pretty damn sure a picture of this moment would be right there in black and white.

Once our plates are full of thick, cheesy slices of ham and mushroom pizza, Tawny hands me two beers from her fridge and we take our late dinner back into the living room. When we settle on the couch, she fixes me with a stern glare.

"No funny business this time, got it? This couch has seen more action in the last few hours than it has in the last four years."

I raise my eyebrows at her, unable to hold back from asking, "When did you buy the couch?"

A faint blush covers her cheeks and she looks down at her plate before mumbling, "Four years ago."

I can't contain my grin at that, or my relief. Fast on the heels comes guilt. I haven't exactly been living a chaste lifestyle all these years and I always assumed Tawny had moved on as well. Not that I want to spend even a second thinking about other guys she might have been with. I'm definitely not about to ruin the fucking fantastic vibe between us right now by asking about her exes.

A couple of hours later the credits are rolling on some action movie we put on. I have no idea what it was about, my mind was too busy thinking about us. She's agreed to give us a month to figure out how this is going to work. I know she's not about to leave the island, not with the inn and her sisters here, but I've got my contracting business well established on the mainland. It won't be easy to just pick up and move my headquarters, and with the number of jobs I have lined up over there, commuting would be insane. I know my dad was always able to find work on the island doing maintenance and renovations, but that's not my style. I've developed a reputation for leading some pretty massive reno's in upscale neighborhoods up and down the coast. I'm not a handyman, I'm an in demand contractor with a team of twelve guys who labor for me and a long list of trusted subcontractors. How the hell do I relocate that to Westmount Island?

I'm torn from this stressful line of thinking by Tawny standing up and stretching her hands overhead. The move lifts her shirt up high enough to reveal her toned stomach and the sight of it is making me hard already. She looks down at me with a soft, loving gaze and reaches her hand down to me.

"Will you stay?" she asks, and there's an innocent and adorable hesitancy in her voice.

I stand up and entwine my fingers in hers, tugging her close so I can kiss her.

"I don't think my heart would let me leave."

We walk, hand in hand, back to her bedroom, turning off the lights behind us. She finds a new toothbrush under her sink and the act of brushing our teeth together is a brand-new experience for us, seeing as we've never actually spent the entire night together. Tawny must also realize the importance of this, because she keeps casting furtive glances my way as if she, too, can't quite believe this is really happening.

Tawny climbs into bed first and I walk around to the other side before pulling off my sweats, leaving me in nothing but my boxer briefs. I slide under the blanket, suddenly feeling weirdly unsure of what to do next. She's lying on her side, looking at me with sleepy eyes, and I realize all I want to do is hold her. It's a long buried fantasy of mine to fall asleep with Tawny Michaels in my arms and wake up the next morning still holding her. Tonight, that fantasy can finally come true.

32

Tawny

I'm surrounded by a wall of heat and hardness and my half-asleep brain can't figure out why. Slowly, gradually, as my awareness increases, I realize it's Mac. *I slept with Mac...*like, slept. Not sex, sleep. It's weird how big of a deal that seems, but we've never spent the night in the same bed before.

Waking up with his arms wrapped around me, my head pillowed on his chest, everything feels perfect. It's early and I can tell by the steady rise and fall of his chest that Mac is still sleeping. I shift myself slowly so as not to wake him, but I want the chance to look at him.

His features are relaxed and I can see the small differences between the man he is now and the boy he was before. The tiny wrinkles around his eyes that tell me he's outside a lot, the strong angles of his jaw, and that faint scruff that felt so delicious between my legs last night. It's thicker now and I wonder if he'll shave it or leave it. Part of me wants him to leave it...my eyes travel down, over his broad shoulders, roped with muscle, to his chest. There's just enough hair on his body to be masculine without looking like a bear, and it's thicker now, too. I like it. My fingers lightly trace down the ripples of his abdomen. The tight, washboard muscles tell me that Mac still enjoys working out regularly. I stop when my fingers reach the waistband of his underwear and simply lay my hand flat on his stomach. *Mine.* This man, this body, it is as familiar as my own.

"If you wanted to keep exploring, don't stop on my account," he rumbles in the sexiest morning voice I've ever heard. I smile against his chest before lifting myself up so I can see his face. His eyes are sleepy and hooded, but I can't mistake the love shining from them. I lean down to kiss him, but he takes over what I intended to be a quick peck.

In one quick move, I find myself on my back with my handsome man, who is clearly now wide awake, hovering over top of me, a wicked grin on his face.

"Morning breath!" I try to protest, turning my face, but Mac grabs my chin and turns it back to meet his. His lips cover mine and he doesn't hesitate to devour me with his kiss.

"Don't care," he mutters in between kisses. I giggle and let myself relax and enjoy this playful morning with the man I love.

After a few moments of kissing and enjoying the feel of each other, Mac rolls away with a groan.

"As much as I want to take this further, I really should get home to my parents. Mom's got an appointment later today and I promised I would take her."

I sit up beside him, drawing my knees into my chest and let my head rest there so I can look at him.

"Did you tell them you were with me last night?"

He waits a beat before he answers. "No, I just said I would be staying with a friend. You want this to stay a secret, so it will. For now." Mac sits up and leans against the headboard. The sheet has fallen away, and his torso is on display, making my mouth — and other parts of me — wet. He is so damn sexy. Part of me hates that my duties at the inn keep me from staying in bed all day, but I've got to get to the inn.

"Thank you," I whisper. "I know you don't want to keep quiet about things, but I really think it's best for now."

His head turns toward me and he takes my hand, brings it up to his lips, and kisses it.

"I'll respect that, but not forever. You're mine, Tawny. And I want everyone to know it. We'll figure out how this is going to work and then I'm going to tell the world that I love you."

His voice is heavy with promise and I shiver. I want that so badly. I want to walk down the street holding his hand, I want to go out on dates with him, I want to kiss him wherever and whenever I want.

I nod, because I'm still too scared to tell him why I want to keep things between us for now. Thankfully, that seems to be enough for him, because he climbs out of bed and pulls on his clothes.

"Can you come back tonight?" I ask, suddenly anxious about when I'm going to see him again.

"I don't know, T. I need to see what my dad needs from me first." Mac walks around the bed and takes me by the shoulders. "Last night was amazing. Falling asleep with you, waking up with you, it's everything I've ever wanted. If it were up to me, I would spend every possible second with you, loving you. But I came here to help my parents and I can't let them down just because I've finally got you back."

I can hear the regret in his voice, but he's right. He needs to be here for his parents, just like I'm needed at the inn. I go into my closet and pull down a maroon dress to wear and some clean underwear. I dress quickly, needing the armor of clothes to try and hold back my desire for Mac.

Eventually, we're standing at the front door of my house and I realize someone could see him leaving my house.

"Mac, how are you going to leave without all of my neighbors knowing you spent the night here?"

Mac chuckles before leaning down and pressing a hard kiss to my lips.

"Guess we just have to take the risk, babe."

He opens my door and walks to his truck without looking back. Once he's seated, he looks up at me and gives me that smile that makes me weak in the knees. My smile. He waves and blows me a kiss before pulling out of my driveway.

Once he's gone, my legs sag and I lean against the door jam for a moment before quickly locking my front door and going to my car. Before I drive away, I cast a quick glance around the street. It doesn't look like anyone was outside to see Mac leave, but in a small town, you just never know. My whole motivation behind keeping our relationship quiet is the underlying fear that Mac's life will take him away from me again. And if that happens a second time, I don't want everyone I know looking at me with pity. I might have wished for support last time he left, but now the pain will be so much greater that I don't think I could stand it if everyone knew Shawn Macdonald broke my heart.

* * *

At the inn, I don't have long to dwell on my night with Mac. We're fully booked this week and the restaurant is busy as well. I'm answering emails, manning reception so my team can have a break, checking on food orders for the kitchen, and dealing with housekeeping issues all day long. Before I know it, it's after seven p.m. and Ella is pushing open the door to my office.

"Hey big sis, got time for me?"

I push back from my desk with a smile. "Always. Especially if it can be over a glass of wine."

We head to the restaurant and go straight to the table that I always keep open in case my sisters come to visit. I grab a bottle of white wine from the kitchen, two glasses, and smile my thanks to my head chef when she passes a plate of appetizers into my hand. Smoked salmon puffs, crispy green beans, and a hot crab dip. Perfection.

Ella and I dig in to the food and the wine. I know why she's here; she wants details on what happened with Mac. She's the one who told him where to find me yesterday, so she must know we were together.

Sure enough, a few minutes in and just as I'm popping a salmon puff in my mouth, Ella clears her throat and gives me a pointed look.

"So, got anything to say about yesterday?"

I shake my head in an attempt to feign innocence, but Ella doesn't buy it. She may be the sweeter of my two sisters, but make no mistake, she gets what she wants.

"Nice try, Tawny. I know Mac came over. How did it go?"

I sigh and Ella must hear something in that one breath because her eyes light up and she claps her hands. "Holy shiitake, he stayed over!"

As a kindergarten teacher, Ella only uses food names to swear. It's annoyingly adorable.

"Yes Ella, my nosy sister, he stayed over," I answer with a roll of my eyes to disguise my grin. Memories of Mac rolling me over and pushing into me brings a flush to my cheeks, so I duck my head down and take another sip of the crisp wine to try and cool myself down.

"Was it amazing? Oh, your first time together in such a long time, it must have been so romantic!" The hearts in Ella's eyes fade as I start giggling under my breath. Her tone is defensive. "What's so funny?"

Romantic isn't exactly how I would describe last night. Emotional, passionate, lust-filled, sure. Romantic? Not really.

"Romance wasn't high on our list of priorities."

Ella's eyes flare wide for a moment before she's giggling, too. I raise my glass and we silently toast each other. *Here's to amazing sex.*

"So, are you guys together now? Like, for real this time?"

I wait a moment before answering. It's complicated and I don't know if anyone else would understand my reasoning or agree with me on my decision.

"Sort of. We're together, yes. I still love him, he still loves me, we're working through the mess that happened. But we're keeping things private for now." It's an honest answer, even if it isn't the complete answer. It seems to be enough to satisfy Ella for now because she just nods.

We continue to enjoy our food and wine, our conversation moving on to how Ella's husband Marcus is progressing with the new community he's developing at the north end of the island. It's going to be beautiful and integrate really well into Westmount Island. Ella's been acting as a pseudo-liaison for the project, making sure the community meets our needs and attracts the right kind of people as residents. People who enjoy nature and a slower pace of life.

Eventually, the wine bottle and plates are empty and I realize far too late that I'm a little tipsy.

"Crap, I don't know if I can drive home," I state, surprised until I realize that those appetizers were the only real food I ate since breakfast. Salmon puffs were no match for half a bottle of wine.

Ella giggles. "Why don't you call lover boy to come and pick you up?"

I snort inelegantly. "First of all, don't call him lover boy ever again. Eww. Second of all, he's helping his parents." But I want to see Mac, even more now that Ella brought it up. My tall, muscled, sexy, Mac...

"I can get Marcus to drive you home," Ella offers sweetly, but I shake my head.

"Nah, I can walk. It's not far." Which is true, nothing on the island is that far. My home is at most a three-mile walk. Easy peasy.

Ella waves at me from the front steps of the inn and turns to skip toward her cottage, conveniently located on the inn's property. Once she's inside, I head out down the long driveway, wobbling only slightly.

Halfway into my walk, I'm regretting my stupid decision. This trip might seem like no big deal in daylight, but when I'm drunk and wearing heels, it's harder than climbing West Mountain.

I feel like an idiot. I'm so caught up in complaining to myself that I don't notice the truck pull up beside me until it's right there, startling me. The window rolls down and over the thunder of my racing heart, I hear the most amazing sound.

"Hey hot stuff, where are you headed so late at night?"

Mac's teasing is filled with warmth and promises, and I eagerly open the truck door and climb in. I crawl over the bench seat and grab his face, pressing a kiss to his smiling lips.

"My hero."

His chuckle fills the cab. "Happy to oblige, but why didn't you call me?"

"I didn't want to bother you." I fasten my seatbelt, then look over at him, confused. "Wait, how did you know to come and find me? I thought you were with your parents?"

"Marcus called me from Ella's phone. Seems like a nice guy. Went on about you two drinking lots of wine and you deciding to walk home. He didn't like that idea, but didn't want to leave Ella, so he called me. I guess Ella told him about us."

"Yeah, she would do that. They're so in love," I say dreamily as my head falls back.

"That wine did a number on you, didn't it, T?"

I nod slowly and giggle. "Yup."

33

Mac

I grin fondly at my tipsy girl. "Well, I'll get you home and settled, then I should get back to Mom and Dad's."

Tawny pouts and I chuckle. She wants me to stay with her and I want that, too. But I do need to get back to my Dad.

"I'm glad I got to see you tonight." I glance over at her and she turns her head to smile at me.

"Me too."

I take her hand in mine and relish the feeling of her fingers wrapped between mine. The rest of the short drive is filled with an easy silence. Tawny sitting in my truck, holding my hand, brings back memories of when we were younger. How exciting it felt sneaking around, stealing moments together. I wish the secret felt exciting this time, but it just hurts. And if I'm honest, I'm worried it means she isn't all in, like I am.

I pull into her driveway, only to realize Tawny's fallen asleep, her head leaning against my truck window.

I gently untangle my hand and climb out, then walk around to her side. It isn't easy, but I manage to get the door open and her seatbelt unbuckled without waking her up. Once she's in my arms, Tawny lets out a little noise before nuzzling under my chin. I chuckle and walk to her front door. Since I don't have a key, I realize I've got to wake her up.

"T, where's your key?" I ask softly.

"Mmm," she mumbles, then burrows in closer to my body.

"Tawny, I need your key," I say again.

"Purse," she mutters, and I look down to see no purse. A glance back at my truck reveals it sitting on the floorboard.

"Shit," I mutter. But there's nothing else I can do, so I quickly carry her back down the path to my truck, grab the purse with one hand, and head back to the front porch.

It takes some juggling and jostling, but somehow Tawny doesn't fully wake up while I get her key out and open the door. I leave it open behind me as I walk down the hall to her bedroom and gently lay her on the bed. She rolls over with a mumble.

I jog back, close my truck door and her front door, then take in a few deep breaths to try and quell my desire. I can't do anything with her right now, she's drunk and asleep, and I've got to get home. But that doesn't stop me from thinking about waking her up with kisses up and down her spine.

When I have better self-control, I walk slowly back to her bedroom. Standing in the doorway, I just look at her. She's lying on her side and her long hair is spread out across the pillows. My eyes follow the curve of her body and it's killing me to not climb in and wrap my body around hers.

Instead, I carefully remove her shoes and grab a blanket from the chair in the corner of her room to drape over her. A gentle kiss to her forehead is all I allow myself before walking back out to my truck.

* * *

MAC

When I get home, my dad is just coming out of the bedroom he shares with my mom. He closes the door softly before coming down the stairs to the kitchen where I am. He pulls two beers out of the fridge, handing me one. We crack them open, leaning against the counter in comfortable silence.

"Your friend get home okay?" he asks innocently enough, but I know he suspects something is up with me and Tawny.

"Yeah, all good."

"You two together now?"

And there it is. My matter-of-fact father letting me know he is all too aware that I'm with Tawny again.

"Yeah."

"Good. Don't screw it up this time."

He finishes his beer, sets the bottle down on the counter and walks out of the room without another word.

I wander out onto the back deck. Last year my mom convinced my dad to splurge on new outdoor furniture, so I sink down onto the cushioned chair with a sigh. Probably should've grabbed another beer, but I'm too comfortable to move now. And more alcohol seems as if might make it harder to figure the shit out that I need to.

I love Tawny and I love the island. That's the easy part. If I'm being honest with myself, I always envisioned returning to the island someday. But I never in my wildest dreams imagined that I could have Tawny again. The life we once dreamt of — where we finished college, moved back to be together, got married, and started a family — had disappeared forever. Or so I thought.

Now that it's all within my reach again, I close my eyes and let the fantasy of Tawny wearing a ring I've given her, pregnant with my baby, wash over me. *Fuck*, she'd be gorgeous pregnant. And there's no one else I want to have a family with. Never has been, never will be.

With my heart easily sorted, all I have left to worry about is my company. I've been considering the idea of bringing on a foreman to handle on-site issues for the last year or so, ever since things started getting really busy. Doing so would alleviate some of the challenges that are inevitable if I relocate back to Westmount Island. But I know I'd still have to travel to the mainland a lot and I'm not sure how Tawny would feel about that. Would she come with me? Technically, she doesn't have to be at the inn every single day, although I can remember from high school how much of a control freak she can be. I'm sure it's no different with her work. Still, she could travel if she wanted to.

I open up my phone, scrolling through the short list of guys I had been thinking of for the foreman position. All members of my general labor crew that I've employed for a while, they're good guys, trustworthy and skilled at their jobs. Truthfully, I would be happy to work with any of them, and promoting one of them would allow me to hand off most of the on-site work, leaving me free to coordinate things from a distance.

But is that enough for me? I enjoy the hands-on work, getting dirty on demo day, and watching things come together at the end. And I'm not sure if there's enough work here on Westmount Island to keep me busy in the way I'm accustomed.

My gaze flicks out over the edge of the balcony and an idea hits me. *Marcus.* Ella's husband has been building a whole new community on the north side of the island, but from what my dad has said, progress is slow as he tries to figure out the nuances of construction. He's a numbers guy, not a brick-and-mortar guy. That's where I could come in. I hope. Before I can second-guess my decision, I open a new text chat, grateful that he gave me his number over the phone earlier, and send him a message:

MAC: Hey Marcus, it's Mac. Would you be open to meeting for lunch tomorrow to discuss a business proposition?

I immediately see the rolling dots that show me he's responding.

MARCUS: Hey man, if you're going to suggest what I hope you're

going to suggest, then yes, I am.

MAC: Not sure what that means, but I think we might be able to help each other out with something.

MARCUS: I think so. See you at Seas the Day at noon?

MAC: Great. Thanks for the opportunity. Sorry to bug you so late.

MARCUS: All good. See you tomorrow.

I put my phone down with a smile. If Marcus and I could work out a deal, things would really start looking up.

* * *

As I sit in a booth at the diner early the next day, waiting for Marcus, I absentmindedly wipe the fingerprints off the laptop that holds my digital portfolio.

I've been busy this morning. I've got interviews set up with my top three picks for the foreman position lined up for tomorrow over video chat and I'm feeling good. My future with Tawny is starting to take shape.

A few minutes past noon, the door opens and the man I've seen walking in and out of Ella's cottage comes striding over. He's got an air of confidence that I admire, even as he's dressed casually in jeans and a tee shirt. I can see the intelligence in his eyes and his grip when he shakes my hand is strong.

"You must be Marcus, glad to officially meet you."

"Mac, nice to meet you, too. I've heard a lot."

Marcus smiles, but I can tell he's all business right now. I took some time to look him up and Marcus Ryder is not a man to mess with. His investment firm is extremely successful and he's made a name for himself by investing only in projects he feels passionate about.

I've heard of a few start-ups that he's refused to help and that makes my request that much more daunting. I don't want to use the sister angle, but at the same time I'm hoping he's motivated to keep Ella happy, and a happy Tawny would lead to a happy Ella. And me being on Westmount Island is critical to a happy Tawny, at least I think it is. Marcus is the key to make all of that happen.

We order food and while we wait, Marcus leans forward and places his forearms on the table.

"Alright, you got me here, what's on your mind?"

I take a steadying breath, then open my laptop to my website.

"Rumor has it your project on the north end of the island is stalled because you're having a hard time finding competent construction crews."

He nods, but doesn't reveal anything else, so I carry on.

"I've run a successful, high-end contracting company for almost a decade. You can see our work here on our website and I've got a list of past clients willing to give testimonials. My focus has always been on home renovations, but we've done new builds as well. Here's what I propose. Hire my company to do your construction work. I've got contacts for every trade you'll need, from an architect who specializes in green homes all the way to the painters and landscapers. I'm confident I can get a crew of guys out here to start as soon as we have the machinery in place. You'll get your community built and I'll get enough work to keep me on the island."

When I finish, I try not to squirm under Marcus's steely stare. He holds my gaze and holy shit, I can see why this guy is so successful in business. I'm not easily intimidated, but he's got me shuffling my feet. Trying to keep calm, I keep my eyes on his. He pulls the laptop over and finally breaks eye contact long enough to look through my portfolio. When he still doesn't say anything, I start filling the silence.

"I can get a physical portfolio couriered over by morning if that works better for you," I say, hoping my nerves don't show. Marcus is critical to my plan. Not only as a potential client, but also as a potential family member if everything goes the way I want it to.

"I don't need to see anything else." He leans back and finally smiles. "I've been talking with your dad for weeks. He's been trying to convince me to reach out to you, but Ella said she didn't think you'd ever come back. Honestly Mac? As soon as I found out you were here, I've been itching to set up a meeting. Consider yourself hired."

I sag back against the booth with a laugh. "Seriously?"

"Seriously, man," he replies with a grin. He reaches his hand over the table and we shake. "Welcome to the family might be a bit premature, but welcome back to the island seems appropriate."

We both laugh and proceed to eat our lunches. Conversation shifts easily to the project, with Marcus outlining his plan for the new community and me chiming in with advice. After an hour, he promises to have contracts ready for me to sign by the end of the week and I leave the diner, walking on air.

All I need now is a foreman, a crew willing to work on the island, and a way to convince Tawny I'm back for good.

34

Tawny

Hangovers suck. Especially when you're a lightweight that doesn't drink often. And working with a hangover? Even worse. But here I am, entering purchase orders for cleaning supplies with a pounding head and a swimming stomach.

Even my hangover isn't quite enough to erase my memory of last night and the memory of how sweet Mac was to me. I'm a bit fuzzy on how he found me, but I do remember him driving me home, carrying me inside, and tucking me in.

This wasn't the first time he's had to look out for me while drinking. Our graduating class held a big bonfire at the base of West Mountain and that was the night I learned just how low my alcohol tolerance is. Mac took care of me, making sure I made it home okay, and even slept on the couch so he could check on me. His love was strong, even as a teenager, and despite our years apart it seems it's only grown.

My phone beeps with a new text message and I pick it up, welcoming the break from the mind-numbing tasks I'm dealing with today.

MAC: How's the hangover?
TAWNY: *grumble grumble*
MAC: LOL still can't handle your booze I see.

TAWNY: Nope.

TAWNY: Thank you for last night. How did you find me?

MAC: Marcus called me. Ella was worried about you walking home. YOU should have called me, babe. We did talk about this in the truck... Don't you remember?

TAWNY: Huh. Nope. Don't remember that at all. I guess I'll have to thank Marcus and Ella too. Walking home drunk wasn't my smartest idea.

MAC: I'll always come for you, T. No matter where you are.

I put the phone down as my breath whooshes out of me. As wonderful as that makes me feel, eighteen-year-old me demands to know why he didn't come for me all those years ago. Sighing, I acknowledge her pain and push it down. I need to focus on growing; I have to move on if I want a future with him. And I do.

Someone knocks on my office door, but before I can say anything, it opens and Mac walks through, a grin on his face and what looks like a breakfast sandwich from the diner in his hands. Even though it's the afternoon, I haven't been able to eat anything because the only food that helps me when I'm hungover is a greasy diner breakfast. The fact that Mac remembers this from the *one* time he saw me get really drunk leaves my mouth hanging open.

"Please tell me that's a bacon and egg sandwich on a cheese scone," I say.

He nods and hands the bag over. "I wasn't sure if that was still your hangover cure, but Kayla brought Toby in for lunch while I was trying to decide what to get you and confirmed it for me."

"You're an angel." I quickly unwrap the sandwich and moan when the aroma hits me. I eat the entire sandwich, then sit back in my chair with a sigh. "Better already."

Mac grins, then walks around behind my desk and spins my chair so that I'm facing him. He leans down and holds my head gently in his hands before pressing a kiss to the corner of my mouth.

"You had a little something right there."

His soft touch sends a shiver down my spine.

"Thanks. I think I've got something right here too," I whisper as I touch my neck. Mac gives me a wolfish smile and that shiver turns to a flickering heat, burning in my core. He kisses my neck, harder this time, and doesn't stop at just one. He kisses me in a trail from the base of my neck up to my jawline and over until finally he reaches my lips. I grab his head and hold him there as we lose ourselves in our kiss and that flicker builds into an inferno of need.

"Mac..." I breathe, unable to formulate a full sentence.

"I need you, T. But not here." Somehow Mac has the strength to pull back, but I can't hide my whimper at the loss of his lips on mine. He leans down and kisses me, fast and hard, before walking back to the other side of my desk. His face is flushed, his shoulders are heaving, and I watch him adjust himself in his pants with a satisfied smile. Knowing I have this effect on him is powerful and I'm sure it's written all over my face just how much he turns me on.

"What time can you finish work?" he asks, a heated promise behind his words.

"I can probably get out by six."

"Perfect. We're going to have a date." Mac smiles, but his words have me nervous.

"We can't go out in public together, Mac," I say quietly.

"Don't worry, we won't. But I do need your house key."

I hand it over without asking any questions. I trust him and now I'm curious about what he's planning. He gives me one more quick kiss, then turns and leaves, closing my office door behind him.

I drop my head to my desk, trying to figure out how I'm going to get through another four hours of work without spending the entire time fantasizing about Mac. Thankfully, the one thing that can kill arousal faster than anything is the mind-numbing repetition of inventory. And that was my Friday afternoon plan. To my relief, it worked. Mostly.

* * *

Shortly after six, I pull into my driveway. Mac's truck isn't here, which has me wondering what's going on. He's got my house key, so hopefully he's here or I'm locked out.

When I try my front door, it opens and I'm greeted with the aroma of something delicious, and the sight of candles flickering down my hallway. Mac appears in the entrance to the kitchen, looking like he stepped off the pages of a romance novel. Dark slacks are perfectly molded to his legs and the sleeves of his blue dress shirt are rolled up to reveal his forearms. To top it all off, he's smiling *that* smile at me, the one that makes my knees week, and holding a single red rose.

"Welcome home, my love."

Tears are forming behind my eyes, because this is just so perfect. It's all of my dreams come true; Mac waiting for me at home, sweeping me off my feet with romance. I drop my bag and coat on the floor, slip off my heels and run to him. He catches me and lifts me so I can wrap my legs around his waist as we kiss.

"I love you," I whisper as our foreheads rest against each other.

"And I love you," comes his earnest reply.

I slowly slide down until I am standing in front of him, but he keeps me wrapped in a tight embrace. I've always loved how I fit in his arms, my head resting in the middle of his chest. I breathe in deeply, feeling his chest rise and fall and his heart beat strongly beneath me. *Home.* That's what Mac is to me, he's home in every sense of the word. He is where I belong.

My stomach growls loudly, interrupting the moment. Mac chuckles and steps back, taking my hand and leading me into the kitchen where the source of that tantalizing aroma is revealed.

"You made shrimp linguine?" I'm drooling. This is one of his mom's recipes and I've always loved it.

He walks over to the stove and stirs something, then turns his head over his shoulder to give me a grin. "Only the best for you."

I settle down on a stool to watch him. "When did you learn to cook? In high school you burned toast."

He turns to me, pours a glass of wine and pushes it across the counter. "After college, I kind of had to learn. Living by myself and not wanting to survive on takeout meant I was begging Mom for lessons over video chat." He looks sad and I know he's worrying about her.

I walk over to him and wrap my arms around his neck. "She'll be okay."

He nods, but his smile doesn't reach his eyes, and when he moves back over to the stove, I know he doesn't want to talk about her anymore. I return to my stool and think carefully over how to phrase my next question. I'm curious about his life all these years, but don't want to seem nosy or jealous.

"Was your mom the only one to teach you to cook?" I ask casually, but Mac sees right through me. He cocks an eyebrow at my question and folds his arms across his chest. The motion makes his biceps stand out against his shirt and I raise my fingers to my lips to make sure I'm not drooling.

"There was no one serious, if that's what you're really asking."

"No one?" I'm skeptical. Ten years without a girlfriend? Seems too good to be true. But Mac just shrugs and nods his head.

"I mean, I dated, sure. But just casual. No one I felt strongly enough about to have in my home day after day. Certainly no one I ever wanted to cook for."

This floors me. For some reason, this confession means more to me than any other declaration of love he could have made.

"Wow," I say softly.

"What about you?"

I shake my head. "No one important. A few dates, but nothing really. It's hard to date on an island where you grew up with everyone."

He chuckles at that. "Ain't that the truth. That was always the thing with us, wasn't it? I've known you since we were kids, everyone knew we were friends, and we didn't know how they would react to us suddenly dating."

I nod. "Exactly. And if we broke up, it would have been so awkward seeing each other everywhere."

Mac stands up abruptly and turns back to the stove. "Yeah, well, that sure as shit turned out to be true." His voice is gruff and I can hear the lingering pain and frustration in his words.

My heart aches. I didn't mean to bring up our past like that and suddenly there's a weird tension in the air. I'm debating whether or not I should say something when Mac takes a deep, audible breath, then turns to me.

"I'm sorry, T. I said we should move on from the past. We're here now and I'm not going anywhere. No more awkwardness, no more pain."

I want so badly to believe him. I want to believe that he's not going anywhere, but I've got to talk to him about his plans, and I need to do it now. Before I'm too far in love with him again to survive him leaving again.

35

Mac

Sure screwed that up, idiot. I wish I could hit myself for saying that. I can't claim that we need to move on and then say shit like that. Tawny's gone quiet and my plan for the evening is quickly going off the rails. I wanted to woo her with a candlelit dinner and then tell her my news from my meeting with Marcus. I envisioned a perfect night, hot sex, and best of all, Tawny finally being fully invested in us. Instead, I stuck my foot in my mouth and made things tense. What a fuck up.

I serve up dinner and carry it to her dining room table, which I've set with roses and candles. It's cheesy as hell, but I'm hoping she likes it anyway. Tawny follows me with her wine glass, so I go back and grab my glass and the bottle. Once we're settled, I raise my glass and look at her. She's glowing in the soft light. How goddamn lucky am I to get a second chance with this woman?

"To us. Past, present and future. We're here now, and I for one, couldn't be happier."

We lightly clink our glasses and dig into dinner. She doesn't say anything after my toast, which eats at me. There's something wrong and I don't know what to do.

The silence grows as we eat, along with my anxiety. When she finally finishes, I stand up from the table and take her by the hand, leading her to the couch. We sit, side by side, but Tawny shifts slightly so she isn't touching me. *Fuck. This is bad.*

"T, what's going on? You've been quiet ever since my stupid comment before dinner."

My words come out more bluntly than I meant, but I need to figure out what is wrong with her, with us. Every second that goes past with this new wedge between us feels like an eternity.

"I know I've been quiet," she says, her fingers twisting in her lap. She finally looks up at me and the uncertainty I see there kills me. "It's not that I don't appreciate what you did tonight, it's, well, it's so sweet and romantic. I just…"

"Just what? C'mon Tawny, talk to me, babe. Please." I'm pleading and I don't care. I can't lose her again. Not now, not when I've finally got her back again. Not when I finally have everything lined up for our happily ever after.

"I'm scared you're going to leave again and I won't survive losing you a second time!" she cries out, flinging her hands in the air before she sinks back onto the couch with her arms crossed over her body.

The silence after her outburst is deafening, but only for a second. Then I'm laughing, but not at Tawny. It's pure relief exploding out from me. It's not the best reaction, and judging by the hurt and anger on Tawny's face, I should stop.

"Nice to know my pain is funny to you," she says angrily, and goes to stand up. I grab her hand and tug her down into my lap, still chuckling.

"No, babe. That's not it at all. I'm sorry I'm laughing. I'm just so fucking relieved to hear you say that." Tawny's arms are still folded as she sits in my lap, stiff and not looking at me.

"Tawny. I'm not leaving. I want to live here, in this house, with you. I want to marry you and have babies with you, and never leave your side longer than I absolutely have to." That's not exactly the way I had planned to tell her this, but I think telling her the truth is more important than making things romantic right now.

She softens in my arms at last and turns her head to look at me, her eyes wide with uncertainty. I can feel her searching my face, looking to see if I'm serious. I am, one hundred percent, and I hope she can see that.

"Really?"

"Really. I met with Marcus earlier today. We're signing contracts this week for me to take over as the lead contractor on the Northgate project. I've got interviews set up with some of my guys to hire a foreman to take over the on-site work on the mainland, and I'm going to move my main office here. My admin assistant has already said she's willing to move. I'm staying, Tawny. For good."

She smiles and her eyes brim with happy tears. She throws her arms around me and buries her head in the crook of my neck. Finally, the tension that was getting so thick between us fades away.

"I take it you're good with that plan?" I tease, and she nods against my skin. I chuckle again and she lifts her head to glare at me.

"You laughed at me. Laughed!" she says, but the accusation is softened by the feel of her lips against my shoulder.

"I know, T. I was so worried about why you were quiet over dinner. Finding out it was because you want me to stay was such a relief, I just started laughing. I didn't mean it as an insult; I'm sorry babe."

She huffs, but I know I'm forgiven. Especially when her fingers twist into the hair at the base of my neck and she pulls me in for a soft kiss.

"You're staying. For good. With me." she says in between kisses, and I nod in agreement to each statement.

"I am. Forever if you'll let me."

"I'll allow it," she replies, her voice full of mock severity. I grin and dive my fingers between us to tickle her sides until she's giggling and smiling, and I can finally breathe knowing we're going to be fine. But when my finger grazes the underside of her breast, her laughter catches on a gasp. The energy changes in an instant, from light and fun to seductive and needy.

I need her, I need to feel her surrounding me, cementing our love and bonding us together.

36

Tawny

Forever with Mac sounds pretty darn good, and my head is spinning from his news. He slowly inches my shirt up and I lift my arms to accommodate what he wants as we continue to touch, tease and kiss each other. I trace his face, his neck, his shoulders with my lips, and I can feel my heart slowly relaxing, memorizing the feel of him. He's mine; I get to keep him. It feels unbelievable, and yet so, *so* real.

Our clothes come off in a rush and soon we're standing in my bedroom, the curtains closed against the outside world. It's just me and Mac, baring not just our bodies to each other, but our hearts and souls as well. Time slows down and so do we. He's leisurely in his exploration of me, his lips and his fingers running over my body, leaving shivers of desire in his wake.

"Mac..." his name comes out in a breathy sigh as his lips coast over the swells of my breasts. His hands wrap around my waist and suddenly I'm lifted in the air. My legs are wrapped around him and I can feel his cock nestled between us, pulsing with his arousal. He sits down on the edge of my bed and lays back, bringing me over his body. My hair is loose and he gathers it in his hands, pulling it gently to the nape of my neck.

"You're so beautiful, T. It's like I'm looking into the face of heaven," he murmurs, as his eyes rove over my face with reverence. His abs contract under my hands as he lifts himself up to kiss my forehead. I'm filled with need as I shift myself off the bed until I'm kneeling between his open legs. His cock is right in front of me and I lick my lips before grabbing it and squeezing lightly.

Mac groans and a drop of pre-cum appears. I lick it up without a second thought. God, he tastes good.

I wrap my lips around the head of his cock, and hollow my cheeks, bringing him deep into my mouth. The sounds he makes encourage me as I work him up and down with my mouth and my hand, alternating between deep sucks and licks and swirls around the tip. The muscle memory of bringing Mac pleasure is coming back to me and I settle into the rhythm I remember drives him wild. Sure enough, it isn't long before he's pulling me up into his arms with a growl. He plunders my mouth, his tongue darting in and out.

"I need to be in you."

"Then do it."

He's got a feral glint to his eyes as he flips me over onto my back,

He looks at me, searching my face for any hesitation and I smile before reaching down to squeeze his cock. I can tell he knows I'm okay with this when he grabs my leg and lifts it over his shoulder. Then with one long thrust, he's inside of me, and I scream out his name.

He slowly draws out before slamming back in again. He's relentless, his mouth latching on to whatever part of my body he can reach — my breasts, my neck, my shoulders — all are defenseless against him. My hands find their place holding onto his biceps, squeezing them tightly as he screws me into oblivion. This is way hotter than sex has ever been between us. This is not your everyday, ordinary sex. This is raw, lust filled, and love fueled. This is the kind of sex that millions of romance novels are written about.

My release is thundering towards me and if I wasn't holding onto him, I might float away. Mac is my anchor, holding me to him. When my body ceases to be mine to control, my voice gets higher and higher as I cry out his name. Mac gathers me into his arms and effortlessly lifts my hips so that he's stroking even deeper. I combust. There's no other way to describe the explosion of sensation that comes over me.

Mac shouts out my name seconds later and with one, two, three final thrusts that go so deep I swear he's touching my soul, he collapses on top of me, sliding just enough to the side so as not to crush me. We're sweaty, our chests heaving, and our limbs are tangled together. It's perfect.

* * *

Waking up the next morning to Mac kissing his way down my body, nestling between my legs and wringing a quick but intense orgasm out of me, feels so good it should be illegal. I want nothing more than to stay in bed with him all day, loving him.

But my sisters sent text messages yesterday telling me they expect Mac and I to show up together for brunch at Ella's cottage today. Marcus, Kayla and her fiancé Sam, and his son Toby will be there, too, and I suspect they've got some sort of interrogation planned. I'm nervous about it and I think Mac can tell.

Eventually he lets me out of bed and we get dressed. It's only when we're standing side by side in my bathroom, me applying make-up and him brushing his teeth, that he finally says something.

"Why are you worried about brunch? You're wound so tight I feel like I need to give you another orgasm to relax." He waggles his eyebrows suggestively and it looks so ridiculous with his face covered in shaving cream that I can't hold back a giggle.

"It's just so ridiculous. I think they're planning to do something dumb like question your intentions. I just wish they would leave it alone and let us be," I explain as I carefully apply mascara.

Mac puts down the towel he used to wipe his face and turns around to lean his hip against the counter.

"Didn't I hear that you basically interrogated Marcus and Sam when they first arrived?"

"That's different. They were strangers. Ella and Kayla have known you as long as I have."

"But they haven't known me as your boyfriend," he says, sounding far too reasonable.

"I know, but..."

I've got nothing and he knows it. Which is probably why he just leans over and kisses my cheek before whispering, "It'll be fine, T." With that he walks away, calm and cool as a cucumber, to get dressed and leaving me to groan in exasperation at the stressed-out woman I see in my reflection.

The drive to Ella and Marcus's cottage is woefully short. For once, I wish the island was bigger so that I would have more time to get myself under control. Part of me knows I'm silly for being nervous, but I can't help it. This is, after all, the first time Mac and I will be a couple in front of other people. That feels momentous, even if the people in question are just my sisters and their significant others.

Mac is relaxed and instead of calming me, it irritates the shit out of me.

When he opens my door and extends his hand to help me climb down from the truck, I huff at his smile.

"Tawny. Seriously, you've gotta relax," he chides gently as he runs his hands up and down my arms.

"Easy for you to say," I mutter under my breath and he chuckles. *Chuckles.* How dare he?

As we're walking up the short path to the cottage, the front door suddenly flings open and Kayla appears, grinning from ear-to-ear.

"Oh my fucking God, it's true. Finally!" she cheers and I roll my eyes as Mac grabs my hand and laughs again.

"Hey, Kayla. Good to see you."

"Shawn Macdonald, it is *really* good to see you with my sister at last."

Apparently, Kayla is dedicated to her 'embarrass the crap out of Tawny' act.

"Well, I have to say it's good to be *seen* with your sister at last," Mac commiserates and I fix him with a glare.

"You hush. We *both* agreed to keep it a secret back then," I hiss.

He just shrugs his shoulders at me and heads inside the cottage.

Toby, Sam's son, comes running up to us, spewing questions at a million miles an hour. I love the kid, but dang, is he exhausting.

"Hey Tawny, is this Mac? Kayla said he's your special friend like she's my dad's special friend. Do you have sleepovers and kiss? That's what Kayla and Dad do. I think it's gross, but they like it, I guess. Did you know we're having cinnamon buns? They're my favorite but only if they have icing. Ella said I can call her Ella when we aren't in school, so I get to call her Ella now that kindergarten is over. She said I might get Mrs. Watson for grade one, I hope I do 'cause she sounds fun."

He runs off and Mac looks at me wide-eyed. "Does he always talk that fast?"

I giggle. "Yep, that was pretty tame, actually. He's an awesome kid, but only has two speeds. Stop and go."

"Fun." Mac replies sarcastically.

We head straight to the kitchen where Ella's fussing over something on the stove top while Sam and Marcus are involved in a conversation about football.

Kayla claps her hands loudly. "Attention everyone! Mac and Tawny are here!"

I groan. "Was that really necessary, Kayla?"

She grins. "Sure was. This is a big day, my dear sister. We've been anxiously awaiting visual proof of Mac and Tawny ever since you told us your dirty little secret. There's no going back now, you're official."

I look at my sister. "We aren't telling everyone. Not yet."

Kayla just rolls her eyes as Ella turns to me with a slightly more compassionate but still curious look. "Why not? What's the harm in going public? You're both adults now, you know what you're doing."

The silence after Ella's question is tense. Mac shifts and puts his hands in his pockets as he looks at me. Yeah, I know, this is my mess, so I've got to be the one to try and explain.

"I just don't want to tell everyone until we're more settled as a couple."

Kayla snorts. Marcus and Sam look beyond uncomfortable with the energy in the room, and I don't blame them. It's awkward.

"Ella, what are you cooking? Smells great." Mac's trying to move the conversation forward and I could kiss him for that. But he won't look at me and when I reach for his hand, he moves out of reach. My stomach sinks. Crap. He's upset.

Ella's eyes dance between me and Mac before she answers. "French toast casserole, bacon, and fruit salad." She turns to Marcus with a soft smile, "Babe, could you take some things to the table outside?"

He nods and Sam grabs a dish as well. "I'll help."

They're gone, leaving me, Mac, and my sisters alone in the kitchen. Kayla clearly isn't done with her attack as she fixes me with a glare.

"Tawny Michaels. Stop being chickenshit. You love Mac and he loves you. What's the problem?"

I don't have an answer that doesn't reinforce the fact that I'm scared. Even now that I know Mac is here to stay, I'm scared. And if I'm honest, I know that isn't fair to him or to us.

"I'm going outside to help the guys," Mac says quietly as he leaves the kitchen without looking at me.

Now it's Ella's turn to give me a hard time. "Tawny, what's wrong? Marcus told me he and Mac are going to work together so he can stay here. He's not going to leave and he's obviously crazy about you. What are you scared of?"

"Honestly? I don't know," I say quietly as I sink down into one of the stools at the kitchen counter. I drop my head into my hands. "There isn't a good reason to keep things a secret. I know there isn't, I'm just terrified we won't work out, and my heart won't survive it."

"That's bullshit and you know it. If Mac can love you after more than ten years apart, if he's willing to move his company and his entire life back to the island *for you,* then *obviously* he's in it for the long haul."

Wow. For Ella to use a real swear word, she must be really worked up about this. Even Kayla looks shocked at what just came out of her sister's mouth.

"What she said." Kayla nods toward Ella, who's standing there with her arms crossed, staring at me.

I let out a sigh. "I know. I know you're right. And I know if I don't suck it up and get over myself, I'm going to ruin this before it even starts. I just…I don't even know how to *be* with Mac in public."

Ella walks over and wraps her arms around my shoulders. "Just let your love guide your actions and don't hide."

I give a weak smile. She makes it sound so simple.

37

Mac

Outside with the guys, I can almost forget my frustration over Tawny's insistence that we stay a secret. Marcus and Sam are cool; I can see us being friends. Toby's a riot and so full of energy I'm tired from watching him.

But even as we talk football stats, half my mind is occupied with thoughts of Tawny. How can I get her over this hurdle of not wanting to go public? I thought she believed me when I said I was in this forever, that I wasn't going anywhere. But if that was true, then why the hell won't she let me tell the world she's mine?

I've done everything I can to convince her this is real for me, but her reticence fires off a voice of doubt deep inside that keeps getting louder. If Tawny can't accept our relationship as real and go public with it, then maybe she's not as invested in it as I am. Maybe I'm setting myself up for a world of hurt.

When we finally climb back into the truck after brunch is over, there's a weird tension between us that I don't like one bit. Deciding to take matters into my own hands, I drive us to the base of West Mountain, to our trail and park.

When we get there, Tawny looks at me with her eyebrows raised.

"You do realize I'm in sandals and a dress, right? Hardly hiking clothes."

"We aren't hiking, T. We're talking."

She drops her head and focuses on her hands twisting in her lap. I reach over and grab one, linking our fingers together. Turning in my seat, I face her and lift the center console up so that the front seat becomes one long bench seat. A gentle tug brings her closer to me, but not close enough.

"Tawny Michaels. I love you. I'm not going anywhere. I'm here to stay. And I want the world to know that, or at least the residents of Westmount Island."

Can't say it much more clearly than that, now can I? If she doesn't agree, I don't know where we stand. My stomach ties itself in knots when she doesn't answer right away and I swear I can see the happy image I'd created of us slipping through my fingers.

Finally, I hear her take a long, deep inhale and blow it out through her mouth.

"I love you too, Shawn Macdonald. So much that I want to marry you someday. And I guess if I'm going to do that, we kind of need to let people know we're dating."

She says it so quietly, so matter of fact, I almost think I heard wrong. But then she turns to me, a tremulous smile on her face, and I realize that she's serious.

A fire kindles inside of my soul. This is the moment I've been waiting for, the moment she finally surrenders to our love.

"Kiss me." The words come out as more of a growl than I mean them to be, but it's taking all of my self-control not to rip her clothes off and take her right here in my truck.

As soon as our lips touch my need for her takes over. I plunder her mouth, swiping with my tongue until she opens for me, our mouths dancing together. She's giving as much as I am and the dam that has been holding back our passion breaks.

"I need to get you home and out of these clothes," I mutter when we finally separate. When I lean back in my seat, I have to adjust myself from the agony of my dick struggling against my zipper. Not easy to do in the front seat of a pickup truck.

Once we're both buckled, I place my hands on the steering wheel and hold on tight to try and stop myself from touching Tawny. I'm so revved up that one more feel of her skin might make me combust. I drive back to her house as fast as I dare and without caring one fucking bit who might see us.

I pull the truck into her driveway and park haphazardly on an angle and I don't care enough to take the time to fix it. Tawny seems just as impatient as I am because I don't even have time to open her door for her, she's out and hustling up to her front door as quickly as she can.

The door closes behind us and it's as if someone fired the starting gun for the race to get naked. Clothes fly everywhere, her bra landing on top of a lampshade making us both laugh for a second in between kisses. We stumble over to her couch and she pushes me down. I sit, my legs spread and beckon for her to sit on my lap. She shakes her head and with a sultry smirk that makes my cock twitch, she drops to her knees in between my legs.

"Tawny."

"Mac," she says in the sexiest voice I've ever heard from her. She wraps her hands around the base of my cock and slides them up and down slowly. The friction is insane, but I want more. I put my hands over top of hers, groaning at the squeeze she gives me.

"I have a better idea, babe. Climb up here." I swing my legs around so that I'm lying on the couch. When Tawny climbs up, facing me, I shake my head.

"Turn around."

Understanding dawns on her and heat flares in her eyes with anticipation. She turns and backs up until her hips are right over top of my face.

"Fuck you're so beautiful."

"Less talking, more licking," she commands, shaking her ass in my face. I slap it lightly, loving this dirty, playful side of her.

"Yes ma'am."

I grab her hips, my fingers digging into her ass, holding her in place as my tongue gives one long swipe up her sex. Her back arches and she moans before dropping her head and taking me in deep. Her hands are holding her up, but I don't miss them, not with how goddamn talented Tawny is with her mouth. I know I won't last long like this, not with the taste of her on my tongue and the feel of her mouth on my dick. *Fuck.* All too soon I can feel the pressure mounting inside of me.

I'm determined to get Tawny off before I blow, so I move one hand in between her legs and slide my fingers inside. That, plus my lips sucking on her clit, has her bowing her body with pleasure, grinding against my face. The vibration from her moans is bringing me dangerously close to my own orgasm but when I feel her leg muscles clench, I know I'm good to go. She comes with a cry around my cock and seconds later I'm coming into her mouth.

Tawny climbs off of me, licking her lips like a cat who got into the cream. She holds her hand out to me, I take it, and stand up beside her. Lifting up on her toes, she pulls my head down close to her.

"That was fun, but I need you to fill me, Mac," she whispers before leading me down the hall to her bedroom and the sight of her hips swaying in front of me calls to me like a siren's song. Even though I just came a few minutes ago, already I can feel my dick stirring with need. I'm insatiable when it comes to Tawny Michaels.

Once we're in her room, she turns and wraps her arms around my waist, pulling me in close. She lays her head on my chest and we simply stand there for a moment. The feel of her naked body pressed against mine is intimate and arousing, and it doesn't take long for my cock to harden all the way. I can sense her smile against my skin and she glances down, then up at my face.

"Ready for more?" she asks.

"I'm always ready for you."

I hold her head in my hands and kiss her deeply. We walk backwards until we hit the bed. She lies down and I move over top of her. My arms are on either side of her head, her hands slip around my waist again, and I'm sliding into her heat like I'm coming home.

Slowly we move together, her hips lifting to meet my thrusts. Our kisses are languid; our bodies know we have all the time in the world. But this relaxed lovemaking can't last forever, not when it's fueled by the fire that burns between us.

Soon her nails are scratching my back and I've got one hand clenched on her hip as we thrust and grind into each other, going deeper and deeper until there's no end and no beginning. Time stands still until Tawny arches her back and cries out my name as her orgasm takes over, and I come roaring after her, this second release taking everything out of me.

I fall onto the bed beside her, panting. *Damn that was a workout, time to up the cardio.* Tawny's breathing heavily, too, and when I turn to look at her, strands of hair are sticking to her sweaty skin. Her eyes are still hooded with desire, but the grin she gives me is playful.

"Shower with me?"

As if she even has to ask.

* * *

Somehow, we manage not to fuck in the shower, but you better believe I go down for another taste of her.

Afterward, as we get dressed, Tawny faces me and puts her hands on her hips.

"We might as well rip the Band-Aid off, Shawn Macdonald. You're taking me out for dinner tonight. In town."

My hands freeze in the middle of buttoning my jeans. She's chewing on her lip, but I see courage underneath the nerves. I walk over to her and with my thumb, gently pull her lip free before kissing her.

"Isn't the guy meant to ask the girl out for their first date?" I murmur against her lips.

She snorts in reply before we both start laughing.

"It's hardly our first date, Mac," she says.

"It kind of is, T. Think about it. We've never actually gone on a real date."

I can see her thinking back to before, when we were younger, and when she reaches the same realization a look of shock comes over her face.

"Jesus, you're right! I can't believe I've had sex with a guy I haven't even dated. I don't put out that easily, you know." Her eyes are dancing and when I grab her around the waist with a mock growl, she shrieks with laughter. I toss her on the bed and climb over her, my fingers tickling her waist while she laughs and shrieks my name. Eventually I stop and lean down to nuzzle her on the neck. Slowly my lips make their way up to her ear, making her shiver. I trace light kisses over her jaw until I reach her mouth.

"You've been anything but easy, Tawny. And every moment has been totally worth it to get us here."

Her hand comes up to hold my cheek and love is brimming in her gaze. I'm so distracted by her beauty that she actually manages to get the best of me when she rolls us over and jumps off the bed with a laugh.

"Sweet words will only get you so far, Mac. Feed me," she teases as she dances out of the room.

MAC

Looks like we're going public.

38

Tawny

"It's the moment of truth, T. You ready for this?"

I nod and let the love I hear ringing in Mac's voice wash over me. It might be foolish of me to hope no one will make a big deal out of us walking hand in hand down the street, but I can't help it. I don't want the attention, but I do want Mac.

He helps me climb down from the truck, but instead of simply holding my hand he wraps his arm around my shoulders, tugs me into his side, and kisses the top of my head.

"Go big or go home, babe," he whispers into my hair with a chuckle.

I swallow down my nerves and let him lead me down the sidewalk of Wharf Street. It's not too busy this evening, but there's Harold, who mans the gangplank at the ferry terminal; he looks at us closely and I can see the surprise register on his face when he notices how Mac's holding me.

We walk in to Seas the Day and Mac's arm falls off my shoulders while he grabs two menus and we head to a booth. *So far so good. Deep breaths, Tawny.*

"Doing okay, babe?" Mac asks, and I'm touched that he's so worried about me, and annoyed at myself that he even has a reason to worry. I paste a smile on my face and hope I look convincing when I reply,

"Totally fine!" Yeah, because that didn't sound hysterical *at all*.

Mac chuckles and reaches across the table to cover my hands with his. He leans down and kisses my knuckles, just in time for Lois, one of the diner's owners, to appear and take our order. Her jaw drops, and it's so comical I actually laugh. Mac takes it all in stride and is able to maintain a straight face.

"Hey there, Lois. Good to see you," he says amiably.

"Shawn Macdonald, nice to have you home," she stammers out as her eyes dart over to me. "And Tawny Michaels. Well. You're here. Together." She looks down at our hands, still entwined together on the tabletop. "Really together?"

Mac lifts his eyes to me and I melt at the happiness he's projecting. "Yeah, Lois. Really together."

"Well, I'll be," Lois says. Then she turns to the rest of the diner and surprises the crap out of us both by shouting out loud, "Shawn Macdonald and Tawny Michaels are here, *together!*"

"Oh my God," I mutter and drop my head to the table in embarrassment as everyone turns to look at us. A few people even cheer.

"Sorry, kids, you have no idea how long we've all waited for y'all to get your heads out of the sand and realize you were made for each other! This day has been a long time comin'," she proclaims loudly.

I lift my head to see Mac nodding and trying to hold back his laughter.

"Well, thanks for that, Lois. We're pretty happy to be here together." He motions to her notepad, trying to move the focus off of us and onto dinner. "Could we order two salmon burgers with spicy fries, please?"

"Oh sure, sure. On the house for you two. This is a big day!" Lois gives us one more gigantic smile before walking away.

"Did that really happen?" I ask in a low voice. Mac snorts under his breath.

"Sure did, babe. No changing your mind now,"

That makes me smile. "I wouldn't dream of it."

* * *

By the time we're finished eating, I'm pretty sure the entire town has been by our table to tell us how happy they are. It still baffles me that none of them seem to know about our teenage romance, but everyone certainly is vocal about their approval of us dating now.

We head back to my place eventually and I'm equal parts exhausted from being on display all evening, and relieved that it went so well.

"See? Nothing to be afraid of," Mac says as he comes around to my door once we're parked at my house. He helps me down and clasps my hand as we walk up to the front door.

"Oh really? Nothing? You know the town is planning our wedding already, right?" I say, meaning it teasingly. But Mac stops, tugging my back into his chest.

"Would that be so bad?" he murmurs.

I shrug my shoulders, because no — it wouldn't be that bad. It would be everything I've dreamed of ever since I was a teenager.

"Tawny," Mac says, and something in his voice makes me turn around. He's looking at me with such love, such adoration in his eyes, it takes my breath away. But it comes rushing back in a gasp of surprise when he drops to one knee in front of me. Reaching into his pocket, Mac pulls out a small black box.

My vision is going blurry with tears and I can hardly believe he's doing this now. But when he opens that box and I see the stunning ring nestled inside, I know it's really happening.

"I wasn't planning on doing this so soon, but now that everyone knows about us, I just can't wait. Mom gave me this ring yesterday and I'm dying to put it on your finger. I've loved you since we were kids,

Tawny Michaels. Even when we were apart, I never stopped loving you. My body has always craved your touch and my soul has always yearned for yours. I was lucky enough to get a second chance with you and I can't let another second go by without making you mine forever. Will you promise to be my best friend for life, my partner for always, and my lover for eternity?"

Tears are streaming down my face and I'm grinning wildly, my eyes darting between the beautiful ring and his beautiful face.

"Got an answer for me, babe?" his voice cracks, and I can see he's crying, too.

"Yes, of course, I'll marry you!" I throw my arms around his neck and we tumble to the ground in front of my house. We're laughing and crying and kissing and everything feels wonderful. Suddenly I pull back with a gasp.

"The ring!"

Mac laughs and slides it on my finger before lifting my hand to his mouth and kissing it sweetly.

"It was my grandmother's. When Mom found out that we were officially together, she insisted I have it. I think she knows you are it for me."

"Mac, really?" I gasp. "It's beautiful. We have to go and see your parents so I can thank them"

"You're beautiful. And I love you so goddamn much. But my parents can wait. This is our new beginning and I want to start our life together the best way I know how."

The smolder in his eyes tells me exactly what he means by that, but I can't resist teasing him.

"Oh? And what might that be?"

With a growl, he's on his feet and sweeping me into his arms. Mac takes me into my bedroom, *our bedroom*, and proceeds to show me just what he means.

I sigh as my heart feels like it's finally home.

* * *

Thank you for reading The Westmount Island Trilogy! If you enjoyed these stories, please consider leaving a review on Amazon.

For bonus scenes from the Westmount Island trilogy, be sure to sign up for my newsletter at www.authorjuliajarrett.com

About the Author

Julia Jarrett is a busy mother of two boys, a happy wife to her real-life book boyfriend and the owner of a rescue dog from Guatemala. She lives on the West Coast of Canada and when she isn't writing contemporary romance novels full of relatable heroines and swoon-worthy heroes, she loves to run, practice yoga, drink wine and read.

You can connect with me on:
- https://www.authorjuliajarrett.com
- https://www.facebook.com/juliajarrettauthor
- https://www.instagram.com/juliajarrettauthor

Also by Julia Jarrett

The Westmount Island Trilogy - Available now on Amazon and Kindle Unlimited
- Falling Fast
- Falling Again
- Falling Forever

Dogwood Cove - COMING SOON
- Always and Forever - Pre-order now, releasing June 2021

The Lucky Strike Lovers Quartet - Available now on Amazon and Kindle Unlimited
- Loving Callie
- Protecting Anna
- Serenading Reagan
- Romancing Melanie

Made in the USA
Columbia, SC
21 May 2021